KU-315-924

03428638 - ITEM

Bronwyn Scott is a communications instructor at Pierce College in the United States, and the proud mother of three wonderful children—one boy and two girls. When she's not teaching or writing she enjoys playing the piano, travelling—especially to Florence, Italy—and studying history and foreign languages. Readers can stay in touch via Facebook, or at her blog, bronwynswriting.blogspot.com. She loves to hear from readers.

Also by Bronwyn Scott

Allied at the Altar miniseries

A Marriage Deal with the Viscount
One Night with the Major
Tempted by His Secret Cinderella
Captivated by Her Convenient Husband

The Cornish Dukes miniseries

The Secrets of Lord Lynford
The Passions of Lord Trevethow

And look out for the next book
coming soon!

Discover more at millsandboon.co.uk.

THE PASSIONS OF LORD TREVETHOW

Bronwyn Scott

MILLS & BOON

All rights reserved including the right of reproduction in whole or in part in any form. This edition is published by arrangement with Harlequin Books S.A.

This is a work of fiction. Names, characters, places, locations and incidents are purely fictional and bear no relationship to any real life individuals, living or dead, or to any actual places, business establishments, locations, events or incidents. Any resemblance is entirely coincidental.

This book is sold subject to the condition that it shall not, by way of trade or otherwise, be lent, resold, hired out or otherwise circulated without the prior consent of the publisher in any form of binding or cover other than that in which it is published and without a similar condition including this condition being imposed on the subsequent purchaser.

® and TM are trademarks owned and used by the trademark owner and/or its licensee. Trademarks marked with ® are registered with the United Kingdom Patent Office and/or the Office for Harmonisation in the Internal Market and in other countries.

For Ro, Catie and Brony.
I love living the fairy tale life with you.

Chapter One

The Elms, Cornwall, family seat of the Duke of Hayle—March 5th, 1824, St Piran's Day

'You can't have the land.' Those were fighting words. The surest way to guarantee Cassian Truscott's interest in a cause was to tell him something couldn't be done. That being the case, Inigo Vellanoweth, investment partner, best friend and utterer of said words, currently held *all* his attention.

Cassian looked up from the map spread before him on the long, polished surface of the estate's library table. '*What* did you say, Inigo?'

The dark-haired Inigo fixed him with a challenging blue stare from his desk near the wall of long windows overlooking The Elms's immaculate gardens. 'You heard me. You can't have the land. The Earl of Redruth won't sell.'

He emphasised his point with a wave of the most recent letter in a series of failed attempts.

Cassian sighed. His solicitors and Redruth's had been meeting all winter to make arrangements for the sale, to no avail. Spring was around the corner and he was no closer to breaking ground on his Cornish pleasure garden than he had been last year. Without Redruth's acres, there was simply no ground to break.

'There's other land, Cass. Perhaps it's time we consider other options,' Inigo pointed out practically. 'There's the acreage over by Truro,' he said, reaching for the numbers on the property, but Cassian cut him off. They'd been over this too.

'No, not land like this,' Cassian insisted, planting his hands on either side of the map, his gaze lingering on the spot marking the coveted thirty-two acres. Damn. He needed that land. It was the ideal location for accomplishing the achievement of his own dreams and for rejuvenating the Cornish economy. The coastal views were spectacular and sweeping, the distance to Porth Karrek or Penzance close enough to engage workers from several of the villages and to access other needed supplies to run such an establishment. 'Doesn't it gall you that the earl won't sell?' Inigo was his partner in the Porth Karrek Land Development Company, yet Inigo seemed less bothered by the downturn of events.

'It's just business to me, Cass.' Inigo gave him a wry smile. 'What do I always say? Don't get attached to money, to things. It makes a person less flexible.'

Cassian looked up from the map and grimaced. 'You think I'm being stubborn. You think I should move on and take the land near Truro.' It might be just business for Inigo, but it was far more than business for Cassian. This project was redemption, a chance to restore a legacy, a chance to do penance to the community for his brother's mistake. It had to be here. Putting it in Truro couldn't accomplish those things. It was too far away from the people he wanted to help.

'Offer Redruth double.' Cassian sighed. He needed that land. He'd invested months in negotiation—he wasn't going to give up now.

'We've already offered double,' Inigo reminded him.

'I know. Double it again. I can't imagine why Redruth remains obstinate. It's not as if he's using the land. It's been dormant for over a decade.' But even as he gave the order, Cassian felt the futility of it deep in his bones. Money would not coerce a man like Redruth, a man much like himself, who had money aplenty to spend, to whom doubling or quadrupling a price was no great stretch. He shook his head, cancelling the suggestion. 'No. Don't offer the money. We'll look stinking desperate and then we'll never get that land.'

Lord, this was maddening. The earl was well-known for his philanthropy in London. He supported numerous orphanages, championed the veterans of the Napoleonic wars and other causes in Parliament and out. Couldn't Redruth see all the good that could be done here at home in his very own environs? It wasn't as if Cassian was asking for charity. He was willing to pay handsomely.

Cassian left the table and went to the windows. He studied the green lawn before him. The sun had broken through the grey skies of the morning marine layer to make for a tolerable afternoon in early March. 'If money won't impress him, what will? He's a hermit except for sitting his seat in London.' Even in London, the earl barely socialised. He left that work to his son, Phineas. Cassian knew the son by sight only since Phineas was a few years younger. As for the earl, Cassian knew nothing of the man except that he craved seclusion and preferred to wield his power from the behind the walls of Castle Byerd.

'It's hard to know how to appeal to such a private man, Inigo. I don't think he's gone out in years except to perform his duties and attend church.' And to host his annual charity ball, the only night of the year the doors of Byerd House in London were thrown open to society. Cassian had attended only once. Usually his father went.

'What does Redruth need?' Cassian mused out loud. 'More importantly, what does he need that he can't get on his own?' But nothing came to mind. Surely the man wasn't unassailable. Everyone had a weakness. 'Did your digging discover anything?' After the last refusal, Inigo had set about investigating Redruth's situation.

'Only what we already know. He is committed to the land staying in the family. I've said it before, but my professional advice is that you look elsewhere for your acres.' Inigo left the desk to study the map. He tapped a finger. Cassian didn't need to see the map to know the spot. 'There are benefits to being near a larger town, Cass.'

Cassian turned from the window. 'No. Absolutely not. That would be to admit defeat. It's too far away to provide jobs for the people here, the people I want to help.' There was nothing like telling a man who had everything that the one thing he truly wanted was beyond his reach. 'The people of Porth Karrek and the surrounding area need economic relief *now.*' His friend, Eaton Falmage and his new bride, Eliza, had begun establishing a string of mining schools to educate the children of miners so that the next generation might have a choice as to how and where they worked. Those benefits would be long-term. But in the meantime, something needed to be done about present conditions and he was determined to do it.

Having been raised on the Cornish coast, he was fond of the expression 'a high tide raises all boats'. An amusement garden could do that by supplying three hundred jobs directly and countless other employment opportunities indirectly for those more intrepid entrepreneurs willing to set up in business on their own. A project of this magnitude could revitalise the region.

More than that, an amusement garden was Cassian's dream, his grand vision to bring new experiences to people who never ventured further away from their homes than they could walk in a day. He'd had the luxury of travel. He'd ridden the ice slides of Russia, partaken in the grand amusements of the French. He'd seen and tasted the convergence of culture and food from all over the world in Venice.

Those experiences had enriched him greatly. He'd learned more from those encounters than he had from his time at Oxford. Why shouldn't others be enriched in the same way? Why not bring those experiences to people who couldn't go to the source? Why should such enrichment be limited to only the very wealthy? It was the philosophy that Richard Penlerick, the Duke of Newlyn, Cassian's mentor and friend, had imparted to him for years, encouraging him to have purpose in his travel. 'Travel for those who cannot. Bring it home for others,' he'd counselled. 'So that one man's experiences might enrich a community.' Richard Penlerick was dead now, the first anniversary of his death approaching in June, but his legacy was as alive as it had ever been in the schools Eaton and Eliza had founded. Cassian was determined to continue the legacy. Damn the Earl of Redruth for standing in his way on the basis of some reclusive shibboleths about keeping the land in the family.

'It's a noble goal, Cass. But are you sure that's the only reason you're holding on so tightly?' Inigo had a way of piercing through the truth to get to even deeper truths, darker truths. Heaven help the man who lied to Inigo. He wouldn't stand a chance. 'Don't tell me this is about honouring Richard Penlerick. You can honour his legacy just as effectively in Truro as you can here.'

Cassian bristled. He didn't like being called out. Inigo knew very well he was sailing in dark waters now, close to the things they never discussed. 'Why don't you tell me what my secret agenda is, then? What, pray tell, am I holding on to?'

'There is no need to be testy. Sarcasm doesn't

become you.' Inigo gave him a hard stare, his voice like the fine, thin, steel of his favourite rapier. Inigo the fencer, with blades, with words. 'Tell me this isn't about Collin.'

Collin. His younger brother. Dead now for five years, yet the single word still had the ability to suck all the air, all the life out of him. Anyone close to him knew better than to pull out that particular skeleton from the family closet. It was the Truscott family's Achilles heel. Ducal families weren't supposed to have such disasters, such tragedies. Maybe his family wouldn't have had one either if Cassian had chosen differently when his brother had come to him. But he hadn't and now Collin was dead. It took Cassian a moment to still his emotions before he could respond. 'What does it matter if it's about Collin? We all have our obsessions, Inigo. Vennor's quest for justice regarding his father's death. I have Collin and you have Gismond Brenley. Don't pretend that you aren't driven to bring down Brenley.'

'The man has been a thorn in our collective sides for years. He deserves a reckoning, for the part he played in Collin's death, for what he tried to do to Eliza Blaxland, for what he's still trying to do to the industries of Cornwall,' Inigo argued.

Cassian gave a dry laugh. 'That's hardly sporting, Inigo. You can justify your obsession, but you won't validate mine? My revenge against Brenley is to build that park, to give workers a choice. They don't have to work for Brenley. They don't have to mine. They can work for me doing any number of things. Then, we'll see what Brenley has to say when he has no work force.' Revenge could be served in a variety of ways.

'Your revenge is only theoretical at the moment, thanks to Redruth,' Inigo reminded him. 'That land is meant to stay in the family. If you're not family, you don't stand a chance.'

'Then I need to become family.' That sparked an idea. Cassian strode to the shelves, searching for his father's copy of *Debrett's Peerage*. Cornish families were tight-knit and old, with lineages that went back to William the Conqueror. He set the book on the table alongside the map and opened it, running a finger along the list of names and stopping beside Prideaux. Perhaps there was some remote connection between the Truscotts and the Prideauxes, or perhaps, failing that, there was some remote cousin in need of marrying.

His finger stilled at the thought. Would he really be willing to marry for the land? It wasn't a preposterous strategy. His own lineage *was* something he could barter with. He was a duke's heir, a wealthy man with a title of his own as Viscount Trevethow. He could, maybe, entice Redruth with that. It was always worthwhile to have a future duke on the family tree. If he did that, though, what would be the difference between him and his last mistress? Cassian suppressed a shudder, unable to shake the idea that such a trade reduced him to a high-class whore and not even an honest one. It would be backhanded to marry without disclosing the truth: that he was the chief owner of the Porth Karrek Land Development Company, which Redruth had already discouraged in its pursuit of the very land available to him in the marriage settlement. Of course, it would come at the cost of Redruth despising his new son-in-law for the deception. Hardly ideal grounds on which to begin married life, to say nothing of what his bride would think of the situation.

Aside from that, however, a marriage between the Earldom of Redruth and the Dukedom of Hayle would be a grand alliance of two old Cornish families, Cassian thought wryly. Many men of his age and social standing married for less. At the end of the proverbial day, he'd have his land—perhaps the rest didn't matter as long as the dream could move forward. But the rest did matter. Achieving the dream by marrying for the land came with great cost, starting with his pride and ending with the loss of other dreams he held close, dreams that might seem fanciful to other peers. He'd like to fall in love with his wife. He'd like his marriage to be as grand in passion as it would be in politics. He'd like his marriage to be more than a contract, although that might be even more of a pipe dream than his pleasure garden.

In Cassian's experience, men of his station were regular targets for matchmaking mamas and pound-wise papas who saw the financial as well as social benefits of such a match. One had to be on constant guard in order not to fall prey to their schemes. His brother and that unholy mess with Brenley's daughter was indication enough that such caution was not misplaced paranoia.

Yet the notion persisted for Cassian that, despite the monumental evidence to the contrary, love inside of marriage *was* possible. His own parents were proof of it. The Trelevens were proof of it, Cador and Rosenwyn Kitto were proof of it as were Eaton and Eliza. Why shouldn't he have the same? Why should he settle for a dynastic contract? Cassian scanned *Debrett's* for the Prideauxes, his eyes landing on the list of the earl's family members.

Countess of Redruth, Lady Katherine Prideaux, née Dunstan. Born 1783. Died 1814.

She'd been young. He'd been little more than a boy when she'd passed. There was Phineas Michael, the son and heir. His finger stopped on the name below it.

Penrose, Margaret. Born 1803.

Inigo's gaze was steady on him. 'You think to marry for it. I see it in your eyes and now you've found the daughter. So many forget about her.' Inigo's eyes narrowed as they studied him. 'No one's seen her. She doesn't go about in society.' Like father like daughter it seemed on that note.

There was a wealth of implication in those words. Cassian shut the book. Perhaps she was the reason for the Earl's reclusive lifestyle. Perhaps there was a reason she hadn't been seen in public. Was she crippled? Burned? Did she limp? Not that those things mattered to Cassian. He was not as shallow as to determine someone's worth based on their physical abilities. But society was. Regardless of her potential afflictions, it seemed Redruth's daughter wasn't bound to be a beauty.

'Certainly, though, her father's title and her dowry are enough to guarantee she has suitors regardless of her looks,' Inigo pointed out.

'But not me among them.' Not yet. Cassian wasn't willing to engage in such manoeuvring. To sacrifice one dream for the sake of the other seemed to demean both dreams. Perhaps it would come to that, making himself into a placeholder for an exchange of titles and lands. For today, he was out of ideas until he could figure out what might persuade Redruth.

Tomorrow, he would write to the earl one more time, outlining all the benefits of such a sale.

Cassian put the book away and stretched. 'I'm going out. I'll ride into Redruth and take in the St Piran's Day festivities while the sun is shining. The town always puts on a good fair. The fresh air will clear my head. Perhaps I'll think of a new angle for getting that land while I'm there.' Maybe he wouldn't need to. Perhaps once the earl read all the benefits that could come from such a project, he wouldn't be so hard-hearted as to reject progress when it came with so many advantages and a substantial offer of cash.

Chapter Two

They were making no progress here. Lady Penrose Prideaux stifled her temper behind the osculation of her fan while Lord Wadesbridge conversed with her father. She knew what was afoot. Her father was matchmaking *again*. At first, it had only been a game to Pen, one she could win. Since she'd turned eighteen, her father had discreetly invited a select few men of good standing to Castle Byerd and, over the past two years, she'd repeatedly found something wrong with each of them. In the beginning, her father had not pushed her to reconsider. But with each rejected candidate the game posed an ever larger obstacle to her freedom. Two years in, it wasn't a game any more, but a threat.

Her father was in earnest over today's suitor, Lord Wadesbridge, who had an estate not far from Byerd. She could see why her father liked him. The latest candidate for her hand had more in common with the earl than he had with her. It wasn't surprising considering Wadesbridge was her father's contemporary, not hers. He was at least twenty years her senior. She knew what her father saw in him: an estate outside Looe close enough to visit, security, stability, sensibility. There wasn't a more stolid man in Cornwall.

If she was an older widow with half of her life behind her, or a quiet, retiring wallflower with no eye towards adventure, she might find Wadesbridge more appealing. But she was none of those things. She was twenty years old and hadn't been allowed outside the walls of Castle Byerd alone for the last decade. Whatever escape from Byerd she'd had over the years, she'd engineered covertly. She was full of wanderlust and a passion for living. She wanted to see the world she'd read about in her father's library, wanted to make her own choices, live her own life. She wanted to do more than support unseen causes for the poor from behind the safety of Byerd's walls. She wanted to help them first-hand. She wanted to travel, to see the places on the maps she studied, to dip her toes in the warm ocean of the Caribbean, to smell the spices in the Turkish bazaar, to ride in a Venetian gondola, maybe indulge in ordering gowns from a French salon, at the very least, to have a Season like other girls of her rank, to dance with a handsome gentleman who wasn't her father's age, to flirt, to fall in love, to meet someone that made her heart pound and her pulse race, who understood her dreams. Some days, like today, she felt as if she'd burst from the wanting of it all. There was so much to do beyond the walls of Byerd and she was running out of time. She couldn't say no to every suitor for ever. Her father wouldn't permit it. If she didn't choose, she had no doubt he would choose for her. He was the most determined man she knew.

'My daughter is honoured by your attentions, Wadesbridge.' Her father shot her a sharp look, jerking her back to awareness. She'd missed her cue. 'She will consider your suit.'

Pen's eyes snapped to attention. What had just happened? She'd drifted for a moment and she was nearly betrothed. Wadesbridge smiled and rose, happy enough to conclude his visit on that note. He reached for her hand and bent over it. 'I look forward to showing you Trescowe Park, my lady. The gardens are at their best in the spring. Your father tells me you enjoy flowers.' She nodded non-committally, not wanting to agree to anything she might regret. She did like flowers, wild ones. She envied them their freedom to grow where they chose, to run rampant over hedges and moors, to climb stone walls and poke through cracks.

'I have a greenhouse that would interest you, my lady.' Wadesbridge was still talking. 'Over the winter, I perfected some grafts with my roses in the hopes of producing a yellow rose tinged orange on the edges. If you'd permit me, I could send a cutting over.'

Wadesbridge was being kind. She could not shun him for kindness, but she wouldn't marry him for it either. Pen responded carefully. If she showed too much interest she'd end up with a room full of cuttings tomorrow and both he and her father would take it as an endorsement of his suit. 'You are too generous, my lord.' Pen offered a polite smile. 'I will look forward to seeing your new rose when we visit and perhaps I can select a few cuttings then.'

It was better to stall any potential outpouring of gifts. She smiled Wadesbridge out, but her smile faded the moment she and her father were alone in the drawing room.

'I don't want to marry him.' Pen spoke first, her voice full of sharp authority.

Her father sighed, looking suddenly weary, his voice tired. 'What's wrong now? Wadesbridge is rich, titled, stable, local.'

'He's old.'

'He's only forty-five.'

'He's closer to your age than he is mine,' Pen pressed. Only ten years separated her father and Wadesbridge, but two and half decades separated her from him.

Her father's dark eyes studied her in frustration. He had a temper too. They were alike in that regard. At the moment, they were both struggling to keep that particular character trait under control. 'The previous suitor gambled, another drank, another had debts. I should think Wadesbridge's lack of vices would appeal after that parade, or is it your intention to find fault with every suitor?' There was accusation in his tone. He was disappointed in her. She hated disappointing her father. She loved him and she knew he loved her. Too much sometimes.

'I want to do something with my life, Father.' She gentled her tone in hopes of making him see.

'Marry, raise a family. There is no worthier calling in life,' her father insisted. 'Family is everything, it is a man's life's work and a woman's too.' But it wasn't the only work of a lifetime. There were other worthy ways to spend a life.

'Maybe, in time I would like those things, but not yet.' How did she convince him? 'I want to live a little before I'm handed off to a husband. I don't want to go from my childhood home to my husband's home without an adventure first. I haven't even been to London for a debut.' Other girls her age, girls like their nearby neighbour, Sir Jock Treleven's daughters, had all gone to London for Seasons. Marianne was having her *second* Season this year and she was only nineteen, a year younger than Pen.

Her father's eyebrows rose in censure at the mention of London. 'The city is far too dangerous. Don't you recall what happened last Season? The Duke of Newlyn and his wife were stabbed to death coming home from the theatre. They were practically our neighbours here all these years and now they're gone. I wouldn't want to risk you. Besides, with your dowry and your antecedents, what need do you have for a Season?' He leaned forward and pinched her cheek affectionately. 'You have no need to hunt for a husband. *They* come to you.'

'I want to choose for myself and to do that I need time and a larger selection, Papa. How can I know what I want in a husband if I haven't met anyone?'

'You should be guided by the wisdom of your elders. I would not allow you to marry someone unworthy.' No, he wouldn't. She would be assured of marrying a decent man, but the thought of wedding a decent man didn't exactly set her heart to racing. What about romance? What about stolen kisses? What about *love*? 'I must insist you seriously consider Wadesbridge.'

'And *you* must seriously consider what I want. Does it matter so little?' She felt as if an invisible noose was strangling her. Her lovely home had slowly become a prison over the years. If she stayed, she'd scream with the futility of her life. She had to get out of here, if even for a short time. She needed a walk, a chance to clear her head.

'I don't want to quarrel with you, Penrose.' His tone softened with love and she heard the old, familiar tinge of sadness that had been present in his voice for over a decade. 'You grow more beautiful every day, Penrose. You look so much like your mother. You have her honey hair, her green eyes, like the Cornish sea at summer. A stunning combination.' Her father was biased, of course. She might be striking in her features, but she was not beautiful. There was a difference. Her mother, however, had been beautiful and life had been beautiful when she was alive, every day an adventure from romping the hills to building hideaways in the vast attics of Byerd on rainy afternoons.

Her looks were a blessing and a curse Pen had lived with every day since the event that had claimed her mother's life, a constant reminder to them all of the woman they'd lost to a violent, senseless act and the very reason her father was so protective. He feared losing her the way he'd lost his wife: instantly and arbitrarily. Pen felt her anger over the latest suitor slipping. It was hard to argue with a man who was still grieving after all these years, hard to hurt a father who loved his children so deeply. She couldn't keep putting the discussion off, though. If she didn't stand up for herself soon, she'd end up married to Wadesbridge or if not Wadesbridge, the next suitor who walked through the doors of Castle Byerd. But not today. She would not fight with her father today. Today, she would do as she usually did and simply escape.

She moved towards the door, and her father looked up. 'Where are you going?'

'Upstairs. I think I'll lie down before dinner. I have a headache,' she improvised. There were festivities in the village, even fireworks this evening, and she didn't intend on missing them, especially if this might be her last time to see them. She wasn't getting any younger and her father's collection of suitors was only growing more insistent by the day. Desperate times called for desperate measures. She could either sit in her room and mope or she could go to a party.

Upstairs, Pen reached under her bed for an

old dressmaker's box that had once contained a gown. Now, it was home to a plain brown cloak, a simple dark blue dress made of homespun wool and a battered pair of half-boots. Pen smiled as she pulled them out one by one as if they were made of the finest silk. The clothes were her treasures. Once she slipped these on, she was no longer Penrose Prideaux who couldn't leave the castle without an army for an escort. Now, she could be whoever she wished: a peasant girl, a farm girl, a girl who worked in one of the shops in the village, maybe even a stranger who'd walked here from another village. These clothes were freedom. She could be whoever she desired, do whatever she desired and no one would be the wiser.

Pen finished dressing and took down her carefully crafted hair, plaiting her long honey-hued skeins into a single, thick braid that hung over her shoulder. She critically studied her appearance in the pier glass, looking for anything that would give her away: a forgotten piece of jewellery or a silk ribbon in her hair. Satisfied that she'd erased any trace of Penrose Prideaux, she raised the hood of her cloak and set off to leave herself behind. Tonight, she would make some adventures of her own before it was too late.

Chapter Three

Cassian loved a good fair and the town of Redruth did not disappoint. It was a point of pride for the town as the nominal originator of the St Piran festivities. Many other towns in Cornwall had their own celebrations these days for the patron saint of tin miners, but Redruth had been the first.

Cassian stabled his horse at the livery, tossing an extra coin to the sulky young ostler left on duty while his comrades had gone off to join the festivities. 'You'll be rich when they come back with their pockets to let,' Cassian consoled him, but the boy continued to pout. Well, he knew a little something about that. He wasn't so far past boyhood himself that he'd forgotten how much he'd looked forward to an outing when he was younger. Fun was sparse in this part of the world. His pleasure garden could change that. It would have entertainments for all ages, unlike Vauxhall, which catered to an adults-only crowd. Children needed stimulation, too, especially when their imaginations were at their most fertile. Growing up, he'd loved adventure stories even though reading had been a labour for him. He'd loved any day that his father or Eaton's father or Richard Penlerick had taken the four of them out riding or exploring. But those days had been rare. Perhaps he'd bring the sulky ostler a pasty when he came back. Cassian's stomach rumbled at the thought of a hot pie, a reminder that he hadn't eaten since breakfast.

Outside in the street, happy townsfolk jostled past as he let his nose lead the way to a pasty vendor. He purchased a pasty and bit into the flaky crust, the savoury meat warm in his mouth. It took the edge off the weather's late afternoon crispness. March wasn't really spring in this part of the world. Cassian wandered the booths, stopping every so often to admire goods that caught his attention. It was at the leatherworker's booth, as he studied the workmanship on a bridle, that he noticed her out of the corner of his eye. He couldn't say what it was exactly that drew him: the swirl of her cloak, perhaps, or the way the woman beneath the cloak moved, all slender, straight-shouldered grace as opposed to the bustle of the fair-goers.

Cassian stepped back from the leatherwork-er's booth to study her. She moved as if she were savouring each sight, lingering over each of the items in the stalls, treating them as if they were luxuries. Maybe they were. Not everyone who came to a fair had coins in their pocket to spend. The hood of her brown cloak was drawn up over her face, her hair. Cassian found himself wishing it wasn't so. He wanted to see this woman who walked through a village fair with such reverence. More than that, he wanted to know her mind; what did the fair look like to her to inspire such awe? How might he capture that for his amusement park? It was precisely how he wanted guests to look when they visited. If he ever got it built.

She moved into the crowd and Cassian followed. Perhaps he would speak to her. She appeared to be alone, an odd condition for a woman at such an event. For all the excitement a fair could bring, there were dangers, too, if one wasn't careful, especially as the day wore on and the men were deeper into their drink. At the edge of the village green the booths gave way to the pens of livestock and the crowd thinned. Here, she halted, suddenly surrounded by a gaggle of children who'd swarmed her.

Cassian quickened his steps in concern. There were too many of them. These were not village children. These were street urchins, some of them older boys who likely followed the vendors from fair to fair. A smaller boy, likely the decoy, said something to her, tugging at her and claiming all her attention. Cassian could guess what he was asking for. The woman hesitated and then reached beneath her cloak and produced a coin for the lad. That would never do. The boys would either beg the rest of her purse from her or come back to steal it later now that they knew where she kept it. From the looks of her clothes, she hadn't the money to spare should she lose whatever her purse contained.

'Hoy there, lads! Be off with you!' Cassian strode into their midst, dispersing them with his sheer bulk. Smart lads didn't mess with men built with height and breadth to match.

They scattered like swatted flies in the wake of his broad-shouldered, baritone-voiced barrage.

The woman straightened, becoming taller, more slender, more graceful than she'd been in the marketplace. 'That was hardly necessary, sir. They were just hungry children begging a coin.' There was a slightly imperious tone to her voice. A proud woman, then, a woman who liked to be self-sufficient. He had two older sisters who had that same tone. He knew it well. A man had to tread carefully where such a woman's pride was concerned. It was a lesson he'd watched his sisters' husbands learn over the years.

'They'll have your whole purse off you if you aren't careful. Those were no ordinary children,' he scolded kindly.

'I know their sort very well. It doesn't make their plight any less pitiable. Out of concern for my fellow mankind, I'll take my chances, every time,' she answered staunchly.

Cassian nodded. 'A noble sentiment, although I doubt they'll extend you the same courtesy when they come back to take your purse. You exposed yourself, you know.' He wished she'd expose a little more of herself, perhaps push that hood back from her face, show him the eyes, the mouth that went with her voice. In his experience, a confident woman was always attractive. He found confidence sexy in the bedroom and out. This woman's confidence stirred him, intrigued him. 'Perhaps I might escort you in case they return.' If he was beside her, he was certain they wouldn't.

'Where might *you* escort me? A dark alley?'

'Would you like me to?' He flirted with a smile. 'There are many things one can get up to in a dark alley, not all of them bad.'

'You might be more dangerous than the gang of boys,' she answered shrewdly. She was enjoying the exchange. 'How do I know you're not in on it with them?' She gave a throaty laugh when he raised an eyebrow in approval of her quick wit. 'See, I'm not as green as you think.' Sweet heavens, the minx gave as good as she got. The open boldness appealed.

Cassian chuckled. 'I never thought you were. I was merely concerned you were too kindhearted for your own good. Might I interest you in a pasty or some other delicacy?'

'I don't even know your name, sir.' She was serious about that. He'd reached the limits of what she'd tolerate. However, he was enjoying her far too much to ruin it by announcing his real name. It would change everything if she recognised it. Even if she didn't recognise it now, she would be sure to recognise it later. A name was power, to be used for or against him. He would not put that kind of power in a stranger's hands.

'What would you like my name to be?' Cassian flirted. 'Choose one for me.' Beneath the hood of her cloak, green eyes lit in liking and understanding. The idea appealed to her as well. His intrigue ratcheted. His lady liked games.

'Matthew.' She chose easily and quickly. 'And what shall you call me?' It was an interesting woman who saw the benefit of an alias, who perhaps was just as eager as he to keep her identity hidden. Maybe because it made the little game between them more exciting, or maybe there was something more to it.

'Must I call you anything? I'd rather know your face than your name.' Cassian cajoled. 'Push your hood back a little farther so that I can see you better.' He was starting to like this game. This was a woman with secrets, a woman who liked her privacy. He respected that. He had secrets of his own.

With her free hand, she pushed her hood back just far enough to reveal hair the colour of caramel and honey and eyes like sea glass, a mouth that was full and inviting. Taken together, her features were starkly, intensely riveting. Memorable. In the right clothes, the right setting, she would be a beauty. Amidst the plain folk of Redruth, she was remarkable, a faerie queen among mere mortals. He understood why she stayed cloaked. Remarkable women drew attention and hardly ever the right sort.

'I saw an opal once the shade of your eyes, but I think Emerald makes a better name.' Cassian let her draw her hood back up. 'That way I can call you Em. It sounds friendlier.'

'Are we to be friends, then, for the night?' They'd begun walking back towards the stalls, the decision to share the evening already implicitly made.

'We shall be whatever you want, Em.' He let his voice linger on the last, the caress of his tone carrying the nuance for him; they could be strangers, lovers, friends. Em suited her, his cloaked minx with her throaty laugh and her bold mystery. He purchased two pasties stuffed with hot, sliced potatoes. He passed one to her and watched her bite into it.

'Oh, that is *good*.' Her eyes closed as she savoured the food, chewing slowly, and Cassian felt himself grow hard at the sight. If she looked this delicious eating a pasty, what might she look like in the throes of taking her pleasure? Her hair loose from its braid, her long neck arched?

A droplet of juice dribbled on her lips and Cassian felt the wicked urge to lick it from her mouth. She smiled coyly as if she guessed the direction of his thoughts, but before he could lean forward, the tip of her tongue darted out to claim the drop.

He wanted to kiss her, this handsome, dark-haired man. A little frisson of excitement raced through Pen at the realisation. She'd read enough novels to know. The drop of the eyes, the lingering gaze on one's mouth. Those were the signs. Only she'd beaten him to it with her tongue.

Perhaps she ought to have let him kiss her? But it was too soon. He'd think her easy. They'd only just met and she'd broken so many rules already: talking to a stranger, walking with him, accepting food from him, flirting outrageously, saying wickedly witty things she'd only ever practised in her mind and taking on a false name. *Em*, he'd called her, only when he said it, she imagined it as M. *M* for mystery, perhaps. Perhaps he might try for a kiss again when they'd known one another a little longer and she could oblige. It was naughtily delicious to think she might get kissed tonight; her very first kiss, and from a tall, dark, handsome stranger at the fair.

They finished their pasties and began to wander the booths, stopping when something caught their eyes: a belt here, a scarf there, a pretty bauble, a scented bar of soap and a never-ending stream of conversation. Matthew was easy to talk to and easy to listen to. He had stories about everything from how the French soap was milled to how many crimps of a crust it took to make a true pasty to how Brussels lace was made.

'You've seen them make the lace?' She fingered a delicate sample in renewed appreciation for the labour. At home in her wardrobe, she had several gowns with lace collars and yokes. She'd not stopped to think of the effort those yards had taken.

'Yes, it's a very elaborate, time-consuming process. It can take months to produce a design.'

She gave a sigh. 'I'm envious of you and your travels! How wonderful to see the world. I'd give anything to leave here, at least for a while. Where else have you been?' They stopped to sniff little vials of perfume. She held up a vial of sandalwood mixed with an exotic scent. She sniffed and handed it to him. 'Try this one. It's very masculine.'

He sniffed and put the stopper back in. 'It's nice. It reminds me of Russia.'

She smiled. 'So, you've been to Russia. Tell me. What is Russia like?'

He winked. 'I will, but first we need sustenance.' He was a bottomless pit, she discovered. The pasty they'd consumed earlier was followed by a sampling of every sweet available as they shopped and talked and he regaled her with stories of his travels. They ate, turning the night into a parade of scones with jam and clotted cream and saffron buns warm from the oven. When they stopped at a stall selling fairings, she gave a laughing groan as he bought a bag of the biscuits and offered her one. 'Oh, no, I couldn't eat another a bite!'

Matthew grinned mischievously and waved a ginger treat under her nose. 'Are you sure? I have it on good authority from my nieces and nephews that fairings are generally irresistible and these are fresh. Try one, for me, please.'

He smiled at her and it seemed to Pen that the crowd disappeared, that the whole world vanished when he looked at her like that with whisky eyes and long black lashes. She was lost. 'Well, perhaps I could find room for one,' she teased.

'Open wide, then, Em.' Her pulse raced as she divined his intentions. He meant to feed it to her from his own hand! She took the fairing from him with her teeth, aware of his fingers lingering on her lips, aware of the spark that leapt between them. Around them, the lanterns began to cast their glow as light faded, the day was changing and *they* were changing with it. There was a charge between them. Matthew's eyes were on her as she swallowed the fairing, searing into her as if his gaze could see into her mind, her very soul, into every fantasy she'd ever harboured of a night like this— a night with a stranger who wanted her, just her; a stranger who knew nothing of her family's tragedy, of her seclusion, her private fight for freedom; a stranger who didn't want her for her money, her land, her family's title, a man not curated for her by her father.

She was aware, too, that the fantasy had to end very soon. She'd already stayed longer than she'd intended. Matthew fed her another fairing and she took this one more slowly, revelling in the brush of his fingertips at her lips as she summoned the willpower for the words that must come. 'I have to go.' Her maid, Margery, would cover for her, of course, but she still had to walk back and that walk would now occur in darkness.

'Soon,' he said, taking her hand in his and beginning to stroll again. 'But not yet. We haven't seen the Venetian glass-blower.'

'One more booth and then I must go.' She could not resist the temptation of a few more minutes with him, a few more minutes of freedom.

The glass-blower did not disappoint. In the

darkness, the flame of his forge was inviting and warm. They joined the semi-circle of on-lookers gathered around the stall to watch him work his magic. Pen gasped as the man blew through a tube and a fragile shape took form at the other end. She'd never seen glass blown and the process mesmerised her almost as much as the man standing behind her. She was acutely aware of him, of his height, of his body so close to hers in the crowd, the breadth of his shoulders beneath his greatcoat, the heat of him rivalling the heat of the glass-master's forge. She felt the gentle grip of his hand at her waist as they watched the demonstration. No man had ever dared touch her so intimately, so possessively, but he did it easily as if his hand belonged there, as if it had a *right* to belong there.

A hungry, curious, lonely part of her wished he had that right, but she knew better. She was an earl's daughter, a woman destined for a match that went far beyond the means of this whisky-eyed stranger. He was not a peasant. His bearing, his confidence was too grand for that with his greatcoat and boots. Perhaps he was a squire's son, a man of decent means, but no substantial wealth, a man who could never be a contender for the hand of an earl's daughter. She could only be his for the night. And who knew? Perhaps he had obligations elsewhere as well? Perhaps he could no more be hers beyond tonight than she could be his?

The glass-blower completed his demonstration to applause and the crowd dispersed. Pen lingered to look at the items on display in the case: a clever glass heart that could be hung as a pendant, a menagerie of little glass animals of all sorts, tiny thimbles and teardrops. 'Amazing,' she whispered under her breath. 'To think that Venice has come all the way to Redruth. What a world it must be.' It was worth it to be late getting back to have seen this and to have seen it with him, her Matthew. She slid a glance his way and smiled. 'I'm glad you insisted I see this.'

He did not look away, his gaze holding hers long after her words faded. 'Will you permit me to offer you a souvenir?' His voice was low and private, for her alone.

'I should not.' Her voice was equally as quiet.

'But you will. Your heart's not in the refusal,' he said softly, gesturing for the glass-blower. 'The lady would like the pendant.'

Pen blushed furiously. It was too much, too intimate, far more intimate than Wadesbridge's rose cuttings. The necklace wasn't fine diamonds or even Austrian-cut crystal. She had a jewel box full of items that were more expensive, but she was cognisant this was a trinket of some expense for a common man. Yet Matthew handed over the coins easily. 'May I put it on you, Em?' He was searing her with his gaze, burning her alive here in public where everyone could see. Did *he* see what he did to her?

She gave him her back, pushing off the hood of her cloak and lifting the thick braid, giving him access to her neck. His fingers were cool against her skin where he tied the ribbon, where they lingered at her neck as he whispered, his mouth at her ear as if they were lovers, old familiar lovers who knew one another's bodies, 'You have the neck of a swan, Em.'

'Thank you.' Was that the right response? What did one say when one's neck was complimented? Somewhere in the distance, music began for dancing as he pushed up the hood of her cloak, covering her hair, his hands lingering at her shoulders.

'Do you insist on leaving? I would ask you to dance if I could entice you to stay?'

She fingered the glass heart at her neck. 'I must go now. Thank you for a wonderful evening.'

'Where are you headed? My horse is at the livery. I can take you.'

Pen hesitated. She was tempted. A horse would be faster than a walk, yet her father's sense of caution and danger was deeply ingrained in her. Here at the fair, they were surrounded by people. Matthew couldn't do much to her here where she could cry out for help. But on a horse, on the dark road…her mother had died on a dark road.

'You're thinking of dark alleys again, aren't you, Em?' He chuckled softly. 'You don't owe me anything for the necklace. I'm not the sort of man who demands payment for trinkets. That wasn't why I bought it.'

'I know,' she whispered softly. She knew it was true in her bones. Fantasy or not, she was safe with him. *Em* was safe with him. Pen might not be, though. She didn't want him getting close to Byerd. He might try to find her there later. She couldn't risk him showing up, exposing her. 'Still, I must leave you here.' She had to insist although it saddened her to see the evening end. She would never see him after to-night. He would become a treasured memory.

But Matthew was determined. 'Can I see you again, Em?'

'I don't know.' She was faltering now, unsure. She hadn't thought further than tonight. How would she manage it again? Not just getting out of Byerd again without her father knowing, but keeping her identity secret? How would she explain if she were caught?

'There's an abandoned gamekeeper's cot-tage between Redruth and Hayle just off the coast road. Meet me there tomorrow at one,' he urged. 'I will wait all afternoon for you.'

She should absolutely say no now. No good could come of meeting a man in an empty cot-tage. Instead, Pen found herself saying, 'I will try.'

'Do more than try, Em.' His eyes glittered dangerously in the lantern light, all hot whisky. 'I want to see you again. Tonight was magi-cal, being with you, talking with you. I want more of that. If you don't come, I'll know you felt differently.' He raised her hand to his lips and kissed her knuckles. A bolt of white-hot awareness shot up her arm. 'Until tomorrow, Em.' Then he let her go, let her have her way to make the journey home alone with her thoughts. Her hand burned from the imprint of his touch, her heart wishing he'd dragged her into a dark alley after all and kissed her on the mouth instead of the hand. Her mind debated whether or not she was crazy enough to keep the rendezvous tomorrow with all its potential risks and whether or not he'd really wait all afternoon for the likes of her. He'd not struck her as the sort of man who had to wait on a woman.

Chapter Four

Em was keeping him waiting. Cassian snapped shut his pocket watch for the third time in fifteen minutes and retraced his steps back across the room to the hearth where his haphazard fire burned, built from the scraps of kindling he'd picked up on the cliffs. A half of an hour he'd been here, lighting a fire, setting out the parcels of his picnic on the scarred table and pacing the floor of the gamekeeper's cottage, first in anticipation, then in a little self-deprecating irony, reflecting on the intrigue this whole interlude raised in him. Certainly, he'd had more sophisticated affairs and yet this one had him vacillating between anticipation and anxiousness. Would she come? Perhaps she wasn't merely keeping him waiting—the very concept implied she *was* coming. Maybe that was a fallacy. Maybe she wasn't coming at all.

Perhaps she'd woken up this morning and realised the insanity of what he'd proposed—that two strangers meet in an isolated location for an afternoon of undisclosed activity. Such an adventure was always more dangerous for a woman. She would be taking all the risk. Perhaps last night had been risk aplenty for her and yet she'd enjoyed his company, that had been plain enough in her smile, her wit, the flash of her sea-glass eyes.

He'd definitely enjoyed her, the delicious directness with which she'd spoken. She'd been quick to challenge him when she thought he was too bold. She'd been open and unguarded when she'd told him of her dreams to travel. Her joy in the vendors had been natural, spontaneous. *Without artifice.* Those two words described her appeal completely. There had been no dissembling from her, no posturing. Everything between them—from eating messy, juicy pasties to wandering the booths—had been organic in a way no London ballroom or exquisitely coached debutante could replicate.

It felt good to put his finger at last on the source of his attraction. However, it felt less than good to realise *why* that had been possible.

She didn't know who he was. If she did, all that naturalness might be sacrificed. She'd be intimidated into curtailing her open speech, into second-guessing what she shared, or maybe she'd realise the futility of meeting him. There was no future for a peasant girl and a duke's heir. Nothing could come of this except enjoyment of the moment, as it had last night.

Would the promise of continuing that enjoyment be enough to compel her out in the light of day to the cliff lands between Redruth and Hayle? He hoped it would be, but hope hadn't been his friend today when it had come to appointments. Today was taking on a potentially disappointing theme in that regard. The Earl of Redruth had written a vituperative letter in quick response to his latest missive. Redruth's letter had outlined his reasons for refusing to sell to the Porth Karrek Land Development Company. Such a project would attract 'outsiders', the earl's letter had cited with contempt. Redruth felt that such a plan would not only bring the desired tourists to the depressed region, but also strangers, people who would take jobs from the people the project intended to help here at home. Moreover, Redruth believed there would be other more nefarious types who didn't intend to work, but who came to prey on the unsuspecting, such as the families taking a holiday thinking they were safe, but instead finding themselves at the mercy of a cutpurse or worse, citing the tragedy of the Duke of Newlyn in London.

The last had boiled Cassian's blood. Redruth couldn't know how close to his heart that arrow struck. Redruth didn't know that the Duke of Hayle and his son, the Viscount Trevethow, along with Inigo Vellanoweth, Earl of Tintagel, and his father, the Duke of Boscastle; all close intimates of the late duke, were the driving force behind the Porth Karrek Land Development Company. Cassian had wanted to write back, to argue that the duke would have been the first to champion such an innovative project to restore the region's economy. But Redruth would not care and such a self-satisfying measure would risk exposing the land company's ownership. Other than being neighbours, Redruth knew little about the progressive thoughts of the Duke of Newlyn past or present. Redruth, in fact, knew very little of what happened outside the walled fortress of

Castle Byerd. It was a pity. His own people would suffer for it.

Cassian threw another stick on the fire in the little hearth and watched it blaze. It was at times like these, where he could not effect change, could not break an impasse, that he felt most impotent. How could it be that with all his resources he could not breach the walls of the earl's disregard? He would try again. He'd find a way. He did not give up easily. He'd not given up when it had proven hard to read while others around him seemed to pick it up naturally. He'd not given up when the deans at Oxford had said he'd never complete his degree in history, a subject that required much reading. Instead, encouraged by his father, his close friends and Newlyn, he'd found a way to appreciate history through travel, to appreciate the world through other more experiential means than solely through texts. Newlyn was gone now, but he'd left Cassian with a legacy of perseverance and success. Hard work paid in rich reward. And, of course, he knew the opposite was true as well. Quitting, giving in, only bred more defeat. He had quit only once in his life. How might things have been different if he hadn't given up on Collin? Might Collin still be alive if he'd made different decisions where his brother had been concerned?

'Matthew?' Em's sweet voice broke into his darkening thoughts. Cassian looked away from the fire.

'Em!' Her presence chased away the guilt that was always present when he thought about Collin. His day was better already just at the sight of her. Her cheeks were rosy with exertion. Her hood had fallen back and her hair sparkled with droplets of mist. Her boots were muddy and her cloak damp. Cassian moved to help her out of her wet garment. He spread it before the fire, noting how thin it was. 'It will be dry by the time you leave,' he promised.

'You needn't fuss. It's only a light mist.' She held her hands out towards the flames, warming them, and Cassian felt a twinge of guilt. 'I hope the walk wasn't too far? I should have asked last night. I should not have presumed.' A slip on his part. He was privileged. He had sturdy boots to wear, a warm coat. He should not have assumed her shoes would be adequate for the task of tramping through the mud or that her cloak was warm enough for her to *choose* to be out of doors voluntarily.

'It wasn't too far. I like a good walk, rain or shine,' she assured him, but her smile was tremulous, her eyes glancing about the room, taking in the door and the two windows as if she might need to know their location for an escape. She wore the same blue dress he'd glimpsed beneath her cloak at the fair. The pretty glass heart was at her neck and it warmed him that she'd worn it. She was much the same Em in daylight as she'd been at the fair, but today she was nervous.

Cassian strove to put her at ease. 'I'm glad you're here. I thought you might not come.' He dragged over the two chairs from the table and set them near the fire.

'I'm sorry I'm late. I couldn't get away as soon as I'd wanted. I hope you weren't waiting for too long?' She sounded flustered as she cast about for conversation. Perhaps she was realising how alone they were, how different today was from last night. There were no lights, no vendors, no fair magic to guide their conversation. It was just them.

'It's never too long to wait for you.' Cassian

absolved her tardiness with the wave of a hand. The wait had been worth it to have her all to himself. Without her cloak to hide her, he could see the details of her face. Not just her eyes, but the minutiae of her: the tiny scar at her chin, the freckle at the corner of her mouth, the things that gave her features nuance and depth, that made them uniquely hers. When one struggled to read books, one learned to read people instead.

'Do you flatter all the strange girls you meet?' She blushed becomingly and dropped her gaze to her lap. 'Why did you think I wouldn't come?'

Cassian stretched his booted feet out before the fire and gave her a winsome smile. 'I thought you might have realised how insane it was to meet a stranger in a cottage.'

Oh, she had definitely realised that. She was still thinking it, in fact, now that she'd arrived and the very space they occupied seemed intent on reminding her of the remoteness of their location and the precariousness of her position. To be caught here would be devastating. Pen fidgeted with her hands in her lap. What did one say to that?

She jumped up from her chair and began to walk the length of the room, expending her nervous energy. 'It is crazy. But you're here, too, so I guess that makes two of us with questionable grips on sanity. Although, to my credit, I did turn around once.' It accounted for being late, that and the rather lengthy debate she'd held with herself on a rock overlooking the sea.

The admission seemed to intrigue him. She felt his whisky eyes linger on her, studying her as she moved about the room. 'Why *did* you come?'

'I had to know, for myself, if this was crazy. I'd never know if I could trust you if I didn't show up.' More than that, she didn't want her father to win. She didn't want fear to win, to steal her one chance at an adventure. But now that she'd come she hardly knew what to do with herself. What *did* one do on a rendezvous? Would there be kisses? More than kisses? She hardly knew the man she'd braved fear and rain to meet in an old cottage. For all she knew, he was a practised rake.

'Do you meet girls out here all the time?' It

was possible she was just another in a long line of clandestine seductions. A hundred horrid thoughts had crossed her mind on the walk, thoughts not just about him, but about her. If he was a seducer, what did it say of her that she was still willing to meet him?

'No.' He sounded insulted by the idea. 'Why would you say that?'

'You've come provisioned, a man with a plan.' Pen opened the picnic basket at the table and sniffed appreciably. There were meat pies inside. Her stomach rumbled.

'We might get hungry. Bring it to the fire and stay warm.' He left his chair and sat on the floor, taking the basket from her as she sat down beside him.

'You mean *you'll* get hungry. You're always ravenous. If I ate as much food as you did at the fair, I'd outgrow my clothes in a week.' Pen laughed, some of the ease of the prior evening returning to her. She'd not realised how much she'd relied on the fair last night to direct their conversation, to give them something to talk about.

'See, you already know me far better than you did yesterday.' He passed her a meat pie.

'You have an unfair advantage on me, I'm afraid. I don't know anything about you.' He slanted her a teasing look. 'I know what we'll do. I propose of game of questions so that by the end of it, we shall no longer be strangers.' He grinned mischievously at her, offering the jug of ale. 'First, the rules. Rule number one: we shall take turns asking each other questions. Rule number two: we must answer with the truth. Our honour requires it. Rule number three: our honour also requires the question cannot be refused. I'll go first.' He stretched out to his full length before the fire, his dark head propped in a large hand, looking indolent and perhaps a bit smug. He was too certain of himself for his own good and too certain of her. Perhaps he was used to women always following his lead. Her mother had always said a gentleman must never be too sure of himself when it came to a woman's attentions. A little dose of humility was a welcome quality in a man.

Pen decided to do something about that humility. '*You* will go first?' she teased. 'What happened to ladies first?' She lifted the jug to her lips and took a swallow before passing it back, wiping her mouth on the back of her hand. How many governesses would cringe if they could see her now? '*I* will start, thank you.' She cleared her throat in mock authority. 'Question one: Why did you notice me at the fair?'

Chapter Five

Matthew laughed at her audacity, a low rumbling sound that shot through her with a bolt of warmth, like his lips on her knuckles. 'You're just going to start with the hard stuff, aren't you, Em? No easing into it with the usual "what's your favourite colour?" or "what do you like to eat"?'

'No, absolutely not.' Pen shrugged, boldly unapologetic. Between the ale and the fire, she was losing her nervousness. Surely, if he'd wanted something from her, he would have taken it last night and forgone the trouble of a second meeting. 'Answer the question, Matthew. You're stalling.'

'All right.' His smile melted her and her boldness was in jeopardy. She'd poked the sleeping bear and now he was going to make her pay. His eyes lingered on her, amber pools, rich and deep, inviting her to drown in him, with him, for him. 'I liked how you moved. Even beneath that cloak there was grace and I liked how you looked at the goods. You had a reverent appreciation for them. I thought to myself, "There's a woman who knows how to enjoy herself, a woman who takes nothing for granted."' His words were as bold as his gaze, searing her with a heat that had nothing to do with the fire and everything to do with the man stretched out beside her. Good lord, she must be as red as one of Wadesbridge's roses.

He smiled, proof enough that she was flushed. 'You asked, Em. Now, it's my turn.' His grin widened and she held her breath. She'd been too daring with her question. He would make her pay. She'd have to be on her guard, careful not to give anything away that might alert him to who she was, or what she was. 'What was your favourite part of the evening?'

She let out her breath with a relieved sigh. There was nothing to fear there. She could answer simply and honestly. 'Watching the glassblower. My turn. What is—?'

'No, wait. That's not fair,' Matthew broke in

with laughing chagrin. 'You have to say more than that. I gave you details.'

'That was your choice. The rule was to tell the truth, not to offer details—that was entirely optional.' It was an option she could have exercised as well. She could have said she'd liked his hand at her waist as they'd watched the demonstration, that she'd liked feeling the heat and power of his body behind her, that it had made her feel safe despite not knowing him. But to say those things exposed her too thoroughly. Wasn't she exposed enough as it was? Perhaps he'd only said those things to trick her into reciprocating.

His amber eyes narrowed in speculation as he gave the issue feigned consideration of the most serious sort. 'Well, perhaps I must concede the point. *This time.*' The glint in his eyes said she wouldn't win that argument twice. He was on to her. She'd have to tread cautiously.

'In return, I'll take it easy on you, for now. I'll ask you something basic. What's your favourite colour?'

'Maybe I won't take it easy on *you*, Em, with my answer.' His reply was low, private, just for her. She loved the way it caressed her name. *Em*. But that wasn't really her name any more than Matthew was his. She couldn't lose sight of that. They might be telling each other bold things beside the fire, but they were still strangers. 'My favourite colour is sea green, the colour of the ocean on a sunny day, the colour of your eyes when they caught the glass-blower's flame, the colour of your eyes right now as you ponder whether or not my answer is flattery or truth.' He was definitely not taking it easy on her. Each answer he gave was a verbal seduction that went far beyond flirtatious banter. A lady shouldn't allow a man to talk like that. But she wasn't a lady, not here. Lady Penrose Prideaux was three miles away in the castle, lying down with a lavender cloth. Only Em was here and Em wasn't a lady. Em was just… Em. Em could allow the indiscretion, although she ought to protest just a bit to keep him honest.

'You shouldn't say such things.' She reached for the ale jug and took another swallow. She might start to believe them, that she was beautiful, enticing, that she could intrigue a man such as Matthew, a man who could have any woman he wanted on charm alone. The words would be easy to believe. She had nothing to compare them with.

'Why shouldn't I if they're true? You're a beautiful woman.' His hand reached out to stroke her cheek and she felt the game spiral out of her control, the conversation becoming one intimacy upon another: the fire, the floor picnic, the long stretch of his body alongside the hearth, the truth game. Even the rain outside had contributed to the cosy familiarity of their grey-skied afternoon.

'My question. If you could only travel to one other place in the world, where would you go, Em?'

She finished her pasty, thinking hard. When she had her answer she licked her fingers. No doubt somewhere in England another governess fainted. 'Venice.'

'Why?'

'That's two questions, sir,' she scolded, but there was no heat in it. 'I am willing to allow you this one transgression.' In truth, she might allow him more than one. Somehow during their questions, they'd moved closer together, their voices choosing to be low and private although nothing required it of them, their questions and answers becoming serious. 'I choose Venice because that is where the world still meets, where east comes together with west. I can find the silks of the Orient there, the spices of the Middle East, and the magic of Venice itself, a whole city built on a lagoon, with canals instead of roads. The best of the world is there.'

'Venice is past her zenith, an ageing queen,' Cassian probed. 'Perhaps you would be disappointed? It stinks in the summer.'

She shook her hair forward over one shoulder and began to comb through it with her fingers. 'No, Venice is like me. I, too, am an ageing queen. Girls younger than me are married, have children, while I am tucked away at home, waiting and waiting and nothing comes.'

'Waiting for what? What do you think will come?' His question was a whisper barely audible above the crack of the fire.

'For adventure, for life to start again or perhaps for the first time. My father is a man full of fear. He fears for me, he wants to keep me safe, but it has turned my home into a prison.' How freeing it was to talk to him, to tell him things she'd shared with no one, not even Phin, out of fear of making her father look bad to others. Perhaps sometimes it was easier to trust a stranger with one's secrets. Matthew didn't know Lady Penrose Prideaux, didn't know the father of whom she spoke, or the legacy of fear she referred to.

Matthew gave her a lazy smile. 'You didn't tell me the whole truth earlier, Em.'

'I told you I came here today to conquer fear, so that I would not be ruled by it,' she protested.

'Like your father? Yes. But you didn't tell me about the adventure part.' His eyes were on her mouth again. 'Am I your adventure? Remember, you must answer truthfully.'

She licked her lips, unsure how to answer. To say yes might be to objectify him. He might feel used. To say no would be a lie. 'I've never met anyone like you who has seen the world I want to see. You are my adventure in the very best of ways.'

'And you are mine.' He reached for her, drawing her down alongside of him, their bodies stretched out before the fire. 'In the very best of ways,' he echoed.

Her breath caught at the nearness of him, the sheer size of him. Matthew was a big man, built like a hero; broad through the shoulders, strong in the chest. Achilles or Odysseus, she thought, straight from the stanzas of the *Iliad*. This was not proper, to lie with a man before the fire, to see his every thought flicker in his eyes, to let him rest his hand at her hip, his thumb massaging low on her abdomen. It was not proper to resent the layers of clothing that kept them separated. But this had never been about being proper. If it had been, she'd never have come at all.

'Have you ever been kissed, Em?' His eyes were on her, intent on her answer. 'Remember, only the truth.' At his words, the game and its remaining questions were forgotten entirely. There was a new game to play.

Her answer was a mere whisper. 'No.' Who would dare to kiss Lady Penrose Prideaux, cloistered daughter of the Earl of Redruth? But here in this cottage, Em was a woman who belonged to no one but herself, who ate meat pasties with handsome men at fairs, who admired Venetian glass-blowers and met with strange men in abandoned cottages to play games of revelation.

'Would you like to be?' came the question,

the dare. It would be easy to close the remaining distance, to part her lips, to issue the invitation he was asking for without a word. But he'd want the words. He would want to hear her consent. 'Would you, Em?'

She brought her hand up to stroke the stubble of his cheek, her own voice pitched low and throaty. 'You are terrible with rules. It's *my* turn to ask the question.'

His eyes darkened, guessing her game. 'Then, ask, Em.'

'Will you kiss me?'

A smile shimmered across his face. 'Absolutely. It would be my privilege.' A tilt of her head, a parting of her lips, and his mouth was there on hers, inviting her to join him in tasting one another. She gave him her mouth, all of it, savouring the remnants of sweet ale on his lips, the tease of his tongue as he explored her depths, the press of his hand cradling her jaw, the deepening of the kiss a reminder of their afternoon, an afternoon filled with simple pleasures, meat pies and conversations, and she didn't want it to end. A purr of desire purled up from her throat as she arched into him, her body wanting more of his touch, of him. She'd never been so warm, so hungry for another's touch. He would burn her and she would flame for him gladly.

She did flame for him, for a while, one kiss leading to another kiss and another as their mouths and hands explored one another. She could have lain there all afternoon, revelling in those kisses, those touches. She would have burned for him if he'd asked, but he did not. Instead, he separated from her, breaking the kisses, the touches, his own eyes dark.

A wave of desperation welled in her. She did not want the kiss to end. If she did not take her chance now, when? His hand brushed her cheek, pushing a loose strand of hair behind her ear. 'It grows late. We don't need to rush. We have tomorrow and the day after that and the day after that. We have as long as we need,' Matthew whispered his promise and helped her up from the floor, but his gaze said he was as reluctant as she to end the afternoon.

He gathered up her dry cloak and draped it over her shoulders, his hands lingering in his familiar gesture. 'Will you allow me to give you a ride home? I have my horse out back.'

She turned beneath his touch, called to action

with sudden urgency at the risk of exposure. As tempting as it was, it was the one thing she could not allow. 'No. Please, Matthew, I must insist on this discretion. You cannot follow me home, not even the briefest of distances.' If anyone recognised her with him, word would reach her father before she even made it home and there would never be another afternoon like this. 'Please, kiss me goodbye here.' And maybe by the time she was home she'd have her wits back.

Chapter Six

He was going to need a new strategy to outwit Redruth and get the earl's attention. The bliss of the afternoon had given him a break from the situation with Redruth, but now it was time to get back to business. All the standard methods of persuasion had failed with the earl. Cassian drained his tankard and called for more as a tavern wench sashayed by with a swing of lush hips and a saucy smile. 'Another for my friend as well.' Cassian winked at Inigo seated across from him at the table. 'We have much to discuss, we've got to keep our throats wet.'

'You're in a good mood despite the setback today.' Inigo eyed him with his usual scepticism. 'You weren't this pleasant when you rode out this afternoon. Your mood was downright foul, if I recall. To what do we owe this change of disposition?'

'Fresh air.' Cassian shrugged non-committally, wanting to keep Em and his secret rendezvous to himself a little while longer. The afternoon had carried a quiet eroticism in its simplicity—two people talking, two strangers moving from the unknown to the known through conversation before a fire. That conversation had led to a kiss and that kiss to more kisses. Cassian didn't kid himself that the setting alone had been the chief contributor to the direction the afternoon had taken. Not just any woman, not just any rainy day would have kept him floating on air hours later. He was too experienced for that. It was *she*, the mysterious Em, who was responsible for his mood. He'd wrapped himself in the memory of her when he'd left the cottage: her mouth, her touch, her voice when she'd whispered her dreams: *'I want to go to Venice. I want adventure.'* He would see her again tomorrow. He could hardly wait. It had been a long time since he could hardly wait to see a woman.

'All right, keep your secrets.' Inigo laughed. 'I can see you're not going to tell me about it.' The serving girl came back with the ales and another round of smiles that turned to a pout when Cassian didn't reciprocate. Cassian slid her extra coins for her disappointment and sent her away. Ales settled, they could return to their discussion without interruption.

'I've tried letters of enquiry, I've tried raising my offer, I've tried outlining all the benefits. None of it has worked. He insists the land remain in the family even though it is unentailed. It was bought by his grandfather and hasn't been used for anything since his grandfather passed.' Cassian threw up his hands. 'I can't decide what upsets me more: that the earl is intractable or that the land is just sitting there rotting for no reason.'

'Well, not really "no reason",' Inigo, always the voice of logic, put in slowly as if he knew the words would be upsetting. 'It's part of his daughter's dowry. Perhaps he cannot simply give it away without damaging her prospects.' Inigo knew money intimately. He made money, invested money, for himself and for others. Better than anyone, Inigo understood people's often intense, irrational attachment to things. Hadn't Inigo called him out on those very grounds yesterday?

Cassian rolled his eyes. 'Her prospects would

be improved twofold if the money received for the sale was put back into the dowry. The company has offered twice what the land's worth.'

'Money can be frittered away, it can disappear before you know it, even a substantial sum like that. Perhaps her father feels that land will last where money will not. He's not wrong,' Inigo put in, playing the devil's advocate.

Cassian nodded, willing to concede the point. 'Perhaps. But that doesn't solve my problem. How do I convince him to sell me the land? He did not care for my plans at all. In fact, I think being open about what I wanted to do with the land hurt my case more than helped it.' Cassian took a swallow of ale and recounted the unpleasant letter, enumerating Redruth's complaints. 'He sees my plans as wholesale corruption, not progress,' Cassian concluded. The thought of not acquiring the land ate at him daily. What would he do if he couldn't break through to the earl?

'He doesn't want to lose control of the land,' Inigo ventured. 'That's what's at the heart of this. Have you thought of leasing the land from him? Perhaps a ninety-nine-year lease like they do with property in London? The land would still be his technically, but you would own any development that occurs on it. The land would be yours for three generations. Your grandsons could tussle it out with his great-grandsons after you're long gone.' Inigo laughed.

'And if he refuses?' Cassian queried, not entirely hopeful.

Inigo arched eyebrow. 'Plan B. I thought we settled that yesterday. You can always marry for it. It would be less of a tussle in three generations if it was all in the family.'

Cassian shook his head. 'I've already thought of that and, no, I just couldn't.' Especially not after this afternoon. He did not want to sell himself, not when there was such honest pleasure to be had with a woman he chose of his own accord.

Inigo leaned across the table and lowered his voice. 'Will you listen before you dismiss the idea out of hand? Consider all the pieces aligning at just this moment before you discard the option.'

'Are you a fortune teller now?' Cassian retorted sharply.

'Do you want to hear the rest of my news or not?' Inigo was undaunted. They'd been friends too long for him to be put off easily. It was what made them such good business partners as well. 'In fact, marrying for the land could be the piece of serendipity you're looking for. I did some more digging today after you left. The earl might not be open to selling the land, but he is open to marrying off his daughter, which could be the reason he isn't keen at this moment to separate the land from the dowry.' Inigo threw a quick glance around the taproom to be sure no one was listening in. 'He's been bringing suitors to Castle Byerd. It's all very hushed up. But Lord Wadesbridge was invited to tea yesterday.'

'Wadesbridge is too old,' Cassian shot back, but he didn't miss the smug gleam in Inigo's eyes.

'Perhaps that's what the daughter thought too. Perhaps that's why there's a dinner party tonight at Castle Byerd with some of the area's finest *young* gentlemen in attendance.' He smiled, pleased with himself, much to Cassian's chagrin. Cassian hated when Inigo might have a point.

'And we weren't invited? Who is finer than ourselves, if we're being blunt? It makes no sense that we're cooling our heels at the Red Dragon while young men of lesser standing are dining at Byerd.' Cassian played the devil's advocate.

Inigo chuckled. 'Actually, it makes perfect sense. I've made no bones about the fact that I've no intentions to marry in the near future and, if Redruth wants Vennor Penlerick for his daughter, the earl will have to go to London to get him, which would require Redruth doing the very things he hates the most: socialising and entertaining. If he wants a duke for her, you're the only real candidate out of the three of us who remains unwed. But it's too soon to go after you. If you'd shown up tonight, you would have intimidated the field. If he wants you, he'll want to draw your attention, make you inquisitive enough to want to meet the girl everyone else is meeting. Men are often attracted to something they have to compete for. It's simple supply and demand.' Inigo looked pleased with his analysis, and Cassian had to admit his friend was probably right. It did not, however, make the prospect more appealing.

'Perhaps I should just let all those swains

have her.' Which suited Cassian just fine. He didn't want to marry for an alliance.

Inigo shrugged. 'That's up to you. All I am saying is that the window of opportunity is open at present. Redruth is eager to marry her off *this* Season,' Inigo pressed. 'If you're going to build that amusement garden here, you need that land now. Time is of the essence for the both of you. Marriage might be the way to convince him. He might not like your plans once he knows you and the land company are one and the same, but he will like your title. *That* hasn't been on the table in your negotiations. It could change everything and it would keep his land in the family where he feels as though he can assert *some* control. I'd wager in a few years' time, when he sees that his perceived harms haven't come to fruition and that you're making money hand over fist *for him*, he'll forget he ever disliked the idea. He'll think his son-in-law is a genius.'

Cassian shook his head, thinking of a caramel-haired minx kissing him beside the gamekeeper's fire with her hungry mouth, and her love of adventure. 'You make it sound so easy. I should simply walk in and trade my title for his daughter's dowry and break ground after my honeymoon.' It would give him everything he wanted.

'It can be that easy,' Inigo replied evenly. 'Other men do it all the time.'

'*Other* men.' Cassian threw the words back at him. 'Since when have we ever aspired to be like other men?' That was the flaw in Inigo's analysis. 'We're the Cornish Dukes, four fathers and four sons sworn to living by a higher code in life and in love,' Cassian reminded him. 'Or have you so quickly forgotten the legacy of Richard Penlerick?'

He'd gone too far there. Inigo's blue eyes sparked and narrowed. 'We all loved Richard, me no less than any of us,' Inigo snapped. 'Of course I haven't forgotten. I have not forgotten how he encouraged Eaton's pursuit of a conservatory or how he supported your endeavour to raise up the economy. Perhaps he would consider an alliance with Redruth a worthy investment for the goal.'

'A marriage without love?' Cassian spat the words with disgust. He was too raw from his afternoon with Em. Discussing the idea of courting another for monetary gain so soon after coming from Em's arms seemed a betrayal of their game in the cottage.

'Perhaps it's all in how you view it. Maybe you've been looking at it wrong? Why should we view the event of a wedding as the apex of love? Is everything else downhill from there? Why not view the wedding as the beginning of the journey *to* love? You have the next fifty years to fall in love with your bride,' Inigo counselled.

'Says the man who doesn't intend to wed any time soon.' Cassian gave an exaggerated sniff. 'Methinks I smell a little hypocrisy in the air.' He gave his friend a half-smile. 'You would have a hard time selling that rationale to Cador and Rosenwyn, or to Eaton and Eliza, or to any of our parents.'

'That doesn't make it untrue.' Inigo grinned, enjoying their debate too much. 'Now, tell me your secret. Who is she?'

'What makes you think a woman is involved?' Cassian felt a sudden wave of protectiveness with regards to Em.

'What other reason would you have to be so irritated over marriage and the principles of love?' Inigo was enjoying this too much. His friend called for another round. 'This one's on me. Tell me everything. How did you meet? How long has this been going on?' At Inigo's grin the tension that had underlaid the heat of their discussion eased. They'd been friends since boyhood, friends for too long to let disagreement sour the evening. They'd disagreed before and they likely would again, but they would still and always be friends.

'I met her at the St Piran's Day fair. We walked, we talked, I met her again today and we spent the afternoon together. She's incredible; she's beautiful, and witty, and she has a voice like smoke, low and throaty. I am meeting her again tomorrow.'

'Does she know who you are?' Inigo's scepticism was in full evidence, and Cassian knew where that line of questioning led. Inigo feared she was a fortune hunter. It was a well-meant sort of protection after Collin's ill-fated romance. But tonight, such caution was unnecessary.

'That's the best part...' Cassian leaned in '... I've taken precautions. We made up names for each other. She doesn't know I'm a viscount, heir to a dukedom. She is simply Em to me and I am Matthew to her. We can be our-selves.' Surely Inigo would understand why the principle of love mattered so greatly. 'Now you see why I can't simply storm Castle Byerd and carry off Redruth's daughter.'

'No, I don't see. You're not simply being yourself. You're being someone you made up.'

'It's not like that. We are still ourselves. *I* am myself, perhaps as I can never be with a soci-ety miss. We can talk and laugh and tell sto-ries and share our dreams. Only the names are false, everything else is true,' Cassian tried to explain, but even as the words came the argu-ment rang hollow.

'That's all well and good as far as it goes. But how far *does* it go?' Inigo asked. 'You can't possibly think anything comes of it. There can't be marriage. Even if the pleasure garden wasn't an issue, there couldn't be marriage.'

'Do you think I don't know that? Do you think I'm some green boy who falls in love with the first woman he lays down with?' Cas-sian snapped with more heat than he intended, perhaps because he knew Inigo was right, per-haps because those were the very thoughts he'd had today and had pushed away. He wanted to think only about today and tomorrow. If he thought beyond the day, beyond the immediate, he'd have to think about losing Em. He wasn't ready to think about that. He'd have to eventually, though.

'No, I don't think that. But I do see my friend perhaps hesitating on the brink of success and I have to wonder why. I have to wonder if this peasant girl isn't a distraction, a convenient foil that excuses him from not moving forward.' Inigo's voice was a low hiss. 'If today showed you anything it was that you are down to two choices. Marry the earl's daughter or build the park in Truro instead.' He paused. 'Or don't build it at all.'

'The last is not an option,' Cassian shot back. 'I know what my choices are, I don't need you to spell them out. I know the cottage affair can't last. But it's not May yet. I have until the Season starts to make up my mind.'

Inigo nodded. 'Fair enough.' A truce had been reached. Cassian knew his duty not only to his family, but to himself and to his brother and he would do it when the time came. But May seemed ages away from the cold March weather. There was always the possibility that Redruth might relent before then.

Inigo pushed back from the table. 'I think I'll call it a night. I have to be at Wheal Karrek early tomorrow to meet with the mine's share-holders to discuss Eliza's latest plans.'

Cassian rose with him, taking the change in conversation as an olive branch. He didn't want to part with his friend on poor terms. 'Eliza is keeping you busy. I thought she'd be back to the mines full time by now.' She'd asked for Inigo's help with the mines six months ago when she'd wed Eaton and become Lady Lyn-ford. It was supposed to have been a tempo-rary arrangement.

Inigo laughed and shook his head. 'Her new mine schools and her new marriage are taking up more time than she anticipated. I've never seen Eaton happier and she positively glows. Her daughter, Sophie, is at Kitto's conservatory now as a day student. I heard her play the other day. She's very talented. Cador Kitto positively drools over her.'

The conversation carried them out into the crisp night air. They talked of the upcoming spring recital in April and Cador's impending fatherhood at the end of the month. Cassian clapped Inigo on the shoulder. 'Thank you for coming out with me tonight. Whether or not I agree with you, I appreciate your advice. As always, it is insightful, old friend.'

Inigo nodded. 'And as always, I am happy to give it. I don't envy you your dilemma. Just remember to think with your head.'

Cassian watched Inigo disappear into the dark before getting his horse and setting out for The Elms. Overhead the stars were bright white points of light in a black sky. At a fork in the road, the left steered towards home, but the right steered towards Castle Byerd and the little dinner party to which he'd not been invited. For several moments he played with the idea of just turning up, but it would accomplish nothing other than to risk further alienating Redruth. Cassian turned his horse towards home. Storming the castle would have to wait for another day. His heart wasn't in it. If his heart was anywhere, it was on the cliffs at the gamekeeper's cottage with Em.

The moment Pen returned to Castle Byerd, she wanted to be back in the cottage. Byerd was abuzz with more activity than it had seen in years. 'For the dinner party, my lady,' one maid said, rushing by with an urn of flowers. The dinner party? This was the first she'd heard of it.

Pen followed the maid into the dining room, a large, formal affair of a chamber that was seldom used. Today, the walnut doors were thrown open, polished silver and china marched the length of the pristine white linen on the table, urns of flowers decorated the sideboards in early spring splendour. The room wasn't being prepared. It was *ready*. For whom, for what? She hadn't done any menus. She counted the chairs. Dinner for fourteen? Pen began to panic. Had she forgotten? Was Cook, even now, wondering what she was supposed to prepare for the guests? Pen furrowed her brow, trying to remember. Had she even seen a guest list?

'There you are!' Her maid, Margery, hurried in. 'Thank goodness you're here. Where have you been? Never mind. It doesn't matter now. A new dress arrived for you and I've already drawn your bath. With luck, it will still be hot. You needn't worry, there's still time to get you ready.' Ready, like the dining room clothed in its best.

'Ready for what?' Pen whispered in half-horror. They never entertained. Yesterday it had been tea with Wadesbridge and now a dinner party. It was as if the castle gates had been flung wide and the world let in.

'For you, my lady.' Margery took her by the arm, leading her to the stairs, her voice low. 'Your father has guests for dinner. All of them with sons.'

Chapter Seven

All of them with sons. Her father was throwing a dinner party and she was the main course, a beautifully dressed lamb led to the slaughter with her hair a high pile of curls atop her head and the rest of her turned out in a gown of shot Parma silk whose iridescence created the impression of being simultaneously equal parts violet and blue. Pen fingered the pearls at her throat anxiously as Margery dabbed the smallest bit of rose-pink salve on her lips. 'There! You look a treat, miss. No one would ever guess you were out tramping the countryside all afternoon.'

No, no one would guess that she'd spent the afternoon sitting beside a fire, eating meat pies with a man whose name she didn't know, playing a flirtatious game of questions. Unconsciously, Pen's fingers drifted from her pearls to her lips. The elegant woman in the mirror didn't look at all like Em, like the woman who'd kissed Matthew in the cottage with her mouth, her tongue, her teeth, her body pressed to his begging for more than a kiss. She would give anything to be back in the cottage now, wrapped in Matthew's arms, a simple dinner on the scarred table. It was a far preferable scenario than facing the glittering formality awaiting her downstairs.

'Careful, miss, or you'll smudge the lip salve.' Margery slid her a sly look. 'We're lucky the fashion is for a more natural complexion these days. No one thinks twice about a lady with a little fresh wind on her cheeks.' Margery pursed her lips when Pen said nothing. 'Whoever he is, miss, your secret is safe with me whether you tell me or not. We've been through a lot since I've been your maid. It's a little late to start with secrets now when you come home with them written all over your face.'

'Was it that obvious?' Pen looked away from the mirror, seeking reassurance from Margery in a moment of panic.

Margery gave her a knowing smile. 'A smart woman knows the signs, miss. Puffed lips, a faraway look in the eyes. You were grinning from ear to ear. I'd never seen you look so happy, or so confused. It was as if you'd fallen from the sky and crashed into reality.' She had. It was exactly how she'd felt. One moment she'd been in paradise and the next in a hell.

There was a soft knock at the door followed by her brother's voice. 'Pen, are you ready? It's time to go down.' The door opened and Phin stepped inside dressed in evening clothes, his walnut hair brushed back from his handsome face with its blue eyes and kind smile. He let out a sound of approval. 'You look stunning. All of Father's preparations will go to waste. I doubt anyone will notice the china and the silver and the food once they see you. The gentlemen won't be able to take their eyes off of you.'

'Perhaps I should change, then, put on something less attractive.' Pen's anxiety rose anew. She didn't want to be the centre of anyone's attentions except Matthew's. Especially when the attentions of those downstairs were driven by avarice. Given that she hadn't met any of the gentlemen here before tonight, it was safe to assume they were here for her dowry—she merely went along with it, a physical embodiment of her father's land and money.

Phin took her hand, misunderstanding the source of her anxiety. 'I know you haven't been out among society much, but you'll be fine. You know your manners and you have good conversation. You've hosted a few of Father's guests—this will be just like that, only there will be more of them. Everyone knows you've been in seclusion.'

He meant it kindly. Phin always met things kindly, but the words rankled and she bristled at the insinuation. 'I am not a wilting wallflower. Seclusion has been Father's choice, not mine. If it were up to me—'

'Yes,' Phin broke in with a laugh. 'I know. If it were up to you, you would have come with me on a Grand Tour of your own. Whatever those gentlemen downstairs think, I dare say they will be pleasantly surprised by you...' he chucked her gently under the chin '...and you, Pen, might be pleasantly surprised by one of them if you allowed it. Hmm?' he said encouragingly with a gentle scold. 'You and Father are the two most stubborn people I know. Make sure you are resisting his efforts for the right reasons. You are young and untried. You know nothing of men. Why not allow yourself to be guided by those who do? You can't think Father would marry you to someone who would be cruel, who wouldn't appreciate you as you ought to be appreciated?'

He ushered her out of the room and into the hallway. 'Most of the gentlemen are friends of mine.' Phin was still offering reassurances, but Pen felt as if she were walking to her execution. 'Father thought you needed to meet young men closer to your own age. He said you felt Wadesbridge was too old.'

That sealed it. She was condemned by her own words. The argument for younger men had been *her* argument and now her father had answered it by serving up a room full of them.

'You're not helping, Phin,' she chided him as they made their way to the curving sweep of the main staircase. Already she could hear muted conversation in the drawing room. 'I want to choose more than my mate when the time comes. I want to choose my own destiny. Father seems to think marriage is the only destiny for me and I disagree. There are too many places on the map to see.' Matthew had not baulked at such a sentiment at the fair. He'd done the opposite. He'd encouraged it with stories of his own travels. Her hand went to her throat, forgetting that she wore pearls tonight, that her blown-glass heart was tucked away upstairs.

At the entrance to the drawing room, Pen paused, taking a deep breath and settling her nerves. She was not afraid to meet these men, she was only afraid of what meeting them represented. Her father had taken her request for younger men to heart, which meant only one thing: after two years of rather sporadic matchmaking efforts, her father was in earnest to see her wed. At her ear, Phin whispered final words of encouragement. 'Don't worry, Pen, I'll be right beside you.'

Phin was as good as his promise. He stayed next to her, escorting her from group to group, making introductions and ensuring that she needn't stay with any one group too long. She was a blue-violet butterfly in a room of neutral colours, flitting from one cluster to another as she tried to keep the names straight. When dinner was announced, she was taken in by Nigel Harrington, heir to the Baron Lynton who seemed to know everything there was to know about goats and cheese, and nearly everything there was to know about fishing.

'But if you want real fishing, nothing beats salmon from Bodmin Moor,' an arrogant blond put in from across the table. He'd been trying hard to catch her eye all night and now she was forced to give it. 'The River Camel is cold, it makes for more fat on the fish, better taste,' the blond counselled. The footmen came and took away the dishes, replacing them with the next course. The conversation continued as the men debated the best rivers, and then moved on to debate the best fish—salmon or trout— with an enthusiasm that stunned her. Surely, they didn't think such a display *impressed* her?

Pen set down her wine glass and took advantage of a brief break in the discussion. 'If only men devoted such passion to the fate of the poor as they devote to their fishing, we might right a many great injustices in this world.' She smiled broadly, hoping to engage the support of the women at the table. Some of the young men, those who lived nearby, had come with their parents.

'That's why they have us, my dear,' Nigel

Harrington's mother spoke up. 'Charity begins at home and the home is the woman's domain.'

'Hear, hear!' the arrogant blond's father toasted and the conversation moved back to trout and salmon. She was relieved when the table turned so she could speak to the gentleman on her other side, a Mr Abel Cunforth, but her relief was short-lived on that front. All he wanted to talk about was himself. At least after the first question, she didn't need to worry about carrying the conversation. In that regard he was as easy to talk to as every other man here was. One simply had to initiate and then the gentlemen picked up the conversation and ran with it. Was this their idea of getting to know her? Or of her getting to know them, not their bank accounts?

Pen smiled and nodded. She made the right noises in the right places. Didn't a single man in this room understand that small talk was more than rolling out one's pedigree and accomplishments? That small talk was about establishing a sense of ease? How did one *feel* when they conversed with someone else? It was about rhythm, about the give and take of the conversation. There was none of that here, only

Mr Cunforth giving and giving facts about himself and her on the receiving end trying to be interested. Not a man in this room knew better. But Matthew had. At the fair and again today, they'd had real conversations.

It wasn't just the kisses she was looking forward to tomorrow, but the continuation of their talks. What would they discuss tomorrow? What might he ask her? What would she tell him? And the reverse as well. What would she learn about him? Talking with Matthew was like peeling back the petals of a rosebud until it was in full bloom. Talking with Abel Cunforth, to the arrogant blond or Mr Nigel Harrington was nothing like that.

What would Matthew think if he saw her in this room, dressed in silk, surrounded by these buffoons? What would he think if he knew she was supposed to marry one of them? Pen took another swallow of wine. He would think she was above his touch. He would think he had no right to her. Would he feel betrayed? He thought Em was a woman who could choose whom she spent her time with, perhaps the daughter of an artisan or a farmer, a woman who could welcome the attentions of a small, landowning squire. He did not imagine himself the subordinate in their relationship in regards to rank or standing, certainly not in experience. He could not find out differently. She liked that they were equals in the cottage. Yet, sitting here as Penrose Prideaux surrounded by suitors left her with a niggling sense of guilt that somehow she was misleading him. But she couldn't tell him or she'd lose him.

'I think the poorhouses do a great service,' Abel Cunforth was saying. 'They offer the poor two meals a day and give them employment to keep them off the streets. If anything, we need stricter laws and less hand-holding of the poor.'

'Have you been to a poor house, Mr Cunforth? Have you eaten the gruel that passes for food?' Pen broke into his political ramblings.

'Why, no, of course not.' Mr Cunforth gave her an odd look so compelling she began to wonder if she really had grown two heads.

'I think if people were paid a wage they could live on in exchange for their labours we might all benefit,' Pen offered. 'I hear London is expensive. I can't imagine earning a pittance *and* being expected to afford rent and food on it let alone clothes or medicines in a big city.'

'Then they shouldn't live there,' was Cunforth's answer.

'It's where the jobs are, sir,' Pen replied. 'How can they support themselves in the countryside when mines can no longer produce and land is being enclosed? What work is there for them? It is my opinion that Parliament is driving the poor to the cities like a herd of sheep.' A footman reached for her wine glass and turned away to refill it.

'Your opinion, eh?' Cunforth was salty. She'd upset him with her thoughts. He wiped his mouth with his napkin. 'Well, perhaps that's precisely why we don't allow women to vote. You'd all be tucking the poor in with beef stew every night if you had your way.'

As the footman made to return her newly filled glass Pen made a deliberately careless gesture with her hand and a fine white French wine drenched the thigh of Cunforth's dark evening breeches. 'Oh, I am so clumsy!' Pen exclaimed, making no move to offer a napkin. She tossed Cunforth a coy smile. 'Perhaps it *is* a good thing I don't vote. We can't have women spilling all of your male privileges to the masses. Looks like you might be the one tucking in early tonight.'

Across the table, Phin shot her a look and mouthed the words 'play nice'. But Pen didn't care. Anyone who set themselves above another simply because they'd had the luck to be born into wealth wasn't worth her consideration.

As soon as the last plate was cleared, Pen wasted no time rising and taking the women to the drawing room so the men could buttonhole the port around the table and congratulate themselves on having impressed her, no doubt certain that she'd been mesmerised by their ability to debate salmon and trout and insult the poor.

This would be her life if she didn't put a stop to it. For two years now, she'd been ignoring the reality, hoping that somehow things would simply change. But if there was going to be any change, it would have to come from her. If she didn't stand up and fight for what she wanted, no one else would. Pen surreptitiously fingered her lips and thought of Matthew. Now there was a man who knew how to treat a woman. She was hungry to be back in the cottage with him. Tomorrow couldn't come soon enough.

Chapter Eight

Pen arrived at the cottage first this time, breathless from a hard walk fuelled by rising distress as much as it was the anticipation of seeing Matthew again. Breakfast that morning had been a disaster with her father asking which of the fine *young* men she preferred and ended with him suggesting another round of dinner parties when she said none of them seemed to suit, or did she want to revisit the merits of an older, more stable gentleman like Wadesbridge? A visit could be arranged to see Trescowe in April. He would send a note.

Pen had barely kept her temper on a leash. She didn't want any of them. That had been the crux of their disagreement this morning. She saw clearly now it wasn't that her father didn't understand her argument. It was that he didn't accept it. He felt she should be guided by *his* choice. Would she never be free except in these clandestine moments? It made the prospect of seeing Matthew, a man of *her* choosing, all the sweeter even as it reaffirmed for her what she'd realised last night: she had to stand up for herself. She could no longer be a neutral party in her fate.

Pen unpacked the basket she'd brought and spread an old checked cloth on the scarred table. She reasoned it was her turn to provide the picnic since Matthew had provided it twice now; at the fair and yesterday. The cloth was faded and the edges were showing early signs of fraying, but it suited the rustic quality of the room. The cottage was no place for pristine white linen even if she could have brought such a thing without revealing herself. Em in her plain dress and cloak was not a woman who had spotless Irish linen. It was all part of the fantasy. Or *the deception*, her conscience prodded. Fantasy and deception were fast becoming different sides of the same coin. Pen preferred not to think about the discrepancy today. If this was a lie, then it was the most exciting, most pleasurable lie she'd ever known.

She laid out bread, cheese, half of a mince pie

she'd found left over in the kitchens and a jug of cider purloined from the cellar. Pen smiled, stepping back to survey her handiwork. The table looked homey with its food and cloth. She rubbed her arms to stay warm and wished she knew how to start a fire, but that would have to wait until Matthew arrived. *If he arrived.* Perhaps he'd changed his mind or something more important had come up, or perhaps he'd realised how silly this was, how futile. Now she knew how Matthew had felt yesterday when she was late. The worry was another reminder that they owed each other nothing, not even loyalty.

His big stallion came into view and the knot in her stomach untied itself. She waited for him in the doorway as he tethered his horse, tying it out of sight from the road. In her relief, it took all of her willpower not to run to him, not to throw herself and her troubles into his arms. He would not admire that. They didn't have that kind of relationship, or any kind of relationship. They were simply two strangers. It was all she could allow them to be.

'Em, how are you? You're early today.' He kissed her on the cheek, pleased to see her, and her anxiety melted. This close to him, she could smell the masculine scent of wind and the earthy odour of a wet Cornish spring on his hair. She breathed it in. There was strength in simply being with him, in having these moments no matter how fleeting, no matter how contrived.

They stepped inside, and he smiled when he saw the table set with her small meal. 'You've been busy.'

'It was my turn to bring the lunch.' His appreciation made butterflies flutter in her stomach, his compliment meaning so much more than the false flattery she'd heard last night at dinner.

'I'll light a fire. You look cold.' His first thoughts were of her, so unlike the gentlemen last night. He set to it with an envious dexterity, producing flint from the deep pocket of his greatcoat. She told herself she watched to remember so she could do it on her own next time, but in truth she would have watched anyway just see him move. He was all strength and grace, so much grace for a big man. The fire came to life beneath his hands, warming the room and adding to the domesticity of doing for one another. It was an intimacy she was unfamiliar with in a house full of servants.

'Are you hungry?' Pen sliced bread at the table, putting pieces alongside hunks of cheese on the tin plates she'd brought. This was all part of the fantasy today—playing house, playing at being a commoner, at living the simple life.

He took off his greatcoat and hung it from his chair. She let herself imagine he was her husband, home from work, perhaps, from the fields overseeing a harvest. 'Yes, I could eat.' He laughed. 'I assume you guessed that. As you've noted, I can always eat. This is quite a step up from yesterday. We're progressing. We have plates today, mugs, a tablecloth, a knife. This is fine living.' He glanced at the fire. 'It would be a shame to eat this excellent food cold. Shall I grill the bread and melt the cheese?' He took the plates to the fire and Pen watched as he arranged the bread with its cheese on top of the grate. Satisfied, he turned to her. 'Come sit, Em. I've had a deuced difficult day. Tell me something interesting to take my mind off it. What did you do last night after you left me?'

Pen took her seat by the fire, that little pinch of guilt she'd felt last evening pinching her a little harder. She could not tell him what she'd done. She hated that, but even more she hated the idea of lying to him, so she said instead, 'Perhaps it would be best if you talked about your difficulty? We might find a solution together.'

He pulled the bread from the fire and put it on a plate for her. 'Very well, my trouble goes like this. There is something I want to purchase, but the gentleman who owns it is unwilling to sell it to me no matter what price I offer.'

Pen bit into her toasted bread and cheese with a murmur of delight. 'Mmm, this is ambrosia.' She swallowed and turned her attentions back to his problem. 'Do you know why this gentleman resists?'

'He doesn't agree with what I want the thing for.' Matthew poked at the fire. 'I've tried persuading him, showing him that my purpose is beneficial to so many, but he only sees the bad. Worst of all, I feel we've reached a point in the discussion where he simply won't listen any more.'

Pen nodded. She knew the feeling all too

well. She'd felt that way this morning at breakfast. 'I know. Sometimes I think my father has stopped listening to me. It's as if he's already decided my fate and he's just going through the motions now to placate me.' The only thing that kept her from believing that in full was Phin, who quite often stood between her and her father when they were at loggerheads, as he'd done last night. When Phin had an opinion, her father listened.

'What do you do when that happens?' Matthew pulled his own bread out of the fire, crisp and golden.

She thought for a moment. 'I find an ally. Perhaps you need one, too, someone whom your stubborn gentleman *will* listen to. For me, it's my brother. Sometimes it's not the message that matters, but the messenger. Two people can say the same thing, but be heard differently. Is there someone this man could be persuaded by? Perhaps he has a son or a friend who also shares your wisdom, but to whom he might be more receptive?'

He seemed to mull the idea over as he ate. 'An ally is a good idea, I just don't think I have one.'

'Then we'll keep thinking of a solution. Surely, between the two of us, we can come up with something.' She stood, brushing her hands on her skirt. 'I'll bring over the pie and cider.'

'You needn't wait on me.' He half rose, setting aside his plate, but she stalled him with a hand to his chest and a smile.

'Sit. You're still eating. Let me. I want to.' She did want to. She liked serving him, talking to him, helping him. He treated her like a partner, someone he could confide in. She was no one's partner at home. At home, she was swaddled, protected, something precious to be hidden away. No one would think of burdening her with their troubles.

Cassian sat back down with a laugh. 'You're bossy.' But he liked that she was assertive and willing to stand up to him, willing to solve problems with him even if he couldn't make use of her suggestion. So many of the women he knew were sycophants more interested in his title and what came with him than in *him*.

She returned with a large slice of pie and something primal stirred within Cassian. A man could find happiness in a simple life: a one-room cottage, four pieces of furniture, one good woman to partner him in life. Who needed ballrooms and titles when one had that? It was a potent fantasy he was spinning and an impossible one. Hadn't his conversation with Inigo last night been about this very subject? The finite limitations of this *affaire*? Dukes and their heirs weren't entitled to simple lives. Their lives were complicated, their alliances complicated; it was all part of their duty, their sacrifice for the greater good.

Despite his vast resources, this woman, like his land, was beyond him; she was a virgin he couldn't marry, a virgin whom he could not take to bed out of personal honour. No matter how low her birth, he would not risk leaving her with a child. Even if he compromised her, he couldn't marry her. Yet he wanted her: her company, her time, her kisses.

'Tell me,' he said once she'd settled in her chair. 'What does your father not listen to you about?' There was something different about her today. Perhaps it was that she was starting to grow used to him, more confident about their companionship, or perhaps it was something else he couldn't put his finger on. Maybe it was that the conversation was different today. At the fair, the conversation had been a general trading of tales. Yesterday had been a flirty game of questions. But today, the discussion was far deeper. This was about real life, things they dealt with in the world beyond the cottage walls, things their real *selves* dealt with. The line between the reality and their fabricated identities was very slowly starting to blur.

She shook her head. 'I don't want to tell you,' she demurred, perhaps in proof of that blurring. To tell would be to bring the other world too close, but Cassian was persistent.

'Why not? I told you about my problem. You can trust me.'

'It's not that.' She rose and collected the empty plates, suddenly restless. 'If I tell you, you will think I am fishing for something, although I assure you I am not.' She paused and set the plates on the table. 'This time here with you is important to me. I don't have much time and I don't want to ruin this.'

'You think telling me will ruin us?' Cassian was doubly curious now and worried. People only used phrases like running out of time when circumstances were dire. A horrible thought came to him. 'Are you ill?' Did she need money for a doctor? For medicines? A bolt of panic shot through him. Was Em dying?

'No, I am not ill,' she quickly disabused him. 'Oh, dear, I've worried you. I think I have to tell you now,' she blurted out the words. 'My father wants me to marry.'

Cassian should have felt enormous relief. To an extent he did. The tension that had welled so quickly in him had evaporated when she said she was not ill, but it had also been quickly replaced at the mention of marriage. 'To someone particular? Does he have the man picked out?' he tried to ask casually. It shouldn't come as a surprise. She was of age to marry, more than old enough, and it was the natural course of events. Yet, he didn't like the thought of his Em, his first-kissed Em, pledged to another.

'No one, not yet. But he's pushing for it.'

Cassian understood why she'd held back. She didn't want him to think she was looking for a proposal. 'It's all right, Em. We don't owe each other anything, no commitments.' This explained her need for the false identity, for the need to return home alone for fear of discovery.

'That's just it,' she said, 'I didn't want you to think you did.'

'We are just Em and Matthew,' he assured her. 'Nothing more.' The thought was less satisfying than it had been earlier, though. Em and Matthew could be nothing to each other. That had always been the case, implicitly acknowledged, never spoken of. It allowed them to be free. But it was less pleasant to contemplate when explicitly addressed. Freedom had suddenly become finite. This would be the ideal time to tell her about London, how he needed to leave at the end of April, but that seemed far off when viewed from the seventh of March, especially when it might end sooner. There might be no need at all to bring it up. He would bring it up, though, he promised himself, if the day drew closer.

She returned to the fire, and he drew her to him, pulling her on to his lap. He smiled, trying to take the new, furtive edge off the afternoon. Only three days in and already the clock was ticking. 'What else is your father stubborn about?'

She wrapped her arms about his neck and settled into him with a warm smile. Perhaps she, too, was eager to chase away reality and return to the fantasy. 'Pets. When we were growing up I wanted a dog badly, but he absolutely refused. No dogs in the house, he'd say. But I was desperate for one. I thought a dog could be my friend. After my brother left for school, the house was lonely.' It was the second time she'd mentioned her brother with fondness; her ally, her playmate. Cassian's throat thickened at thought of Collin. They'd been allies and playmates once too.

'I had great images of how it would be—my dog would wander around beside me, romp outdoors with me, lay by my bed at night, a constant companion, just like in the stories.' There was such wistfulness in her tone, Cassian suddenly wanted to shower her with a litter of puppies. Eaton's dog, Baldor, a magnificent hound with a nose for truffles, had just sired a new batch born a few weeks ago. She would love them.

'Since you didn't have a pup, how did you entertain yourself?' He liked the feel of her on his lap, her body against his. It was easy to talk to her, to listen to her. She was interesting and she didn't even know it. She had no need to dissemble and no desire to do it.

'I played with maps. You go to faraway places, but I dream of them. Seeing them on a map helps make them real.' She wasn't as low-born as he thought. Somewhere in his mind, a silent warning bell began to clang. A brother sent to school, access to maps, the ability to read, a father who wanted to arrange a marriage. These were not the acts of a peasant or an artisan. Yet she seemed to want for certain things. Her dress and cloak were the same each day and they were showing their wear. *And she's a virgin*, his conscience nudged. Might she be the daughter of gentry down on their luck?

If it wasn't out of respect for the game of Em and Matthew, and out of respect for her need for privacy, he could probably determine her identity if she were gentry. It was tempting to try. But that would end the game. She didn't want to be exposed any more than he did. It was for the best. Knowing the truth of their identities would complicate things, especially now. If her father was eager for her to marry, and if her family was truly down on their luck, he'd look like a plum from heaven if they knew who he was. These two false names of theirs was all that kept the fantasy in place, a fantasy they were both desperate for, some time out of time to hold back the world.

He whispered against her ear, breathing her in, all sweet honeysuckle and rose water, 'Let me tell you a secret. I had an awful night last night after I left you, full of disappointments, and all I could think of this morning was getting to you. If I could get to you, if I could get here, everything would be better.' He kissed her earlobe and heard her breath catch. 'I was right. Everything *is* better even if it's just for a short while.'

He moved to take her mouth and she gave it, fully, deeply, as she'd given it before, passionately for a woman who'd not been kissed until yesterday, until *him. She was all his.* What a heady thought that was. He was the only one who had kissed her, who had tasted her like this, who had held her like this. It was an idea darkened by the thought that to be the first meant he wouldn't be the last. In the end, he would lose her to a faceless suitor yet to be named, one who was already on the horizon.

Em's hand was soft on his face. 'Are all kisses like this? Consuming? Burning?' she whispered against his mouth.

'No, definitely not.' London debutantes didn't kiss like this with their whole bodies and mistresses didn't kiss like this, with every honest feeling burning in their eyes.

'Perhaps we should start here next time.' They were talking between kisses and it was quite the loveliest conversation Cassian had ever had. Em's hip moved against him at his groin. There was no hiding his arousal, no protecting her from it. 'I do this to you?' Her eyes registered wonder and shock at the hardness she found there.

Of its own accord, her hand seemed to find its way to the space between them, seeking him. Cassian put a stop to it, delightful as the prospect might be. 'Careful, Em. I am no saint. It would be too easy to take what you're offering and worry about regrets later.'

'Maybe I don't want to be a saint either,' Em pressed.

'You should at least think about it first. Those are easy words in the heat of the moment,' Cassian cautioned. He shifted her from his lap in a pretence of stoking up the fire. He was going to need some relief and soon.

'Don't worry about the fire, I have to go. It's later than I thought.' Em was already at the table, packing up their lunch and sounding flustered. He'd hurt her feelings.

He went to her and wrapped his arms about her, pressing a kiss to her neck in reassurance. 'It's not that I don't want you. I do. I want you more than I've wanted any woman in a long while. But I know the cost and I would not make you pay it for something that can never be more than it is now, a fantasy, a moment of escape from our real lives and selves.' He kissed the length of her lovely neck. 'I can take you part way on my horse.' He was reluctant to let her go, to step outside the door and back into that reality.

'No, I can't allow that.' She turned in his arms, her face alight with the same worry as yesterday, asking for the same promise as yesterday. 'Promise me you won't follow.'

'I promise. I won't follow you.' He thought he understood her fear better today. 'But you have nothing to fear from me, Em.' He whispered his wish. 'What would you say if I said I wanted to know the real you, Em?'

'I would say you already do.' She wrapped her arms about his neck, her hips pressed against him once more. 'Everything I've told you is the truth.'

'Except your name.' The one thing he wanted to know most. But he could not give his return.

'I didn't tell you my name. You gave me one,' she corrected. 'We have truth between us, Matthew, let that be enough.' Enough to bind them together? Enough to bring her back for as long as they could both stand it before inevitability tore them a part?

He nuzzled her neck. 'Can you come in two days?' He had business that required him in Bodmin. There was some disappointment in knowing he couldn't come tomorrow. It would be an eternity until Thursday, until he could return to heaven. 'I want to take you on an adventure. We'll be careful. No one will recognise us.' He assured her, knowing how important that was to her.

Her face lit up at the prospect. 'Where? What shall we do?'

He kissed her once more in promise. 'You'll have to show up to find out.'

Chapter Nine

He took her to Mutton Cove to see the seals. They were lucky. The rain had stopped and an early spring sun had found its way out for the afternoon, although she would have loved going even if it had been wet. She would have gone anywhere just to spend time with him. Pen rode behind Matthew on his horse, her arms wrapped tightly around his waist, her cheek pressed to his broad back, her body warm from the heat of his own despite the breeze. She was hardly noticeable sitting behind him, which was exactly what they'd intended. No one would pay them any mind.

At the cove, a sailboat awaited them, borrowed from a friend, Matthew explained. It was small but seaworthy, something a fisherman might use, or—the naughty, rather adventurous thought crossed her mind—a smuggler.

'The best way to see the seals is on the water.' Matthew grinned and handed her on board before shoving the little craft off the beach and into the surf. He splashed in beside her, the little boat skimming the quiet waters with Matthew competently at the sails.

'Is there nothing you can't do?' Pen admired him from the bow, the hood of her cloak thrown back, her face turned to the fresh air. Matthew merely smiled at her and shrugged out of his coat. He settled beside her in the bow seat, content to let the sailboat bob at will in the cove.

'Do you like your surprise?' He stretched out his long legs as they looked back at the empty beach. There were no seals yet.

'I love it. The wind in my face, the fresh air, no one around for miles.' She let her smile say it all. 'You have no idea what it means to me to be free for just a few hours.' Yet, she wasn't entirely free. Her smile faded at the realisation.

'But?' he prompted. 'Something is amiss?' His arm was about her, and she snuggled against his side.

'I'm not really free, even in these moments. There is so much I wish I could tell you, but I can't, not without giving away too much.' She paused, gathering her courage. 'Sometimes I wish we hadn't made the rule about names.' What would he say to that? Did he feel stifled too? Were there things he wanted to tell her, but couldn't?

His hand stroked the length of her arm. 'It's a type of freedom, though, Em. Knowing our real names creates a different set of limitations.'

All except one limitation. Pen sighed. Real names meant this could last, that she could find him. 'I wish we could stay here for ever. The water is peaceful.' There were no worries here. She didn't have to think about her father, or the suitors, or what she was going to do for the rest of her life. She looked up at Matthew. 'How long do we have? Not just today, but how long…?'

He pressed a finger to her lips and shook his head. 'Whatever it is, it won't be long enough. Do we have to think about it now?'

'Yes, I think we do. I want to know. I want to drink every drop of joy out of the time we have. I don't want to be surprised one day to find you gone. I want a chance to say goodbye.'

Matthew turned his body horizontally and

settled her against him so they lay along the length of the bow seat, the sun and the breeze brushing across them in pleasant strokes from the sky. 'I promise you, I won't leave without saying goodbye.'

'And I promise you the same.' She smiled up at him. 'May I tell you something? I haven't been to the beach for years, not since my mother died. She used to take me and my brother in the summers. I haven't been anywhere since she passed away.' It was the most personal thing she'd told him or anyone. Now that she'd started, she couldn't seem to stop. All the thoughts, all the grief that she'd kept to herself over the years, trickled out in carefully chosen words. 'At home, we never talk about her, not really, not beyond the odd remark about how much I look like her. Her death is why my father is so afraid,' Pen said quietly. 'Nothing's been the same since she died. Sometimes I think we all died with her.'

Then I met you. How will I ever go back to how things used to be?

Matthew's lips brushed the top of her head. 'My brother and I used to come here and swim in the summer.'

'You have a brother?' She hugged the idea to her, adding it to the facts she had about who he was.

'I did. He died.'

Em sighed against him, drowsy from the rocking of the boat and the heat of his body. 'So you know exactly how it is.' It was a tender but bittersweet thing to have in common with the man she was falling in love with. 'Would you tell me about him?'

Tell me about him. Cassian's throat tightened at the invitation. He'd not meant to say even that much about Collin, but he wanted to tell her, here in the boat, with no one around. It seemed the perfect place to do it, to whisper his secrets. Why not tell her, this woman who knew what it meant to lose someone, what it meant to never be able to share that grief? Her hand was drawing light circles on his chest, her fingers tracing him through his shirt, relaxing him as surely as the bob of the boat and the light breeze off the water. His throat eased and words came. 'Collin was my younger brother. He was dashing and reckless, fearless.'

He chuckled, remembering his brother. 'He'd

dive into the water and swim with the seals. He'd swim so far we'd have to sail out to retrieve him. We'd warn him to stay close, but he'd never listen. Even in real life, he preferred to swim in deep waters. It didn't work out for him as well as swimming with the seals.'

'What happened?' She looked up at him.

'He made some poor choices in business and in love. Both played him false. People were hurt because of his decisions.' That was the condensed version, but it was the only one he could bring himself to tell. 'One night he walked out into the waters off Karrek Sands, swam out to the Beasts and never came back. His body washed up a few days later.'

The family had put about that he'd been caught in the undertow—the water was tricky around the Beasts—but Cassian knew what had really happened. Collin had just given up. He was to blame. He should have stopped Collin from going out that afternoon. He should have cancelled his own appointments when Collin refused to stay home. He should have followed him. He should have stopped Collin long before that afternoon. He shouldn't have let Collin invest money with Brenley. Looking back, there were so many places in the timeline where he should have stopped Collin, should have made him listen, and he hadn't. Collin was stubborn and he'd let his brother learn from his mistakes.

'I'm sorry, that's terrible.' She leaned up over him, kissing him lightly on the mouth. 'Thank you for telling me.' She held his gaze. 'Life is precious, it should not be wasted, yet I feel as if I've wasted too much of it, until I met you. You are so alive, so vibrant, and I feel that way too when I'm with you. Thank you.'

His hand moved behind her neck, sweeping aside her hair. 'You make me feel alive, too, Em. More than I've felt in a very long time.' He took her mouth, their bodies shifting, hers moving beneath him, his moving over her, covering her, life and desire surging between them, demanding to be celebrated. But he had to be careful. He could not fall in love with her. This couldn't last. It served no purpose beyond the moment, yet he wanted…

She moaned beneath him, her hips rising up to meet his, her legs parting for him as if he were always meant to be there at the cradle of her thighs. Her eyes captured his. 'I want you, Matthew.'

'I cannot take...' he began to refuse, to counsel caution while he had any sense left. She was untouched and he could not marry her.

'But I can give.' She moved against him and he was nearly lost, so thoroughly did she arouse him. 'No matter what happens, Matthew, I want this first time to be with you, a man I choose.'

He kissed her hard on the mouth, his lips skimmed the column of her neck as he made his way down her body, every ounce of him wishing she were naked and every ounce of him thankful that she was not. It would be impossible to resist her then, impossible to find the intermediate ground on which he could satisfy her desire without ruining her. 'I will give you pleasure, Em,' he vowed fiercely, his hands sweeping beneath her skirts, pushing back the fabric, parting her undergarments until she was bare to him, her curls glistening in the sunlight. 'Sweet heavens, you're beautiful.' His own voice was hoarse with desire.

Her core was all dampness and want, yearning for his touch. He took her then, with his mouth, his lips, his tongue, his teeth, at the most private part of her. She was gripping him hard, her hands tangled in his hair, her legs wide for him. Em made a little sound in the back of her throat, his own body clenched in answer, moved by her ardent, open response. His tongue flicked over the tight nub within her folds, and she cried out at the exquisite pleasure of it. Again he licked and again the pleasure surged and ebbed, pushing her towards release. Soon it would be inevitable.

'I want…' she articulated only half a sentence before she lost the capacity for speech, her body focused entirely on pleasure and only pleasure now. But he knew what she wanted. He was pushing her towards a cliff, a place where she might fly, where he might give her a little more of that freedom she craved. He felt the moment she gave herself over to it, the point at which she let him push her all the way, until she claimed her release in a cry that filled the sky.

He might have held her for hours, both of them drowsing in the aftermath of the afternoon's intimacy, if it hadn't been for the seals. A thump against the boat had him upright and alert, his first thought that they'd drifted too far and hit something. But there was no need to worry. The seals had come out to play at last and one of them had bumped against the little boat. 'Em, come look.' He shook her awake gently. 'Seals.'

Em loved the seals, she loved watching them cavort in the water, diving and gliding through the waves. He brought out the dried fish and she revelled in tossing them into the water and watching the seals swim after them. When she laughed, her entire face lit up, taking simple joy from this simple pleasure. Cassian didn't think London offered a finer entertainment than this. Em tossed the last fish and wiped her hands on her skirts. 'I suppose this means it's time to go?' They still had to sail the boat in and make the ride on horseback. Cassian nodded and turned the boat around.

Neither of them spoke as they made the return trip to the beach, but Cassian could feel her eyes on him as he worked the sails. This afternoon had been more than he'd bargained for: more revealing, more passionate. At the beach, he took her hand and didn't let go. They were together now in a way they hadn't been at the start of the day. They'd shared important pieces of themselves with one another, exposed a part of their souls. He'd not intended that to happen. He was usually so guarded, so careful with how he shared himself and *what* he shared of himself. But Em had broken through those defences with a simple question.

He helped her up on Ajax and settled himself behind her, selfishly wanting to keep her close for as long as he could. He wrapped his arms about her, his thighs about her, and chirped to his horse. It was getting harder to leave her and yet more likely that he must. His trip to Bodmin for an ally had not born fruit. But he still had time. The Season was weeks away yet. Anything could happen between now and then.

Cassian had no sooner thought that than 'anything' did. A rider came towards them on the road. Em's hood immediately went up and her body tensed between his legs, even as her head went down, her face completely shrouded by the hood. He did not know the rider, but apparently she did. Cassian nodded politely as the rider passed, throwing them a sceptical look. But Cassian did not stop.

'Who was that?' he whispered as the danger passed.

'Someone my father knows,' she whispered, still shaken by the close encounter.

She did not remove her hood for the duration of the ride, nor did she relax until they reached the cottage and he helped her down.

'He didn't guess who you were.' Cassian rubbed her arms reassuringly. 'Everything's fine. You spotted him before he spotted you.'

'But if I hadn't?' she asked sharply. 'Do you know what would have happened if he'd recognised me?' She shook her head. 'Of course not. You can't possibly know.'

The rest went unspoken, but Cassian heard it loud enough: *Because you don't who I really am and I don't know who you really are. This is what happens when time out of time meets reality. The two cannot mix.*

Cassian kissed her solemnly. He did know what would happen. She would be shamed and he would be forced to move on because dukes' heirs didn't marry country girls, gentry or not. That was not how he wanted it to end, not after today. 'We would have sorted it out.' At least they would have tried. 'Don't let it ruin today, Em.'

She smiled at that, some of her usual confidence returning. 'Nothing could ruin today, not even that.'

Despite the brave words, the rider on the road did serve as a warning to them both about the dangerous nature of their game. They stuck close to the cottage after that, venturing out only to the nearby meadows for long walks along deserted stretches of land, sometimes walking to the cliffs, watching the sea and talking, always talking, except for the days when all they wanted to do was kiss, to push the boundaries where pleasure and propriety might intermingle.

The cottage became their sanctuary in the weeks that followed. They stamped the little interior with their presence. The faded cloth and tin plates were joined by a chipped vase of wildflowers on the table and a pan for boiling tea water. A pile of neatly stacked wood stood next to the fireplace, old mismatched cushions taken from the Prideaux attics made the chairs more comfortable and a clean, worn quilt covered the bed in the corner. This was a place where they could be themselves, where they could share their secrets—all secrets but one.

Or perhaps two...

Cassian felt a change in her as April progressed. The tension in her grew apace with their passion, their interludes growing more heated, more intense. 'You're hiding something, Em? What is it? It's no good denying it, it's written on every inch of your body.' They were lying on the bed, wrapped in each other's arms, stripped down to their underthings in the warmth of the afternoon. It was as close to naked as he could afford to let them get. He didn't dare more, knowing that the end was near. He'd not broken Redruth. He would have to go to London, but he'd put it off until the last minute. Did she guess? Was that the reason for her tension? He'd tasted desperation in her kiss.

The bed ropes creaked as she lifted up on an elbow to look at him, her green eyes shadowed. 'Do you remember when I said my father wanted me to marry?' It was one subject they had expressly not revisited since the first time she'd mentioned it. 'There's a man he wants me to consider.'

His only thought was that he wasn't ready, never mind that she'd warned him weeks earlier. Somehow, he'd convinced himself he would be the one who'd have to walk away. The London Season and his chance to pursue his amusement garden loomed closer than ever on the calendar, forcing his hand. But it was her hand that was being forced now.

'Will you consider him?' Cassian's words were hoarse even as he strove for neutrality. He was already jealous of this unknown man and yet this or something like it had always been unavoidable. He and Em weren't meant to last.

Her next words spilled out in an apologetic rush. 'I'll tell my father no, of course, that the man is too old.' She bit her lip. 'I just wanted to be honest. I thought you should know.'

'What does he do?' Cassian imagined a merchant perhaps of some means. Her father probably considered it a great opportunity to have his daughter wed a man already established in business. Cassian could offer her nothing, not simply because he was a viscount and she was a girl from an ordinary background, but also because he could only make her unhappy. There would be no joy for her in being a viscountess. She would be under scrutiny for ever, for every little thing she didn't know, every rule she inadvertently broke or overlooked, every faux pas she made. There would be no pleasure for her in that. He would not ruin her that way. He wanted the Em who adored feeding seals, who lay with him beneath the sun in a rocking boat.

'He grows flowers.'

Ah, a gardener then, someone who might work at an estate or who might have some small patch of land of his own. 'Is it a good match?'

'Not for me.' She smiled at him, her fingers touching his face as they lay close together. 'I want something different. Something more than an older man who is dedicated to his roses.'

'Can you refuse him?' he asked. She'd said she would, but was that possible? Her father seemed a very determined man.

'In truth, I don't know. My father is very stubborn once he sets his mind to something.'

She gave a soft laugh that warmed him. 'He's like your reluctant gentleman. Perhaps they should meet.' She sighed. 'I don't want to go, Matthew, but the afternoon has slipped away again.'

'Come tomorrow? We'll go down to the beach.' Time was suddenly of the essence. There were a finite amount of tomorrows left between them.

She shook her head. 'I can't. Tomorrow...'

'...you go to see *him*, the man with the flowers,' Cassian finished her sentence, something fierce and competitive taking up residence in his stomach. But what could he do? He was a man with a false name. He was powerless.

She nodded. 'I'll come the day after.' She drew a fingernail down his chest, her hand hitching at his belt, her lips hovering close to his. 'And we'll make love, promise me. I meant what I said that day on the boat. I want it to be you, no matter what.' The desperation was back. She thought this was the end or very nearly so.

Cassian swallowed. 'Em, I don't know if that's wise.'

She silenced him with a kiss. 'You can't say no. It will be my birthday. You have to oblige.'

'Shall I bring you a present?' he teased, a thought already coming to him, something she'd like beyond anything, aside from love-making.

'If you like.' She snuggled against him. 'Do you know what I really want? I want to lie fully naked with you. I want to feel your hands, your mouth, on my skin. I want to put *my* hands on *your* skin, I want to know *you*, your body, your name, your *real* name.'

Cassian pressed a kiss to the top of her head. 'You can have all but the last.' It was hard to refuse. How many times had he wanted the same? To throw caution to the wind and an-nounce himself to her, to know who she was. But to do so would be akin to eating the apple in the Garden. Once they knew who each other was, they'd be cast out of their little Eden. It was further proof that she thought this was ending. She thought names at the last couldn't hurt them. She was wrong. Cassian rose from the bed and put on his breeches. 'I think we need to keep this one secret, Em.'

Chapter Ten

'I know a secret.' Phin was all smiles in the drawing room before dinner. It was just the two of them. Father hadn't come down yet and there were no guests tonight, much to Pen's relief. She didn't think she could handle another night of feigned politeness.

'What is it?' A jolt of worry took her. Perhaps that *was* the secret? She scanned the room quickly, looking over her shoulder at the entrance for fear she might see a phalanx of gentlemen lining up for her attentions.

Phin laughed as he read her thoughts. 'Not more guests. It's just the three of us tonight.' His smile widened. 'We're celebrating your birthday early.'

'Oh. That's lovely.' Pen knit her brows together. 'Why? It's just two days away.'

'That's the other surprise, the one I won't

tell you. Father would kill me for letting that particular cat out of the bag.' Phin cocked his head, his gaze lingering, inspiring a different worry in Pen. Did he guess she was meeting someone? She smoothed her skirts and played with the fan in her lap. Surely, what she'd been up to with Matthew didn't show in any way? She'd been careful to school her thoughts since the first night when Margery had caught her. 'I thought you'd be more excited than that,' Phin probed. 'Two extra days of birthday presents are not to be sneered at, yet you seemed underwhelmed, Pen.'

Pen looked up and forced a smile. 'Not at all, at least not at all if such largesse wasn't coming from our father. I'm merely wondering what he wants, how does this suit *his* plans?'

Phin frowned at her, disappointed with the cynical direction of her thoughts. 'He wants your happiness. Are you not pleased with the efforts he's made these last weeks? You've had the elite of Cornwall served up to you so that you may make your choice.'

'And tomorrow we're off to visit Wadesbridge,' Pen put in with less enthusiasm. 'We're back to where we started.'

'We wouldn't be if you'd pick one of them, show an interest. Toss Father an olive branch, Pen. He's trying,' Phin encouraged.

'If I toss him an olive branch, he'll take the whole bush and have me wedded to the first man I blink at. Did he put you up to this?' Pen sighed, disappointed in her anger and in lashing out at the least guilty party among them. Her brother meant well. 'I'm sorry, Phin. It must be difficult for you playing the liaison all the time.' She was reminded of the advice she'd given Matthew about his stubborn gentleman. Had Matthew found an advocate? She would ask when she saw him. Two days from now. Despite the promise of birthday celebrations, the two days stretched before her endlessly.

'Are you well, Pen? You've seemed distracted of late.' Phin wasn't done with his scrutiny. She'd have to try harder to not give herself away. Margery had noticed and now Phin thought he was on to something.

'I'm fine. It's been a difficult few weeks.' It wasn't entirely a lie. The last month had been difficult as well as fantastic. She just wished the fantastic part didn't need to be her own secret.

Their father joined them and all personal conversation was set aside in lieu of small talk about the estate until dinner was announced, but Pen did not miss the undercurrent of excitement that jumped between her father and Phin. Whatever her surprise was, they'd planned it for her and it clearly pleased them. It would please her, too, Pen decided, looking around the table at her little family. Tragedy had shaped so much of their lives. Wasn't it time for a little joy to do the same?

'Well, Daughter, you will be twenty-one soon.' Her father approached the subject as the meal ended, a pleased look in his eyes. 'You've done as I've asked this past month, considering various candidates for your hand. But perhaps the process is still too contrived for your purposes.' He smiled kindly and for a moment Pen saw the father she'd known in early childhood, a more carefree version of himself, a happier version. 'Penrose, you've mentioned how much you long to see something of the world and your desire to go to London. So...' he slid a glance at Phin and winked '...we have decided to give you a London Season for your birthday. We leave tomorrow. Your maid is already packing.'

Pen stared. Her father was beaming, looking entirely pleased with himself, and Phin was grinning from ear to ear. They were expecting her to say something. They'd just served up one of her wishes, a wish any girl would be delighted to receive. 'B-but,' she stammered, trying to organise her thoughts, 'I can't possibly go now.' If she left, she wouldn't see Matthew. She cast about for a reason to stay. 'What about Trescowe? Aren't we promised for a visit?'

'We'll stop there and continue on.' Her father was in high humour as he solved the little problem.

'But I need time to prepare. There are purchases I need to make.' She didn't have enough gloves or stockings for London and probably not enough dresses despite the influx of new ones for the dinner parties.

Again her father beamed. 'Buy them in London. You'll have two weeks to shop to your heart's content before the Season truly begins. You see, I've thought of everything. There's no reason not to get in the coach tomorrow morning and enjoy yourself.' He was waiting for her to say something, probably 'thank you'. 'Well? Aren't you pleased, Pen? It's what you wanted. We'll find you a fine husband in London.'

'She's stunned.' Phin leapt into the breach, covering for her lapse even as he slid her a questioning look. 'I never thought to see you speechless, Pen.'

'I'm overwhelmed.' She managed a smile. 'Thank you, truly, both of you.' Phin, no doubt, had probably argued quite hard for this chance. It was unfair of her to not appreciate it now. They couldn't possibly know how their gift broke her heart.

The rest of the meal passed in a blur. Her favourite dessert, a chocolate ganache cake, was brought in. Cook must have worked hours on it. Her brother and father laughed and talked endlessly of London; which entertainments they would take in, the people they would meet. Talk of balls and parties, decorations and food, flowed over her, but left her untouched. She made the appropriate noises, smiling and nodding in the right places. She ate the chocolate cake. She must have since her plate was empty. But all the while her mind was elsewhere.

How could she send word to Matthew? How did she leave a message for a man whose name she didn't know? That no one knew? If she could get to the cottage, she could leave a message there. But how to do that? She'd have to go tonight, in the dark. It would be almost impossible to get out of the castle and impossible to get back in, to say nothing of the risks of injury. In the dark it was easy to lose one's way, to turn an ankle in a hole. She'd not make it back home then.

Perhaps she could send someone else in the morning? But who would that be? Only Margery could be trusted with the errand and Margery was expected to travel with her. There would be no opportunity for a trip to the cottage. By the time Pen excused herself from the table, claiming the need for a good night's sleep, her heart was breaking. Her mind had moved on from thoughts of how to get to the cottage, to accepting the reality that she would not be able to reach Matthew. What would happen in two days when Matthew showed up and she didn't? All this time, she'd worried he would disappear suddenly, but it was she who would break the pact they'd made at Mutton Cove.

He would be hurt. He cared for her. Would all that caring turn to hate? Would he feel betrayed? Would he think she'd decided to wed the man she was visiting? Or would he understand that none of this had been her choice? That events had transpired that were beyond her control? Would he forgive her?

Would she forgive him if he simply stopped coming? That was a difficult question to answer. They'd accepted what they had couldn't last for ever, but they'd intended to say goodbye. Perhaps he'd think the worst of her. He would never know how much these weeks had meant to her, how alive she felt when she was with him.

In her room, Margery was busy packing, full of energy, her excitement at odds with Pen's melancholy. 'Isn't it wonderful? London, at last!' Her smile faded. 'What is it? Aren't you happy, miss? It's what you've wanted.' Margery set aside the pile of gowns in her arms and came to her, taking her hands. 'It is your young man, is it not?'

Pen sank down on an empty patch of bed.

'I'll never see him again. There's no chance to tell him, to explain.' But to explain what? To see him again would require she disclose everything. 'He'll think I left him,' Pen said forlornly. There would be no more kisses, no more of this afternoon's decadence, there would be no hope of lying with him skin to skin on the faded quilt. 'I was supposed to meet him there for my birthday.' She bit her lip as tears threatened. 'He was bringing me a present.' It would have been something thoughtful, something that spoke to the quality of their relationship.

'Perhaps it's for the best. It had to end some time,' Margery consoled softly. 'I know it hurts now, but this way it's over quickly and there will be no messiness. You'll be gone. He can't follow you, can't find you, can't make trouble for you.'

'I know.' Pen had been over all the silver linings in her mind, but that didn't make it better. Those linings were tarnished. She *wanted* Matthew to find her, but he was lost to her. 'Margery, make sure you pack my glass necklace.' She would keep it with her always as a reminder of what it had felt like to be loved for herself and what it had felt like to have a heart so she wouldn't be tempted to risk it again.

Em's birthday present, fifteen pounds of wriggling puppy, squirmed under Cassian's arm as he approached the cottage. It had been a feat of no small magnitude to carry the puppy on his horse. But the look on Em's face would be worth it. It was a rash gift, one she couldn't keep. But he would keep the puppy for her. The gift was the experience, a puppy of her own for the afternoon. They could take it walking in the meadow and it could gambol at her side just as she'd imagined growing up.

Cassian stepped inside the cottage and smiled. He'd arrived ahead of her. Good. He set the puppy down on the floor. He wanted time to set the fire and lay out the picnic. He'd packed something special for her birthday. He wanted this afternoon to be perfect, quiet and private, a celebration just between them. They'd been together nearly five weeks and he was aware time was running out. Soon, he'd have to make good on the promise he'd made to tell her. It looked like he'd have to go to London, after all. There'd been no breakthrough with the earl. Tomorrow. He would tell her to-morrow. He'd would let them have today. One more brilliant day in the sunshine of their fantasy.

Half an hour later, the food was ready, the fire had warmed the room, but there was no sign of Em. The puppy snuffled at his boots and Cassian reached down and scooped him up. 'Just a few more minutes, Oscar.' He took the pup outside to do his business and came back in. The minutes came and the minutes went, collecting into an hour.

He got up and carried the puppy to the door, looking down the path for any sign of her. Perhaps she'd been delayed. Perhaps he should walk out and meet her on the road somewhere. But how could he? What direction did she come from? What might be the nature of her delay? Had she been unable to get away? Had she fallen ill? He wished he knew more about her. Right now he felt as if he knew nothing of her, nothing useful that would help him. He knew how she felt in his arms, how she kissed him, how she liked doing for him. He knew that she liked puppies, that she had a small family, that her father was stubborn. He knew that she liked melted cheese on toast, that she wanted to travel the world. But none of that would help him. If she didn't come to the cottage, she would be lost to him.

Cassian went back inside.

He waited another half an hour before admitting she wasn't coming. 'That's all right, Oscar.' He put out the fire and tucked the puppy into his coat against the cold and damp. 'We'll try again tomorrow.' Perhaps her visit with the gardener suitor had been delayed, perhaps she hadn't been able to get away. It was her birthday, after all—perhaps her family was celebrating. Cassian carefully rewrapped the food. Most of it would keep until tomorrow.

He came again the next day and the day after that, puppy, food and all, until the bread dried and he ran out of excuses for her delay. He had to face facts. Em was not detained. She simply wasn't coming. Cassian sat at the table, head in his hands. Was this how it ended? Suddenly and without warning despite their pact? One afternoon they'd been lovemaking on the bed, promising to do decadent things to one another, wishing for tomorrow to come quickly, promising one another to be here, and the next she was gone. He thought he'd have more time. A couple of weeks at least, time for them to prepare for goodbye together as they'd promised each other at the cove. He wasn't set to leave for London until the end of the month.

Why hadn't she come? A hundred horrible scenarios played through his mind. Did it have something to do with the gardener? Had she chosen him or been compelled to marry him? Had her family decided to keep a closer watch on her now that she might be betrothed? *To another.* The thought nearly made him sick. He didn't want to think on it: his Em belonging to another, kissing another.

He'd known an end would come—he could no more keep her than she could keep the puppy. So why did it hurt so much? He'd been wrong to think anonymity would protect his heart. He'd thought he couldn't fall in love with her, at least not fall too far. But he'd been wrong there. He'd fallen far enough for her leaving to sting. Damn, but the Truscott brothers were ill-fated in love. He'd been prepared and armoured, he'd warned himself against such a thing, and it *still* hurt. His brother had not been half as prepared when he'd fallen for Audevere Brenley, Sir Gismond's daughter. It was no wonder Collin had been devastated when she broke with him just weeks before their wedding. The Brenleys had played his brother false on all fronts.

From his vantage point of the cottage table, Cassian had a new perspective on how that loss must have felt. It also gave him a renewed determination to make sure he didn't let sorrow drag him down. He had to let go. It was time to say goodbye. Cassian took a final look around. The fire where they'd sat, the bed where they'd lain, where they'd flirted with lovemaking. He saw memories and he saw irony. He'd spent his adult life guarding against unscrupulous fortune hunters who would seek to use him as Brenley has used his brother. But in the end, it was love that had done him in. Well, best to learn that lesson now.

Cassian took the note he'd written out of his coat pocket and propped it on the table against the chipped vase with its dried lavender. If she ever came again, at least she'd know he'd been here, that it hadn't been his choice to leave her like this. Beside him on the floor, the puppy whined. Cassian reached down a hand and stroked the puppy's soft head. 'It looks like it's just you and me, Oscar.' As cute as the dog was, the idea lacked a certain appeal.

Cassian rose and gathered up the pup. It was time to do his duty. He'd had a lovely spring reprieve, his project had been given every chance to succeed and it hadn't. Blind, arbitrary hope had failed to produce the results he'd wanted. Now it was time for hard work and sacrifice. They would not fail him. He stepped outside and closed the door behind him with a firm thud. Em was officially in the past. All there was to do now was to move forward. He needed to focus on his amusement garden now and courting Redruth's daughter. He could be married by autumn and he could break ground on the pleasure garden before another year passed. He was back in the game. The thought ought to have buoyed his spirits. It did not.

Chapter Eleven

The Redruth ball was well underway in all its glittering, chandelier-lit glory when Cassian arrived. He paused at the entrance to the ballroom. At his age, stepping over the threshold of a debutante's ball meant one thing: he was declaring himself interested in marriage.

Beside him, Inigo clapped him on the back in well-meant support. 'This is a momentous evening. It's a big moment. You're the first of us to really throw their hat in the ring. Eaton skirted the issue altogether marrying in Porth Karrek on the sly. Vennor can use mourning as a shield a little while longer.'

But not Cassian. He had no shields. Nothing protected his dreams but himself. If he didn't go after that land with every weapon in his arsenal, the dream would be lost. To not at least try smacked of cowardice. Tonight would be the first engagement in his campaign. He would dance with the daughter and see where it led. Campaign, engagement, arsenal. These were war words, not love words. He ought to have a less violent view of tonight's foray.

Cassian tugged at his ivory waistcoat and straightened his shoulders. The past three weeks had led here. There had been flurry upon flurry of activity since the night he'd committed to coming to London. There'd been packing to see to, appointments with his tailors, arrangements for rooms at the Albany so he wasn't underfoot at his father's town house and, most importantly, there'd been acquiring the interview with Redruth. He'd met three days ago with the earl to discuss courting the daughter and to garner an invitation to the ball. The earl had been pleased his daughter's presence in London had attracted the attentions of a duke's heir.

Cassian disliked the arrangement. He disliked being valued for his assets and titles. Even more, he disliked having to use that card to get what he wanted. Furthermore, he disliked the necessity for duplicity. The Earl of Redruth had no inkling that Viscount Trevethow was the man behind the Porth Karrek Land Development Company, the very company that Redruth had refused to sell to. Yet, when those avenues had failed to acquire what Cassian wanted, what choice did he have? He felt the scales of good teeter, balancing his deceit against the greater good. The people hurt by his brother's poor business sense were counting on him. Surely that outweighed his motives for courtship.

'Well, once more into the breach.' Cassian slid Inigo a look as they stepped inside. They wound their way around the perimeter of the ballroom, stopping to chat with friends as they made their progress towards the Earl of Redruth. Cassian was in no hurry and he certainly didn't want to look desperate. He wasn't desperate and nor was he nervous as Inigo seemed to think with all his 'throwing his hat into the ring, momentous occasion' talk. He felt nothing. His attendance here tonight was a professional business decision, nothing more. He wanted the land and he needed a different kind of currency to get it.

His memories of Em carried a dulled edge these days. Those weeks in the cottage seemed like a dream now, something that had been vivid once, but had begun to fade. Even the image of her; all that caramel hair and those sea-glass eyes, blurred into something unreal by necessity. He couldn't move forward if he focused on the past. What kind of a husband would he be if he spent his life mourning a woman whose real name he didn't even know? There might not be a grand passion in this marriage of convenience he sought, but he hoped there might be something milder, respect, perhaps, that would grow over time. That would have to be enough. The greater good would be served.

'Which one do you think she is?' Inigo nudged his elbow as they watched the dancers. So many smiling, hopeful faces. None of them Em's. A dangerous flash of her flared to vivid life past the dulled edges of his memory.

If you were here, Em, we'd dance beneath the chandeliers as if they were the stars in the sky, we'd stroll the gardens, I'd steal a kiss.

Em would look stunning in a silk gown of seafoam to match her eyes, an opal pendant at her neck, her hair done up high to show off the length of that neck. His Em would be a swan among these downy young ducklings.

These were dangerous imaginings. Duty had no time for them. 'I have no idea.' Cassian pushed the thought of Em away. He wished he shared Inigo's enthusiasm for the venture. 'Is this what it's like to invest other people's money for them?' he joked. 'I suppose it's easy to be excited when the risk isn't yours.'

Inigo frowned, missing the humour. 'Oh, no, investing other people's money is positively nerve-racking.'

'And contemplating marriage to a stranger is not?' Cassian laughed in spite of himself. 'Perhaps that's why I brought you along. It's all about perspective.' He'd come to grips with that perspective over the past few weeks. In order for his dream to thrive his other dream would have to die. He would give up a romantic's marriage for a practical marriage in order to honour one man's legacy, to avenge his brother and to right wrongs. It was what the greater good demanded. Dukes lived to serve that hungry beast. It was the code the Four Cornish Dukes lived by.

They nodded to a group of young girls as

they strolled. Four sets of eyes followed them along with a trail of giggles at their attentions. 'Speaking of perspective, it seems your presence tonight has brought a certain level of excitement to the evening,' Inigo pointed out. 'I wonder how many people Redruth rushed out and told you'd be here? You've been in town for three weeks, but you haven't been out yet. Redruth can claim he was your first stop. Quite the coup for him.'

Cassian shrugged. 'This wasn't the first stop. The Trelevens' musicale was and I'll be sure to tell anyone who asks.' They'd spent the early part of the night with their neighbours from home, Sir Jock Treleven, his wife and his five unmarried daughters, all of who were talented musicians. Vennor had been there as well. It had been a quiet, low-profile way to start the evening. 'I wonder who will be the talk of the town tomorrow? Sir Jock with his smaller but tasteful and more exclusive affair with three ducal heirs present, or Redruth's ball?'

'Redruth is usually a hermit. Everyone will be attracted to this anomaly of his. I doubt the Trelevens will even get a mention in the columns,' Inigo offered honestly. 'But you will be mentioned for certain. Everyone is already looking at you. Once you dance with Redruth's daughter, no one will want to look away. I wager you'll be in the betting books at White's by morning.'

Cassian grimaced. 'If you think you're raising my spirits, you're failing. Just so you know.'

Pen was miserable. Everyone was watching her. Talking about her. She was the centre of every conversation. She didn't even have to guess at what was being said. Pen knew. She'd walked in on one such discussion in the retiring room, some silly girls being indiscreet with their gossip.

'There's the girl who is making her debut at twenty-one.'

'There's the girl no one has seen for years.'

'I wonder what's wrong with her?'

Curiosity could be a cruel thing.

She'd exchanged the prison of Castle Byerd for the glittering prison of London of her own accord. She stood with her father and her aunt amid the splendour of the Byerd House ballroom; the chandelier dusted, the floor polished to a walnut gleam, surrounded by silks and

jewels and all she could think was 'This is all
my fault.' She'd asked for London and she'd
got it. Her father had spared no expense for
her debut. Food had been delivered in endless waves today: cakes from London's finest
pastry chefs, chocolates in the shape of Castle Byerd and crates of champagne that had
been chilling since early this morning. There
were flowers, too, white roses in cut-crystal
vases tied with pale pink ribbons everywhere
in the house, except for the one bouquet of
roses tinged with yellow-rimmed petals which
had already arrived from Wadesbridge. It was
set in pride of place on the mantel in the drawing room, perhaps as a subtle reminder of what
her fate would be should London not inspire a
different choice.

Her father had very subtly drawn a line in
the sand with his birthday gift. He'd given her
London, as she'd asked. Now, he would expect something in return—that she choose a
suitor, that she make a commitment to marriage. If not, a suitor would be chosen for her:
Wadesbridge, solid, predictable, stable, close
to home, far from her dreams. It would make
her father happy. He would have succeeded in

keeping her safe until he could hand her off to a husband.

There would be no travels, no grand adventures, no danger. No *passion*. She could not imagine Wadesbridge's kisses exciting the same response as Matthew's, could not imagine lying on a faded quilt with Wadesbridge, yearning to be naked, yearning to put her mouth on him as he'd done her. Surely, Wadesbridge or whomever she selected would not expect her to do such a thing with them, or expect to do such a thing to her. She didn't want to think about it. She only wanted to think about Matthew: his hands, his kisses, his touch, the way he talked of seeing the world. Pen swallowed hard and fought back a sudden rush of tears.

In the weeks she'd been in London, she'd spent hours pondering how that visit had gone. How long had Matthew waited for her? Had he gone back to the cottage after that? What had he brought her for her birthday? What might they have done in the cottage that afternoon? More kisses, more mouths—would they have consummated their relationship as she had wanted? Once, she'd thought such a thing inevitable. Every time they'd met had led them closer to that conclusion. She'd wanted to. She'd made up her mind. She'd wanted a memory to hold against all the nights to come.

Pen fingered the glass heart tied about her wrist on a pink ribbon with her dance card. She was decked out in her mother's tiara and diamonds, but the glass heart was the most precious thing she wore tonight. She'd wanted it with her, a talisman, perhaps, to bring her luck, to keep Matthew close a little while longer. Her dance card was filled with the names of strangers, men only interested in her dowry.

Men, perhaps, like the Duke of Hayle's heir who was claiming the seventh dance. She could picture how delighted her father would be over that—a duke's heir dancing with his daughter and a man from their part of the world at that. It quite positively put Wadesbridge in the shade. She ought to be relieved. But she wasn't. What did it matter who she danced with or who she married if it wasn't Matthew?

At the thought of Matthew, her gaze unerringly picked out the tallest dark-haired man in the room and not for the first time that night. She'd noticed him immediately even though he'd arrived late. He hadn't been in the receiving line—she would have remembered. But her gaze, it seemed, had made a habit out of looking for him once her memory had decided he reminded her of Matthew with his height and his breadth. His shoulders were exquisite. She wished she could see his face, or maybe not. If she saw it, she would have to give up the fantasy. It wasn't Matthew. He was perhaps country gentry, not the sort at all to mingle among the glamour of the *ton*. That didn't stop her, however, from thinking about how different this ball would be if Matthew *were* here, how she'd look forward to every dance in his arms, how he would look at her if he could see her in this ballgown, her hair done up, his common girl transformed into a princess. He would tell her she was beautiful and she would believe him because Matthew didn't flatter.

Matthew didn't lie.

She would not be the only one transformed. How wonderful Matthew would look in evening clothes, a tail coat cut to his physique. No woman in the ballroom would be able to keep her eyes off him. Not even the presence of Hayle's heir could compete with Matthew.

Her father nudged her elbow. 'Trevethow

is coming, my dear.' Her stomach sank. The dreaded seventh dance was here, the one with the much-anticipated heir to the Duke of Hayle. Of all the dances, she was looking forward to that one the least. Trevethow was bound to be a pompous cad. Tonight, when people weren't talking about her, they'd been talking about him. Apparently, he was handsome and rich and every woman in the room was dying of love for him, never mind he hadn't been to any grand balls yet this Season. It was enough to make the girls swoon to know he was in London, that they might run into him at any time, on Bond Street, at the Park.

'Trevethow is the big fish tonight. Penrose, please, be nice to him. He would be a good match, perhaps the best we could hope for.'

She only half-heard him. The tall man she'd spied throughout the evening was on the move. Her gaze had found him again and it was far more interesting to watch him than it was to listen to her father enumerate the benefits of an alliance with the house of Hayle. Pen stilled as the tall man drew near, her breath catching at the growing possibility that the tall man who'd captured her attention *was* Trevethow. Someone touched her arm to ask a question and Pen stepped aside for just a moment to answer.

'Allow me to introduce my daughter, Lady Penrose Prideaux.' Her father tapped her elbow, reclaiming her attention. Pen turned, her gaze and her mind struggling to register who stood before her. It was her tall stranger from tonight, but there was something of the familiar about him, sans greatcoat and dusty boots, but the same broad shoulders and square jaw, the same warm amber eyes. Pen's stomach plummeted and her mouth ran dry while her thoughts were assaulted with a hundred realisations, the foremost among them was that Matthew was *here*, the very fantasy of her thoughts brought to life in vivid physical reality. How? Why? What did it mean?

Pen's shock was overwhelming as he bent over her hand and kissed it, the little glass heart dancing on the ribbon about her wrist. His eyes were no longer the warmed whisky she remembered, but hard amber flints instead, full of their own shock. 'Lady Penrose, how charming to meet a neighbour so far from home.' His words were edged in an irony meant just for her. So he knew. He recognised her too. So much for the protections of secrecy.

Other realisations assailed her in a relentless barrage: not only was Matthew here of all places, he'd lied. The son of a country squire was in truth a duke's heir! He'd gone slumming, hoping to turn a simple country girl's head with all those pretty lines, all the professions of affection. Had he just said them to steal kisses? All this time while she'd been in London worrying over Matthew, worrying over the hurt she might have caused him, he wasn't hurting in the least! He was attending balls and asking permission to court earls' daughters. He'd not been languishing for her. While she'd felt guilty about dancing with other men tonight, he'd been coming to court a faceless girl he'd never met with deadly intent, simply because she was Redruth's daughter.

He'd already been to visit her father, he'd already asked to court her. He'd made his intentions known to her father. He quite obviously had one goal in mind, which begged the horrible question: How long had he known he was going to court Redruth's daughter? Had he been contemplating it during their time together? Had he known the whole time he would be going to London? Had he always known *exactly* when their affair would end? It seemed so. He'd known it would never last beyond April because he would be gone.

The other set of realisations were not flattering: *she'd* been played for a fool and that was all her fault. She'd been naive to believe in his protestations of affection, that she could trust him, that she *meant* something to him. Noblemen toyed with common girls all the time. Had it all been a game to him? What had he meant to do? Set her up as his mistress? Or perhaps not even that courtesy. Perhaps he thought to marry well and keep a little country mouse on the side.

Worse, what did he mean to do now with that information? Her mind ran wild with dark speculation. Would he use their secret affair to coerce her to the altar? To take away all choice? What if he told her father she'd been gallivanting around the countryside meeting strange men under aliases? There would be no place for her to hide if that happened. Her father would insist on marriage.

He managed a cold smile so unlike the smiles

she was used to, his voice tinged with irony as he said her name. 'Lady Penrose, I believe this dance is mine.'

Chapter Twelve

He'd found Em. For just one brilliant, sparkling moment, when she'd turned around, the world had been perfect. If only he could have held on to that singular moment, frozen it in time, Cassian would have gladly lived in it for ever. But then he'd seen her eyes, seen her look of stunned surprise turn to something akin to loathing and fear and the moment passed, perfection shattered by the hammer of reality. Em didn't want him here. Em hadn't wanted to be found. Em had left him. Only it hadn't been Em leaving him, it had been Lady Penrose Prideaux, the woman who held his land. It could not be worse. How could he marry the woman he had loved for her land? How could they recapture what they'd once had when everything about them reeked of rank distrust?

Her hand lay on his sleeve, barely brushing

it as he led her on to the dance floor, as if she could treat him as a ghost. 'You used to like touching me,' Cassian whispered low at her ear as he placed his hand at her waist and moved them into position for the waltz.

'Not you. Never you. Only Matthew.' The ice of her tone matched the ice in her eyes as the music began and they started to move. 'I should slap you for your deceit.' Her hand curled into the fabric of his coat where it lay on his shoulder. For a moment, he thought she might do it. It would be deuced unfair of her since *he* was the wronged party.

'As I recall, you were the one who left me.' Cassian took them through a turn at the top of the ballroom with a nod to a passing couple.

'You were always planning to leave and you said nothing! I told you from the start my father wanted me to marry,' she hissed through gritted teeth.

'Smile, Lady Penrose, people are watching. They've talked of nothing else all night but your debut and my presence at a ball for the first time this Season. You can imagine what they'll talk about now that their two favourite subjects are united as one.' This was not the way he'd envisioned finding Em, of dancing with her, of having her in his arms again.

But this wasn't Em. This was someone else entirely, someone he didn't know. This was a woman who'd no doubt found Matthew dispensable, a man of no consequence compared to the match she was expected to make. She'd discarded him without a thought. There'd even been a man in mind, not a gardener as Cassian had originally thought, but a man of rank. Yet she'd kissed him, touched him, seared him with hot looks and hotter promises, all the while using him to cuckold another.

Be fair, his conscience prompted. *You participated willingly. She told you her father wanted her to marry.*

But it stung. She'd used him and discarded him without saying goodbye. She'd broken their pact and now she wanted to call him to account. He should resent her, but he couldn't bring himself to it, not without reason. Not until he heard her story. This woman in his arms wasn't Em and yet Em was inside those sharp green eyes somewhere. He just had to get her out from behind this wall she'd built. He couldn't do that in the middle of a ballroom with the *ton*'s gaze on him unblinking, assigning nuance to every move.

'We can't talk here.' Cassian put his mouth close to her ear, breathing in the vanilla sweetness of her, a scent he thought he might never smell again. 'Meet me in the library. We need privacy.'

She pulled back, fixing him with a look of pure disdain. 'So that you can compromise me? You forget I know what happens in private with you.' Her words carried a bite. Is that what she thought of him? Em would never have thought twice about being alone with him. Em would have relished every moment. But Em had no reputation to protect, no consequences to think about should they be caught. He understood: Lady Penrose Prideaux had everything to risk.

'Please, give me five minutes. There are things we must say to one another, questions that need answering.' Five precious minutes to change their trajectory. 'If you don't give me those five minutes now, I will be back tomorrow and the day after that. You will not be rid of me until you hear what I have to say.'

Logic flickered in her eyes as she weighed her decision: to see him now for five minutes alone, or to allow him to come back where his time might be unlimited, where he might have a chance to speak with her father. 'All right,' she said, relenting. 'The library. But only for five minutes.'

Victory lit him up from the inside. Cassian returned her to her father and bowed over her hand. He made his way casually to the library, stopping to talk here and there with friends, making sure no one would align his disappearance from the ballroom with hers.

The library was thankfully dark, signalling its emptiness. Cassian turned up a lamp and stirred the fire. He poured himself a drink while the mantel clock ticked off the minutes and he waited. By the time she arrived he'd begun to doubt her intentions. She'd made this promise before and broken it. 'You're late,' he ground out from his chair by the fire.

'How can I be late? We didn't set a time.' Penrose shut the door behind her but kept her distance. Perhaps their dance had affected her more than she'd let on, perhaps she was the one who didn't trust herself with him. One touch, one kiss and she'd crumble. But there was too much to settle between them before he could contemplate such actions.

'Forgive me my doubt, but you have something of a track record in the absentee area.' Cassian rose and poured another drink. Redruth kept excellent brandy. The clock chimed half past eleven.

'Your five minutes are starting.'

'Then let's cut to the chase. Why did you leave me?' Cassian fixed her with a stare over the rim of his tumbler.

'Why does it matter? What we had between us was never going to last. We were going to leave each other sooner or later.'

'But why *then*? We had plans.' He wanted to melt the glacier of her exterior with a reminder of the heat that had passed between them, of what he'd done to her, of how she'd felt when he'd done it. Surely, she didn't think the passion between them was usual? 'You'd wanted to—'

Pen's cheeks flamed in the darkness. She cut him off sharply. 'I know what I wanted. A gentleman wouldn't mention such a thing.' It was a wanton desire, one she'd not likely forget.

He moved nearer, closing the distance between them, his voice a sibilant seduction in the firelit darkness. 'You lied to me. You told me you would come and you didn't.' His voice lulled her toward confession, his words dragging her back into the fantasy where Em and Matthew could ignite each other with a touch. Beyond him the fire crackled and popped.

Pen shook her head. 'When I made you that promise, I meant to come.' She covered her mouth. No. She would not explain to him. Em might have explained. But Em and Matthew were no more and neither was what had existed between them—that had been as great a fiction as their names. She'd made a grievous mistake and now her little adventure had come back to haunt her. 'No, I won't apologise.' Pen straightened her shoulders and fixed him with a stare, hardening her resolve and summoning all the reasons he was dangerous, all the reasons she detested him. He was everything she wanted to avoid in a husband. 'You're acting like the wronged party here, but I never lied to you. Even as Em, I told you my father was pursuing a match for me. You knew.'

'I thought it was a merchant, a tradesman. When you mentioned the roses, I thought perhaps a land steward, a landscaper. You led me to believe—' he fired back but she was quick to interrupt.

'I never told you that, I never misled you. You did that all by yourself, drawing whatever conclusions you wanted.'

'What else was I supposed to think?' Anger was growing now. The viscount had a hot temper. 'You let me think you were a commoner. You knew that's what I thought and you allowed it to go on.'

Pen gave a snort of disbelief. '*Who* was in disguise? It was not only me. You presented yourself as a squire's son with your dirt-caked boots and your greatcoat and your windblown hair. You weren't half as put together as you are tonight. Where were your silk waistcoats and watch fobs then?'

'One does not wear such finery when tromping the cliffs of Cornwall. I was unaware there was a dress code for that.' His eyes narrowed, scrutinising her, and she felt a flush of heat go through her. 'Besides, those were our rules, Pen. *Anonymity was our rule.*' Her heart raced a bit at the use of her name, her real name. She could not afford the attraction. 'We wanted our secrets. Do you deny it?'

No. She couldn't deny it. The fantasy had been intoxicating, only now did she realise how far out of her depth she'd been. 'I never thought...' She couldn't finish the sentence without admitting her stupidity. Even in the dim light of the room, her cheeks betrayed her with remembrances of the things she'd done with him, of the things he'd done to her, thinking she would never see him again, that she'd never need to be accountable for them.

Cassian—that was his name, wasn't it? It was how he'd been introduced to her tonight. Cassian Truscott, Viscount Trevethow. It was strange to think of him that way—chuckled softly. 'Never thought what? That we'd both be masquerading as someone we were not? Never thought your little indiscretion would come back on you?' It was exactly what she'd thought. Never mind the false names. She'd thought there was truth in how he'd presented himself. Even if she didn't know his name, she'd been confident she knew what he was.

He reached for her, close enough now to touch her, his hand skimming her cheek. Her body thrummed at his caress, remembering other touches, other caresses. She had to keep herself in check. She could not repeat her mistakes. 'Can we get past this, Pen? I know you were surprised to see me again tonight just as I was surprised—*stunned*—to see you. I'd given up hope of finding you again.' His voice was low, intimate. 'I was devastated when you didn't come. I waited for hours that afternoon. I went back for three days hoping you would be there. I didn't want to believe you'd left me. But now, we've found each other and this should be a happy occasion. We don't have to pretend any more. We can be ourselves, we can continue to explore what we can be together. Pen, what I'm saying is that I forgive you. I want to try again.'

The cad! How dare he make this disaster out to be of her making? She'd almost been drawn into the fantasy, almost. Pen swatted at his hand, pushing it away. 'Do not touch me. Do not think you can waltz in here, ask me to shoulder the blame and then offer me forgiveness I've never asked you for as if this is all my fault.'

She was blazing now, but with the heat of an anger that had nothing to do with the warmth she'd felt earlier. 'There is a liar in this room and it's not me. I've been nothing but honest about having a match being made for me, about going away to visit the man my father chose for me. But you were never honest. You made all these protestations of love when we were together and tonight you profess to have been devastated when I didn't come, but here you are in a ballroom hunting a wife and contemplating marriage just weeks later. Those are not the actions of a devastated man in love.'

He stood there, unmoving. There was no reaction and that only made her all the angrier. 'Say something, Cassian. Argue with me, shout at me. Hate me.'

But Cassian did none of those things. He was perfect in those moments; perfectly controlled, perfectly contained. He looked every inch the duke he would one day be while she was acting nowhere near a lady. 'I don't want to argue with you. I don't want to shout. I don't want to hate. I want you to see the good in this. Matthew and Em had something special and now Cassian and Pen can have that too. You can have Matthew, Pen. He's not gone.'

She shook her head. She would not be taken in again. What did he want from her that he

was willing to set aside his anger and his earlier sense of betrayal? 'No, I can't. Matthew
doesn't exist. He never did and that means the
man I thought you were isn't the man you are.'
She'd nearly given herself to a pretence. She'd
had a lucky escape even if she hadn't realised
it at the time. What would have happened if
her father and Phin hadn't whisked her off to
London?

'What is that supposed to mean? If Matthew
doesn't exist, then how do you know anything
about me? You can't have it both ways.'

'I know you're here and I know *why* you're
here. You are no different than any other man
in the ballroom tonight. Do you think any
of them care about me? They care about the
Redruth alliance and the dowry that comes
with it. When they dance with me, they're already calculating how they can pay off their
debts or they're wondering why I've been hidden away in Cornwall for years. I'm a thing to
them, a curiosity.'

'Not to me, you *know* that,' Cassian insisted.
'What about Mutton Cove and the things we
told one another?'

'What I *know* is that you played with me in

the gamekeeper's cottage, knowing that you would leave at the end of April. You started the affair knowing full well the Season would take you away. Dukes' sons dally with common maids all the time, intending to discard them.'

'That's not how it was,' he broke in, but she stalled him with a shake of her head. She wanted to believe otherwise, but the facts wouldn't allow it. Her heart was breaking all over again.

'It's exactly how it was. I was nothing to you then but a plaything and I am nothing more than that to you now. Viscount Trevethow came to court me sight unseen. You had an audience with my father, the two of you arranging my life without any consideration for how I might feel about it, all so that my father might have husband with a title for his daughter and so that you might have an alliance you find in some way useful. That is all the proof I need that you are no different than any other man here tonight. The one thing I thought Matthew could be capable of was liking me for me. You've taken that away.' That was what hurt the most about this whole debacle. She drew a breath and smoothed her skirts, calming herself. 'You've had more than your five minutes. I need to return to the ball. I would like you to leave the premises when you've finished your drink.'

She walked to the door and slipped out into the hall without a backward glance, letting her anger sustain her. It was better than giving in to other emotions. She felt as if someone had died. Matthew, and who she thought he was, was gone. Cassian Truscott could never replace him. He must be resisted at all costs. He might look like Matthew, but he did not share the values she'd associated with Matthew. She would not take a husband that was settled on her by her father, but that wasn't Cassian Truscott's greatest sin. His greatest sin was that he was supposed to have been different from the others and he wasn't. He'd gone to her father without even knowing who she was. He'd been willing to buy her sight unseen. It reduced her to a sack of potatoes in the market place, something to be bartered and traded while he'd pretended to have a different code of honour with a different girl in the cottage.

She would not set herself up for failure and

heartbreak. She didn't want to marry a man who would hurt her. She knew already Cassian Truscott had the power to do that. She'd loved that man in the cottage and that man had moved on to another woman, a woman he'd never seen, with no regret. She could not give her heart again to such a man, knowing what she risked. He would hurt her over and over again. He would say whatever it took to win her in the moment, but he could never be true. He'd proven it tonight.

Chapter Thirteen

He'd not proven himself worthy of her. She'd dismissed him for a cad, a man who was pursuing her only for her money, and she wasn't entirely wrong. He had come courting the Redruth girl for those very reasons. Cassian was still reeling from her set-down the next morning over coffee in his rooms at the Albany. He deserved everything Pen had said last night. He couldn't recall the last time or *any* time a woman had not responded favourably to him. The evening could not be termed as anything other than an utter failure.

'Another resounding success for you, old chap!' Inigo strode into the dining room and slapped the newspapers down on the table, pages already creased back. 'One night back in action and already you've made the columns. Allow me to read aloud.' He cleared his throat dramatically. '"Viscount T. set hearts to fluttering and tongues to wagging when he took to the floor at Earl R.'s long-overdue debut ball for Lady P. with said lady in his arms." Then there's this charming little mention.' Inigo reached for another newspaper.

Cassian shook his head. 'Stop. It was a disaster, Inigo. She's all but refused to see me. She threw me out of the ball.'

Inigo pulled up a chair and poured a cup of coffee, becoming instantly serious. 'Well, at least no one knows.' He nodded towards the papers. 'Everyone thinks a St George's wedding is imminent. So, she's refused you. We can work with that. Once she knows you, I'm sure she'll find you charming and your height less overwhelming. You can cut an intimidating figure, Cass.'

'That's the problem. She does know me.' Cassian leaned close to whisper, 'Inigo, she's Em.' There was some satisfaction in watching Inigo's face process the information, moving from confused to dawning realisation to stunned.

'Oh, damn.' Inigo whistled low. 'I'm not sure if that's lucky or not.'

'It's *not*,' Cassian growled. 'I've found her, but she wants nothing to do with me. She thinks I was merely toying with her in the cottage, a nobleman taking advantage of a commoner. Worse, she feels now that I'm here pursuing a wife so soon after our encounter that nothing I said was true, that my feelings were a sham just to seduce her, that I'll say anything to get what I want.' Cassian pushed his plate away—what little appetite he'd had was gone. Guilt was eating at him hard: guilt over Pen, guilt over Collin. He couldn't satisfy one without being untrue to the other. 'It seems I've become the unscrupulous fortune hunter I've guarded myself against.' That thought had haunted him long after he'd left Byerd House.

'May I? If you're not going to eat this?' Inigo reached for the discarded plate still full of warm food. 'Your cook does the best eggs.'

'I'm glad someone can eat,' Cassian replied pointedly. 'The rub is that for a moment last night, when I saw her face, I thought everything would be perfect. We'd found each other and we could pick up where we left off. Then, everything fell apart. The only things I'm picking up now are pieces. I need to win her back. I need her trust.' He needed Em.

'You need her land.' Inigo waved his fork.

'I need her attention before I can contemplate that. How do I pursue a woman who doesn't want to be pursued?'

'You go back. If you don't go back, she'll know you were all fluff and no substance. But...' Inigo dropped his voice conspiratorially '...if you go back, she'll know you're willing to fight for her, that you're serious.'

Cassian chuckled. 'I told Eaton something similar when he was certain he'd lost Eliza. It's a lot easier to give advice than it is to take it.' He fixed Inigo with a sombre stare, his mind working. He had to show Pen the man who was concerned for his people, for his region, a man who was willing to create an industry, to create jobs and income, a man who was willing to come down out of his ivory tower and put his privilege to work for others. Most of all, he needed to show her the man she'd fallen in love with at the cottage. 'What time is it?'

Inigo flipped open his pocket watch. 'Half past eleven. Why?'

Cassian set aside his napkin and rose. 'That's just enough time.'

'Time for what?' Inigo looked up from polishing off the plate.

Cassian grinned, feeling more optimistic than he had in a long while. 'To win her back.' Lady Penrose and her aunt held at-home on Thursdays from three until five. He had four hours to make himself presentable and to acquire the appropriate 'accessories' for his visit. He'd have to time his entrance just right. If her attitude last night was a solid indicator about her husband hunt, she wasn't enamoured of it. She'd had a cynical view of why the young men had flocked to her. Cassian would bet she wasn't looking forward to an at-home the night after her debut. It would be crowded with sycophants. By quarter past four, he'd wager she'd be looking for a way out and he'd be there to provide one. Even the strongest damsel needed to be rescued sometimes. He called for his manservant. 'Send to the stables, have the horses and Oscar ready at four.'

Pen felt her pasted-on smile start to waver as yet another gentleman paid homage to her eyes, her hair, her gown, her laugh, with insipid words designed to appeal to her. Flattery did not impress her. Honesty impressed her and that had been in short supply. She'd almost welcome the man who'd burst into the drawing room and declare in loud terms, 'I'm here for your dowry, Lady Penrose, and you can come along too.' At least she'd know where she stood with that man. She had to be honest, too, though. That man, should he exist, might be welcomed for his truthfulness, but she wouldn't marry him for it any more than she'd marry Wadesbridge for his kindnesses. It didn't change the fact that she wanted to marry a man of her choice for love, his antecedents and her dowry be hanged.

She glanced surreptitiously at the clock. It was four. An hour to go. It might as well be an eternity. The minutes seemed to drag. Her jaw actually hurt from endless smiling. Her brain hurt from trying to remember all the names. She'd danced with most of these men last night. They'd sent bouquets this morning until the house was bursting with vases full of roses, carnations and lilies of the valley filling up every available mantel and tabletop in the townhouse. Her father had beamed with delight when the morning papers had joined her name with Cassian's. Her father would be disappointed when her aunt reported Cassian was the only one not among the crop in the drawing room today.

As to her own disappointment, Pen wasn't certain. Part of her had hoped he might come even though she'd been quite clear last night that she didn't want to see him again. Part of her was glad he'd taken the set-down to heart and stayed away. But no part of her believed that was the end of it. So, here she sat, waiting for the other shoe to drop, as if discovering that Cassian was Matthew wasn't shocking revelation enough.

Even this afternoon, with time to process that reality, it was still stunning. He was not lost to her after all. Oh, how she'd felt last night when she'd seen his face and knew it was him, not a mirage! For a moment, it had been a miraculous discovery. There'd been a split second of pure joy before reality had swept in, bringing with it all the consequences of what his presence meant: for him to be here meant he'd not been honest with her and he was dangerous to her. He could expose what they'd done in that cottage and she'd be ruined. Furthermore, he wanted something from her father enough to court her sight unseen. That in itself should be frightening. Logic proposed she ought to be glad he hadn't come to the at-home.

But it wasn't that simple. Her heart, her body, disagreed with what her mind recommended. Last night in his arms, she'd been hard put not to press herself against him as they waltzed, convention be hanged. It had been torture to be close to him, but not close enough to feel the hard muscles of his chest beneath his clothes, to not be able to lay her head against his shoulder, to feel his arm around her, folding her to him. She'd had to resist those temptations not only for propriety's sake, but for her own sake. He would take advantage of those feelings and the stakes were so much higher now. Marriage. For ever. Her father would be ecstatic. His daughter, a duchess! He would gloat that Father knew best after all. Yet, her eyes still drifted to the doorway and she had to remind herself of all the reasons Cassian wouldn't come through it.

The largest reasons of course was that Cassian wouldn't come today after that scathing set-down and that was as it should be, needed to be. Second, she didn't *want* to see him. At least that was what she told herself as she raised her fan to hide a yawn. Young Daniel Strathearn on her left was telling another story about his grandmother. He was very fond of his grandmother. This was the fourth story this afternoon. What she would give to be whisked away. She wondered if she could plead a head-ache and leave her aunt to manage the rest? But, no, a headache would land her in bed with one of Cook's odious possets.

There was a commotion at the drawing-room door, enough to excuse glancing away from Daniel Strathearn. Her fan stopped oscillating and her breath caught. Cassian had arrived. He'd come, after all. Her set-down had been nothing but a paper tiger and he'd charged right through it, which meant he didn't believe there wasn't anything left to say. That both consoled and concerned her. He wouldn't have come back if he didn't want something.

Her aunt caught her eye with a quiet look of approval, a little smile of delight on her lips. In fact, every woman in the room, every cousin, every sister, every mother who'd accompanied their male relatives here today to make the visit look more altruistic, was smiling as he wove through the room. How could they not? He put every man in the room to shame. He was taller, broader, better dressed, more at ease. More everything. There was an energy that rolled off him and permeated the room. He made no secret of his intentions. All that masculinity was headed straight for her. Pen held her nervous hands still in the depths of her skirts. What did one say to a man she'd sent out of the house the prior night?

He bowed before her, dressed for driving in immaculate in nankeen riding breeches, polished tall boots and coat of claret superfine with pristine linen beneath a cream waistcoat that sported a pattern of twining poppies. His jaw was new-shaven and his hair brushed back, exposing every sharp angle of his face: the strong jaw, the hawkish length of his nose. His whisky eyes were on her, a challenge on his lips. 'Lady Penrose, you look a tad wilted today. I hope last night didn't take a toll on you.'

Wilted? Did he just say she looked wilted in a room full of men who'd been praising her beauty? There was a moment's silence as if the rest of the room couldn't believe what they'd heard either. 'Perhaps we might rectify that with some fresh air.' His eyes sparked. 'May I interest you in a drive? You're nearly done here. I'm sure the gentlemen won't mind me stealing you since they've had you all afternoon. My phaeton is waiting outside.'

Escape! Even if it was with Cassian. She was desperate enough to take it and perhaps it was the chance she needed to determine what his intentions were. If there was to be a battle between them, it was best to know her enemy. Pen glanced at her aunt for permission. 'Air does sound wonderful,' she prompted, earning a nod from her aunt. She put her hand in Cassian's and let him lead her from the room while her guests looked on in varying degrees of disappointment.

Cassian's phaeton was a gorgeous bright blue lacquered affair with a black leather seat and pulled by two matched blacks jingling in their harness. They were groomed to perfection, coats gleaming and blue plumes dancing from their head gear. Hours of effort had gone into preparing the horses and the equipage. His tiger in blue livery rode on the rear bench beside a large wicker basket. 'We'll be noticed by everyone we pass,' Pen commented as he handed her up to the high seat. Perhaps that was what he intended, to be as conspicuous as possible. She wasn't sure she liked that.

'That's the point.' Cassian grinned as he vaulted into the driver's seat and picked up the reins. 'I want everyone to know I went driving today with Lady Penrose Prideaux.'

'The wilted flower of the *ton*? Are you sure you want to be seen with her?' Pen queried.

'I had to say something to get you out of there.' Cassian turned the horses into the traffic. 'We'll take a turn through the park.' That was what she feared; that he was a man who might say anything to get what he wanted. Had that been the case at the cottage? Were his words just pretty persuasion?

'Why did you come at all? I thought I'd made myself clear last night. Are you a glutton for punishment?'

'I'm a glutton for *you*.' Cassian slid her a look that melted her resolve. 'I came because I don't want to give up on us. Matthew and Em had something special. Maybe Cassian and Pen can have that, too, but we have to discover it, to discover each other all over again or perhaps for the first time. Now, we can do it without pretence. We can be ourselves, all our cards are on the table. We don't have to hide.' He was so impassioned in his plea, she wanted to believe him. But she couldn't, not yet.

'Why would you want that? You were clearly ready to settle for less.' She'd already accepted him at face value once before, to her detriment, she feared. She couldn't afford to do that again.

'Because I didn't have a choice, Pen. You were gone. I had to move forward.' They turned into the park, joining the line of carriages parading down the lanes, and Pen tried to summon the loathing, the sense of betrayal that had given her strength last night, but found her defences lacking.

'And you chose Redruth's daughter to move forward with. Why?' The best she could do was wariness and caution. She needed her answers. He made it sound easy, but it wasn't. There were things they couldn't change, like the fact that he was willing to marry a woman he'd never met after he'd professed love to another. She needed a loyal man. Could he be that?

'Redruth is close to home. It made sense for me to seek a Cornish alliance. I'm not out to hurt you, Pen.' Cassian steered the phaeton into the park, choosing to enter through the Kensington Gate at the north-west corner as opposed to the much busier Cumberland entrance.

'Where are we going?' Pen twisted in her seat, looking around and noting the relative absence of people, of horses and carriages. The public had suddenly become quite private.

'The north-west enclosure, some place where we can talk. It will be less crowded and I have a surprise for you. Do you trust me?'

'I don't know.' She was suddenly at sea. Did she dare trust him again?

'That's not a no, so it's a beginning. I'll take that.' Cassian parked the phaeton and called for his tiger to hold the horses. 'We'll walk from here. Horses and carriages aren't allowed in the enclosure.' Cassian climbed down and came around. He reached up for her, his hands at her waist, and swung her down with an impressive ease that was not lost on her. She was nothing for his strength and she relished the feel of his hands on her, confident and warm. She'd missed his touch. 'First things first, there's someone who wants to meet you.' He tucked her arm firmly through his as led her to the back of the phaeton and the big wicker basket. It rocked as they approached and a sharp bark escaped.

'Oh! What is it?' Pen exclaimed, startled by the sound.

'Your birthday present.' Cassian reached inside and lifted out the pup. 'This is Oscar. I brought him with me when I went to the cottage. I'd wanted to give you a day with a puppy. Here, hold him.' Cassian deposited him into her arms as the puppy wiggled.

This was no good at all—how dare Cassian not play fair? One look at those dark puppy eyes and she was lost. How was she to resist Cassian and a puppy, too? 'I can't keep him,' she stammered.

'I know.' Cassian grinned boyishly. He fastened a leash around Oscar's collar. 'I'll keep him for you.'

'I'll be forced to visit you,' Pen pointed out, another unfair move.

'Yes, exactly.' Cassian took the puppy and

set him on the ground. 'Now, Lady Pen, would you like to walk your dog?'

Oh, she did! This was a childhood dream come true. She shouldn't accept it, she *knew* he was bribing her. It scared and exhilarated her. He'd brought the puppy all the way to London. She furrowed her brow and stopped. 'Why did you bring the puppy to London if you didn't know I'd be here?'

Cassian stopped too. 'Because I missed Em that much and the puppy was a way to keep her close. Why do you wear that glass heart?' She reached up to finger it with her free hand.

'Because I miss Matthew,' she admitted. 'But that doesn't mean…'

'I know what it doesn't mean, Pen,' Cassian said softly. He ushered her and Oscar through the front gates of the enclosure, his hand light at her back. 'There are benches inside where we can sit.' He laughed, a low, familiar chuckle at her ear. 'I know a game we can play. Twenty questions. Maybe you've heard of it?'

'Like old times?' Pen asked, immediately wary, not only of him and the easy assumptions he made with his hands and his words, but also of herself and the ease with which she'd gladly glide back into the old behaviour if she wasn't vigilant.

Cassian shook his head, his gaze resting on her. 'No, like *new* times. I don't think we can go back, Pen. We can only go forward.' But the past *would* come forward with them. It would always be between them, reminding them of the potential for passion, for loss, and the consequences of risk, both the good and the bad. 'Give me a chance to know the real you. Give yourself a chance to know the real me before you decide to throw happiness away with both hands.'

Chapter Fourteen

Pen could see why he'd chosen this spot. It was peaceful and green. There was a pasture with deer and cows to one side and a keeper's lodge to the other. The Serpentine served as one border and Kensington Gardens served as another. Within the enclosure, two springs contributed to the country coolness of the space. 'Would you like a glass?' Cassian offered as they strolled past an old woman sitting at a table beside the springs. Oscar gave her a friendly high-pitched puppy yap. 'One of the springs is a mineral spring.' Cassian stopped and fished out coins from his pocket for two glasses. 'You should try some. The water is always cold. Perfect for a warm day like today.' He gave her a glass and they went to the spring to drink.

Pen sipped the water, tentative about the

taste. She smiled, pleasantly surprised as the cool water slid down her throat. 'It's so much more refreshing than hot tea. What's the other spring for? Is it mineral water, too?'

'People come to bathe their eyes from it. I don't know if it works. Do you have weak eyes? Should we try?' Cassian laughed and the sound made her smile. This was the man she'd wandered the St Piran's Day fair with, to whom everything was an adventure.

'I'll pass on that today. My eyes are fine.' She could feel herself starting to relax, starting to remember how it was between them, how easily they talked, how comfortably they moved together. Surely those things weren't lies? Remembering made it easy to forget the wariness she'd armed herself with, the knowledge that this man, who wasn't dangerous to Em, was indeed dangerous to Pen. She needed to determine how dangerous and in what ways.

'I think the enclosure's gamekeeper has the best job in the world,' Cassian nodded towards the lodge with its picturesque gardens. 'To be able to live here, surrounded by the feel of the countryside, and still be in one of the world's most vibrant cities. Anything he wants or needs is within his grasp without sacrificing tranquillity.' He gave her a smile. 'How do you find your first time in London?'

'In a word, overwhelming. There are so many rules, so many people, so many things to do and to see, and everything seems to require a change of dress to do it. Phin is determined that I see it all. He's taken me everywhere: the Tower, Astley's, Gunter's, we've seen the cathedrals, the British Museum, the art at Somerset House. I've shopped on Bond Street incessantly and excessively. I've never had as many clothes or needed as many.' This was safe conversation. It was personal but not terribly probing. There was nothing dangerous in it, no disclosures, no secrets.

They stopped beneath a shady oak. Cassian brushed off the bench, freeing it of tree debris for her to sit. Em would not have cared, but Em hadn't worn expensive Bond Street gowns. 'Can't have you ruining your dresses,' he teased. 'London suits you. There's an adventure around every corner. Isn't that what you wanted?' Oh, there it was, the danger, in just a few words, there was the reminder that she'd shared her innermost thoughts with him. That he was the keeper of her secrets, the things she told no one else.

'It does suit, in a way.' She was contemplative as they rested, enjoying the view of the pasture as Oscar romped in the grass. 'But London takes some getting used to. It's thrown several things into sharp relief for me.'

'Like what?' Cassian whispered the prompt, coaxing the intimacy to life between them, overriding her misgivings.

'Do you truly want to know? They're rather dark things.' She cocked her head and fixed him with her green stare, challenging him. 'Along with the adventure, there's also noise and danger lurking around every corner, especially for a woman.'

'Is that your father speaking or is that you?' Cassian queried to her surprise.

'You remembered.' She softened, touched that he'd recalled the story she'd told him in the cottage. 'Perhaps it's both. However, I wonder if it's really true or if that's a construct men have made up to keep women dependent. Even in London, a supposedly civilised city, I can't go anywhere without an escort. Apparently, even a gentleman of my own class can't be trusted to not be a ravening beast, unable to control his urges in my feminine presence. My very femininity is enough to tempt him. To make his lack of control my fault is ridiculous.' She sighed.

'You're safe with me, Pen.' His hand was warm on hers, his thumb stroking her knuckles. This was her opening and she took it.

'Am I? It occurred to me, after the shock of seeing you again had settled, that I might be in the greatest danger *from* you. You would only have come back today if there was something you wanted and you have the power to get it.' She let her eyes linger on him, watching his face for any reaction, that she was right. 'The cottage, Cassian. You could blackmail me with it.'

A slow smile spread across his face. Apparently, he found some humour in her very serious suggestion. 'And you could blackmail me with the same. Have you thought of that?' He raised her hand to his lips and kissed her knuckles. 'Perhaps *I* am the one in danger? Perhaps, now that you know who I am, you will go to your father and say I compromised you. I know many girls who would do it to be a duchess.' He chuckled. 'Yet, I risked coming back today.'

'But *I* wouldn't do such a thing!' Pen protested, aghast at the thought. In her fear and in her haste, she'd not thought of that.

'Maybe that's why I risked it. Because I knew you wouldn't any more than I would do it to you,' he assured her with a laugh. 'What suspicious minds we have, Pen. No wonder we decided on false identities.'

But it was no laughing matter to Pen. She studied his face for a moment, a thought coming to her. 'Is it because of your brother? You mentioned he was thwarted in love.' It would have been a high-born alliance, she could see that now.

'In part.' Cassian shifted on the bench and crossed a leg over one knee. Ah, the topic made him uncomfortable. Well, good. It was his turn for a change. 'He fell in love with the daughter of a man he made investments with, only she was a decoy. He loved her, but her love for him was not real—it was an act to draw him in. It destroyed him. I would prefer to avoid such hardship if I could.'

'Is that possible, though? I don't think love

works that way. Love is hard, it demands sacrifice. If it was easy, the poets would have nothing to write about,' Pen said softly. 'I am sorry for him and for you in the losing of him.'

'I'd most likely be cynical any way, just as you are.' Cassian offered her a wry smile. 'It's not much fun being hunted. It's why I could not give you my real name.' She'd not forgotten how the women in the drawing room today had looked at him, with naked hunger in their eyes. They would devour him if given the chance, all for his title, with little thought for the man who bore it, the man who could build fires and sail a little boat among the seals of Mutton Cove. What she would give to be back in Mutton Cove now, with him.

'No, it's not.' She gave him a meaningful stare.

'Do you think I'm hunting you?' he asked quietly.

'Like you, I have to assume everyone is hunting me,' she answered. 'We are just animals in the great cage of London. The longer I'm here the more I realise I've confused adventure with freedom and what I really want is the latter. I want to be free. Free to make my own choices, to go where I want to go, to marry how I want to marry. To be who I want to be.'

'Is that why you went to the fair?' They were talking softly now. Birds chirped in the background.

'Yes.' The old intimacy flared to life between them, stoked into being by his touch, his voice, his words, the very nearness of him a source of support and solace. She offered him a smile tinged with mischief. 'Do you want to know a secret? The fair wasn't the first time I sneaked out of the castle.'

Cassian laughed, a low, deep rumble just for her. 'You minx. Where do you go when you sneak out?'

'To the hills. I like to walk and pick flowers and look for the little animals.' She looked down at their hands. 'How do you do it? How do you convince me to tell you all of this? Whenever I'm with you everything just comes out: my secrets, my fears, my hopes. I don't talk to anyone the way I talk to you.' And maybe she shouldn't. She didn't want to give him any more power than that which he already had.

'I'll take that as a compliment.' His eyes were on her. She knew that look, the one that lingered on her eyes and caressed her lips, just before his body leaned in, his head tilted to capture her lips, his mouth on hers, reminding her. A little mewl welled up in her throat as his hand cupped her jaw, encouraging her to open to him entirely. 'I mean to prove myself to you, Pen. I want you back,' he murmured between kisses. In those moments, she wanted that too. She wanted to pretend that he had no other agenda, that there was no danger here on the bench, just pleasure, just them and that a man could love her just for herself. Later she would remember all the reasons to resist.

The first invitation arrived the next morning along with a bouquet of wildflowers. The flowers had looked out of place in their simplicity against the enormous bouquets sent by others, but they meant the most, just to her. Even in this bouquet they had their privacy, their secrets. The flowers were a reminder of their visit to the enclosure. They were also proof that he'd listened. He'd remembered that little detail from when she'd confessed to sneaking out of the castle. 'Put them in my room, please.' She handed them off to a footman while her father was still agog over the invitation.

'The theatre, my dear, tonight if we're free. We are, of course. I'll have your aunt cancel any plans. We'll go. It will be a show of force. All of London will see that we approve and encourage Trevethow's attentions.' Her father handed her the note so she could read it too. After all, it was addressed to her. '*Pizarro* at the Covent Garden Theatre, it's a tragedy.' For a moment her father looked dubious. 'Hopefully it's not too bloody for you? Daniel Egerton plays Rolla and is said to do a passable job.'

'I'm sure I will enjoy it,' Pen put in quickly before her father could change his mind. They'd not been to the theatre yet and Pen was excited to go, no matter what the show, a treat that was marred only by her father's satisfaction. He was getting what he wanted—a suitor handpicked by himself.

'London will enjoy seeing the two of you together again.' Her father returned to his breakfast. 'What do you make of him, Pen? I have great hopes for Viscount Trevethow, although it might too early to disregard a few others. Viscount Wilmington, for instance. He's been most insistent. Your aunt said he was overtly disappointed yesterday with your disappearance. He told her he felt you should not have left with Trevethow.' He'd also been quite overt about his intentions with the largest bouquet of them all usurping Wadesbridge's pride of place on the drawing room mantel.

'I think it's too early to discard anyone.' The last thing Pen wanted was the field narrowed. Narrowing fields meant funnelling *her* towards making a decision.

'Still, being seen at the theatre with Viscount Trevethow will certainly boost your cachet.' He smiled. 'A duchess, Penrose. Just think how proud your mother would be if we could pull it off.'

Pen only smiled. She didn't want to argue with her father although she disagreed. She did think of her mother. Was that all her mother would have wanted for her? To marry well? That wasn't the mother she remembered. Her mother would have wanted her to marry for love, for happiness. Her mother had been full of laughter, she'd had little use for rules and society. She'd insisted on raising her own children instead of turning them over to a bevy of nurses and governesses. She'd hated leaving them for time in London with her husband. She'd invented games and taken them on picnics in the hills and told them stories; Cornish fairy tales or tales she invented as they looked up at the sky. Her mother was fearless. She climbed rocks with Phin and swam in the ocean. She filled Castle Byerd with colour, with life. Then one day she was simply gone, taking all that colour and life and laughter with her. But her mother would never have meant for her to live imprisoned by fear. Her mother would have wanted her to live vibrantly, and Pen would, starting with the theatre.

The theatre was bustling with life as Cassian's carriage pulled to the kerb in front of the Bow Street entrance, taking its turn to disgorge its passengers. Cassian handed Pen down, watching her face light up as she surveyed the Doric-columned facade. Cassian felt as if a shaft of sunlight had warmed him from the inside out. She stood still for a moment, letting humanity swerve around her as she studied the building. 'They've modelled the theatre after Minerva's Temple, haven't they?'

she exclaimed, recognising the likeness. 'I saw a picture once of the Acropolis in a book about Greece.'

'I knew you'd like it.' Cassian tucked her hand through his arm, feeling inordinately pleased. This was one adventure he could give her. There were other plays and other theatres, but he'd chosen this one on purpose for her appreciation of such details. He might not be able to take her to Greece, but he could show her a bit of Greece right here in London.

He loved her enthusiasm. Inside, she wasn't afraid to look around as she exclaimed, 'I know it's not polite to gawk, but I want to see everything!' And everyone wanted to see her. Cassian kept a strong hand at her back, ushering her up the grand staircase on the left, stopping every few steps to greet people. Her enthusiasm was contagious, everything fresh and new through her eyes. When was the last time he'd been interested in the Box Saloon or the coffered ceilings or even noticed them? But with Pen, it was all brand new. He fed her excitement with stories and bits of information whispered at her ear. 'The theatre was rebuilt after a fire in 1808—this one is larger than the original.' Or, 'There were riots here when the seat prices were raised to cover the building the expenses.'

She looked over her shoulder at him with a smile. 'Are you as well informed on every subject?'

'There are some subjects I'd like to be better informed about,' Cassian flirted, his eyes dropping to her lips. Too bad her family was near. He'd like to steal a kiss right here in the box for all of London to see, claiming her as his own. But for now, it was enough to be here with her, to give her this night, to prove to her that he was worthy and to hope that all else would follow.

He settled her in a seat at the front of the box and saw to her family's comfort before taking the seat beside her as the lights went down. Under the cover of darkness, he felt her hand grope for his. A moment later her head bent to his with a whisper. 'Thank you for this.'

His heart swelled at the simple praise even as his mind counselled caution. Would she thank him later? Would she believe all this truly had been for her if she found out about the land? This was the shard of guilt that had lodged itself in his conscience as he'd planned his campaign. His heart wanted her back, land or not. But his mind, his dream, his legacy, the guilt he needed to assuage over his brother, needed to win her. She was the key to his land. Without that land there was no pleasure garden, no boost to the Cornish economy, no jobs for hundreds of unemployed workers, no atonement. Perhaps he should tell her about the land. But how could he? This new burgeoning trust between them was too fragile. He couldn't tell her. Not yet. There would be a better time, a time when she would understand, a time when she would know that he cared for her apart from the land. If she knew too soon, it would only prove to her what she already thought was true: that he was no better than any other suitor come to trade titles and money in a political alliance.

Those suitors came in droves at the intermission, crowding the box to such an extent that Cassian felt obliged to move the party out into the Box Saloon so that no one was crushed. Viscount Wilmington was one of the first to arrive, levelling daggers at Cassian for his interruption yesterday. 'You've stolen her from us twice now, Trevethow,' he joked loudly enough for the other gentlemen nearby to hear in hopes of garnering an ally with his feigned bonhomie. 'It was a bold move, taking her for a drive in the Park. Perhaps I might try it myself.' He arched an enquiring eyebrow Pen's direction. 'Might I steal you away for the last act, my lady? My box has a rather unique view of the stage.'

Cassian was prepared to intervene, but Pen was cool beside him. 'I think you've misunderstood yesterday's events, Lord Wilmington. No one steals me. I make my own decisions about where I spend my time and with whom.' She smiled to take away the sting.

Wilmington gave a curt nod. 'Another time, then. If you enjoy the theatre, I also have seats at Drury Lane.' He bowed and made his farewells.

Cassian watched him retreat with careful eyes. 'He is quite intense where you are concerned.' He might have made an enemy. He'd have to ask Inigo about Wilmington tomorrow. What was the source of Wilmington's interest in Pen? Was it just the competition of the

Season or did it stem from something more? The lights dimmed in warning for the final act and Cassian returned Pen to her seat. She'd been a revelation in the Saloon. Despite her claims of being overwhelmed by London, she'd handled the attention well, just as she'd handled it splendidly the night of her ball.

Cassian leaned close. 'Have I told you how beautiful you look tonight?' She had opted for a gauzy gown of rose-gold with satin striping. The effect was stunning. She looked softly alluring, managing at once to present the image of the debutante while also projecting intelligence and sharp wit. It was no wonder every man in the theatre had been drawn to her. Her hair was twined with a rope of pearls and behind one ear was a small, pink wildflower. 'You're wearing one my flowers.'

'Yes. It was the most thoughtful bouquet I received. Wherever did you find them?'

'I rode out to Hampstead Heath.' He grinned. 'We should picnic there and you can pick flowers to your heart's content. Shall we? Tomorrow? I'll call for you at one.'

'Don't we get to discuss this?' she scolded.

But Cassian simply smiled as the stage lights went up and replied, 'No, the play is starting and we wouldn't want to be rude.'

Chapter Fifteen

This was progress; lying on a blanket in the sun, the smell of sweet grass in the air, watching Pen weave a flower chain while bees buzzed, Oscar napped on the blanket and the May day behaved perfectly. Beyond them were her maid and his tiger, but they had privacy enough should they want to behave less properly than the weather.

Pen held up a necklace of daisies. 'There, I've made a lei in honour of King Kamehameha's visit to London.' The newspapers had been full of the Hawaiian King since his arrival on the eighteenth. But he'd been confined to his suites at Osborn's Hotel until King George could receive him, or *chose to* receive him as some less favourable news reported. Some papers suggested the English King had no intention of meeting the Hawaiian King, or the Sandwich Island King, depending on which paper one read.

'Are you interested in meeting them?' Cassian propped himself up on one arm. 'Secretary Canning is giving a reception for them in a few days. The Foreign Office has taken over the visit since the King drags his feet on meeting them. Canning has invited several dukes, Wellington included, along with the Duke and Duchess of Hayle and their son.' He watched her eyes light up as she grasped his intentions.

'Really? I could meet them? People from halfway around the world? People from a place I've only read about?' She gave him an infectious smile. 'Perhaps I should make some more English leis.' Then she sobered and reached out a hand to touch his. 'I fear you are spoiling me. First the theatre and now this.'

He took her hand and threaded his fingers through it. 'Why do you fear it? I mean to win you back, Pen. I am serious about that. You told me the other night at the ball that I was not worthy of you, that I was no better than any other sycophant in the ballroom. I want to prove to you that I am better, that I am worthy of you and your dreams.'

'Please don't.' Pen tugged at her hand and he let it go, feeling as if a shadow had scuttled across the sun. 'It's not just that. I don't want to be traded in marriage. I don't want to be a pawn between my father and a man he's chosen for me, or my husband's pawn because my marriage settlement possesses something he wants. Marriage should be more. It should be trust, and honesty, and respect and love built between two people who *want* to share a life together, not just live in the same house.'

Yes! Yes! Cassian's soul wanted to cry out a chorus of yeses. Wasn't this exactly what he sought in a mate? What he thought he'd lost when he'd come to London to claim Redruth's daughter? Someone who wanted those things, too? But her next words dampened that enthusiasm. 'I don't know that you and I can have that, that we can get there after everything that's happened, not just between us, but with my father. He chose you, the Viscount Trevethow. He picked you out for me. And you picked out Redruth's daughter sight unseen. You were going to choose her over Em, always. No matter what you say about love, you chose duty first.'

This was the argument he dreaded, the one for which he had no good answer. He had chosen duty over love when he'd come to London. Even if he hadn't lost Em, he would still have chosen duty. How would she feel if she knew about the land? Perhaps he wouldn't have to tell her, if they chose each other voluntarily, if she fell in love with him the way Em had with Matthew? It was the coward's way out, but it was also the only way in which he could have both Pen and the land.

He reached out and smoothed back a strand of caramel hair that had fallen in her face. He didn't want to quarrel with her today, not with the sun out and this rare peaceful moment of privacy between them. London made it deuced difficult for them to be alone. He didn't want to waste the opportunity. He picked up the lei in her lap and changed the subject. 'How did you learn to make these? They look difficult.'

'They're not that hard.' Pen plucked two daisies and handed them to him. 'Copy me. First, you need to break off some of the stems to shorten them. Then, you can take your fingernail and make a slit right here on the stem.'

'With a fingernail?' Cassian arched a brow at the request and she laughed.

'Or a knife if you have one. Ladies so seldom carry knives, you know. We must make do with what's on our bodies.' She passed him a second flower. 'Now, you slide the stem of this flower through the slit, and repeat until you have a chain long enough.'

Bodies, slit, sliding and repeating.

Cassian shifted on the blanket. Daisy chains had suddenly become a rather sensual activity. 'Who taught you how to make them?' He was more interested in watching her face as she worked than in making his own. The task absorbed her entirely.

She looked up with a soft smile. 'My mother taught me. We used to make them when we went walking at home.'

Ah. The hills. The place she went when she sneaked out of the castle. 'And now you walk the hills alone.' The afternoon became intimately quiet, the buzzing of the bees in the nearby lavender more pronounced in the stillness.

'I'm not alone. I feel closest to her there. It's where I have the most memories of her.'

'You miss her.' It was a statement. He could hear the longing in her voice—it was a tone he recognised too well. 'What happened?' Their fingers were flirting with one another again, slowly moving to the middle ground between them on the blanket. He reached for her hand. Sometimes touching helped people to open up, to feel safe with their disclosures.

She didn't pull away. 'My mother was travelling to Truro to meet her sister. It was a sudden visit. Word had come early that afternoon my aunt, who was expecting a baby, was doing poorly and the child was imminent. My father was busy with the estate and couldn't accompany her on short notice. He asked her to wait, but my mother felt she couldn't delay. It had been a difficult pregnancy and my aunt was older.' She looked up at him, the memory giving her gaze a far-off look as if she was seeing beyond him into the past. 'It was one of the few times I'd ever heard them fight. My father denied her nothing and in the end he didn't deny her this. He called for the coach and off she went. But the quarrel had delayed departure and part of the journey would be made in the dark. Her coach was set upon by highwaymen.' Her voice caught and Cassian waited as she gathered herself.

'You needn't say any more,' he assured her. He knew how hard it was to talk of the dead, how stirring the memories stirred other aches as well.

'There's little more to say. The coachman and the outriders were killed defending her. One of them lived long enough to report my mother had drawn a pistol on the leader and shot him through the shoulder. She'd gone down fighting.' Pen smiled a bit at that. 'I wouldn't have expected it any other way. My mother wasn't afraid of the world or of anything or anyone in it. She always said, "Live your life, Pen, and don't worry if anyone else likes it. It's not their life."' She sighed. 'It's not easy to do that. I wish it was.'

Cassian heard the unspoken regret behind her words. Just the opposite had occurred. Pen's life had become the life her father chose for her. She wasn't free to explore the world. The world beyond Castle Byerd was limited to books and atlases. 'Did they ever catch the highwaymen?' Cassian asked quietly.

'No. It's been ten years. There's no likelihood of that now. Perhaps they've been caught by someone else and found justice that way. Criminals don't last long. That's what I have to believe, at least, if I want consolation or if I want to move forward and not be paralysed by fear.'

'Like your father?' Cassian prompted. He was starting to see now how large of a role fear had played in her life in the years. Fear had been her ruler whether or not it had been her choice. So much had been decided for her out of fear.

'Yes. My father regrets not stopping her. He regrets he wasn't able to catch them, that he didn't go with her.'

Cassian nodded. 'I felt that way when Collin died. I should have been there to stop it. I don't know if that kind of regret ever goes away.'

'That regret is eating him alive and the rest of us. He's taken that regret out on me, ensuring that nothing will happen to me. If he can keep me safe, then somehow he is making up for not keeping her safe. In the meanwhile, in his attempt to save my life, he's robbed me of it.' Her words were raw with resentment. At last, here was the source of the cynicism he'd heard as they'd walked in the enclosure at the Park, the bitterness he'd heard the night they'd quarrelled in the library.

'So you sneak out of the castle to remember, to escape, to live.' He saw more clearly what he was up against: her desire to choose her mate was more than selfish defiance. This was about reclaiming the freedom she'd been denied. She'd been locked in a castle for ten years like a princess in fairy story even if it had been done without malicious intent. Now, she was breaking free, only to risk being tied down again the moment she'd tasted that freedom. From that perspective it seemed almost cruel to have brought her to London, to let her taste freedom only to snatch it away.

Cassian leaned in, claiming her mouth in a sweet kiss. 'I can show you the world, Pen,' he promised.

'I know,' she breathed, her lips brushing his in return, the fire between them starting to ignite. The world was more than places…it was passion and pleasure. 'That's what scares me. How can I go back in the cage after I've seen it?' They were kissing in earnest now; mouths and tongues competing with words, air coming in ragged breaths.

'You wouldn't have to go back.' Cassian rolled her beneath him, his gaze intent on her face watching for any sign of capitulation.

'Don't make promises you can't keep, Cassian,' she warned softly. 'A duchess is the most gilded cage of all.' But there was no heat to the argument. The only heat was that which sprang between them on the blanket and warmed them overhead. Nature's heat, passion's heat, but not anger's.

'My duchess may do as she pleases.' Cassian nipped at her neck, feeling her pulse race beneath his mouth, his own desire rising hot and fast for this woman, for this moment. He would make her any promise.

'May she?' Pen's words were laced with sensual purpose. She pressed a hand to his chest. 'Shall we test that theory? Lie back.'

'Pen, what are you doing?' Cassian said warily, but it didn't stop him from complying. She gave him a wicked look full of meaning and he went hard. Dear sweet heavens. She meant to use her mouth. It took only the insight of a moment to understand her intention. She

worked the fall of his riding breeches open, her
eyes already wide at the prominent evidence of
his arousal. There was smug pride in her gaze,
too, a woman's pride that she could rouse him
so effortlessly. Perhaps there was surprise too.
'I had no idea a man could be so big, so hard.'

'Does it please you that I am?' Cassian le-
vered upwards on his elbows and stole a kiss.
Gone were talks of dead beloveds and regrets.
This afternoon was for the living.

She leaned up over him and kissed his mouth.
'What do you think? Now, hush. I have it on
good authority it's rude to talk when the show
is starting.'

'Show, is it?' He couldn't resist one last tease
as she wiggled down the length of him, her
mouth closing around the tip of his shaft, the
heat of her lips reducing him to a moan. Dear
lord, she was good at this. It just proved one
didn't need experience when one had curiosity
and ambition, and Pen was ambitious in the ex-
treme. She explored him with her tongue, lick-
ing at his length, lapping at his tip, tasting and
testing, as if he were a fine, well-aged vintage
and she a connoisseur who knew that one did

not gulp such a wine, but sipped it, savoured it. Which was all well and good up to a point.

She'd licked him to a frenzy. He dug his hands into the folds of the blanket, feeling the give of the grass beneath the fabric, his head arching to the sun, his eyes closed tight, the cords of his neck exposed and taut, every muscle in his body exerting themselves in a bid for restraint. He was not alone in the struggle. From his thighs, her own breaths came in ragged pants, her artful seduction degenerating into the primal. He gave a sharp groan as her teeth bit too hard in her excitement. Her head came up for a fleeting second. She was a wild thing, her hair falling forward, her eyes green fire before she took him again, working his length with her mouth until restraint could be held no longer. He let out a warning growl, giving her time to move away and take him in hand instead before he spent quite thoroughly against her palm, against his thigh, his stomach.

'Fireworks,' Pen murmured as she took a handkerchief from him. 'Or a great fountain.'

'Do you like fireworks?' Cassian adjusted his breeches, drew her up to him and settled her against his shoulder. Her efforts had left him pleasantly drained and drowsy. He wanted to hold her, wanted to feel her warm body against his.

'I like yours,' she teased gently.

'Tuesday is opening night at Vauxhall. I have a supper box. There will be dancing and fireworks and a hundred other entertainments. Will you come?'

She lifted her head. 'My father says Vauxhall is full of danger.'

'He can come with us. Perhaps if you're with me, he'll feel there is less to fear.'

'I think you are the danger.' But she didn't mean it. There was only joking in her words this time as she snuggled against him, her hand comfortable and familiar on his chest. For a moment they were Em and Matthew, lying together once more in the gamekeeper's cottage, content just to be. No, Cassian thought drowsily. Today they'd become more than Em and Matthew. Em and Matthew had nothing to lose, nothing to risk by being together. It was easy to share secrets with a stranger. But Cassian and Pen had much to risk and they had shared any way. It was a significant step forward towards winning her trust.

'I wonder what my mother would have thought of you?' Pen traced a circle on his shirt and Cassian regretted the invention of clothes. How wondrous it would have been to feel her finger on his skin, to lie beneath the sun naked with her, to feel the sun's heat on their bodies. Her finger stopped tracing and he could sense her gathering her thoughts. 'I talk to her a lot, not just when I'm out walking. Do you think that's crazy?'

'No.' His hand played idly through her hair, lifting it and dropping it. He liked lying her with her, listening to her think out loud. What a precious gift this was, a gift he thought he'd never have again.

'I think losing someone close changes your relationship to them. They're gone, but they're not gone. They're with you, in your mind, in your heart. Does that make any sense? Have you ever lost someone close to you besides your brother?'

'Yes. Last year, I lost a mentor, the Duke of Newlyn, Richard Penlerick.'

'I heard of it.' Pen rose up to look at him. 'You were close to him?'

'Our families were close. My father was life-long friends with him and he was like an uncle to me, a mentor. He encouraged me to travel, to pursue my dreams. I hear him sometimes in my head, telling me to go on, to not give up although I've done a terrible job of pursuing those dreams, of honouring his legacy.'

'Tell me your dreams. What are they? I want to hear every last one of them.' She smiled at him, a sun-dappled Circe in her yellow muslin and the temptation was great to lay all of his dreams at her feet, to see what she'd make of them, but the practical dreamer in him warned he could not risk it, not yet. Today had been perfect, he didn't dare tax that perfection any further.

He reached for her hand and kissed it. 'Perhaps I will tell you at Vauxhall with fireworks overhead.'

'I will hold you to that.'

'And I will hold you.' His arm tightened about her and he breathed her in, all vanilla and sunlight and daisies. Somehow, against the odds, he'd find a way to make this dream and the others come true.

Chapter Sixteen

The reception did not disappoint. The Gloucester Lodge gardens were beautifully lit, the scene of ladies and gentlemen strolling beneath the late-night glow serene as soft strains of summer music played in the background. Later, there would be a performance from the Life Guards band, but for now, all was a fairy land and she was part of it. Pen smiled as she looked about. When she thought of all that had happened since she'd come to London, she had to pinch herself.

'I can't believe it's all real,' she murmured to Cassian as they joined the promenade about the gardens. Most of all, she couldn't believe he was real.

It's too good to be true, whispered the unbelief in her head. *He wants something from Redruth and you're the key.*

'Believe it.' Cassian laughed, her enjoyment of the reception pleasing him.

'I'm not sure I dare for fear it will disappear. I'll wake up and discover it's all a dream.' She laughed up at him, but her words weren't entirely in jest. The last time she'd believed in him, he'd been snatched away without warning.

'Lord Trevethow!' A tall man with long dark hair drawn back called to them from beside a fountain where he stood with an elegant woman who nearly matched him in height. 'I thought I might find you here tonight.' The man's English was perfect, although his voice was tinted with an accent.

Cassian nodded the man's direction and ushered her over to make introductions. 'Prince Baklanov, Princess Klara, allow me to present Lady Penrose Prideaux. Lady Penrose, this is the esteemed Prince Nikolay Baklanov and his wife, Klara Baklanova. The Prince is lately of Kuban, formerly a captain in the Kubanian cavalry. Now he runs a riding academy in Leicester Square. His wife is the daughter of the Russian ambassador to Britain.'

'I'm pleased to meet you, Your Royal Highnesses.' Pen managed a curtsy, feeling overwhelmed. Of course a prince and a princess were just sitting here out in the open. It simply added to the magic of the night.

'Do you know of Kuban?' Princess Klara asked. 'Most people don't.'

'Yes, it's in the south of Russia. It seems very wild and magnificent.' Pen could see it in her mind on her maps where east met west along the border of the Ottoman Empire. She could picture the port at Ekaterinador and the long strip of the Kuban River running inland towards the capital.

'Magnificent. That is exactly the word for Kuban,' Prince Nikolay said approvingly. 'Most call it desolate but they don't know any better. I like her, Trevethow.'

Cassian placed his hand over hers, his gaze sliding towards her, warm and adoring. 'I like her too.' Then he lowered his voice. 'How is Prince Shevchenko? I heard it was a near-run thing. An abominable business in Shoreham, I'm afraid.'

Nikolay nodded, all seriousness. 'He and his new bride are well away. They've sailed off into the sunset, quite literally, but his neck is

242 *The Passions of Lord Trevethow*

intact and the officer in charge of the farce will be court-martialled.'

Pen didn't pretend to understand, but Cassian nodded his approval. 'I'll miss Shevchenko. He always had good vodka. You will, too, no doubt. There's only you left of the Russian Princes to do the diplomatic duty when called upon.' Cassian chuckled. 'I think every foreign prince in the city has been called upon to turn out tonight and the diplomatic corps as well.'

'Yes, the Foreign Office was insistent there be a Russian presence here tonight so that nothing looks underhanded,' Nikolay affirmed. There'd been great speculation in the newspapers about whether or not the Hawaiian King meant to seek British protection against a Russian attempt to establish a settlement in the islands.

Two other men, Sir Liam O'Casek and Lord Preston Worth with their wives, May and Beatrice, strolled over to join the group and introductions were exchanged before Cassian politely disengaged from the group, whispering to her, 'There are others I want you to meet before the royals arrive. My close friends, Inigo Vellanoweth, the Earl of Tintagel, and his father, the new Duke of Newlyn, Vennor Penlerick, and my parents.'

That particular group was gathered by a rose arbour near the French doors that led indoors, well positioned to be one of the early groups to meet the King. Pen hesitated as they approached. This was different than a chance meeting on the path. Meeting foreign royalty was exciting. Meeting Cassian's parents was daunting. She smoothed the skirts of her pale blue silk gown. Cassian squeezed her hand. 'You look fine. They will adore you, as I do.'

There was another round of introductions. Inigo Vellanoweth was dark and cynically enigmatic with a sharp wit. Vennor Penlerick was golden and charming. He used that charm like a shield, Pen thought, a shield to keep others at bay along with his grief. Not unlike Cassian. It was rather intriguing to watch the two of them together. She'd not thought of Cassian as having a shield. He was always easy to be with—he drew people in with that ease, and made it easy for others to talk to him.

Perhaps that ease was Cassian's shield. He was all dazzle and grand gestures; the theatre box, tonight's reception, the upcoming tickets to Vauxhall. But behind the glamour of his invitations, he seldom talked about himself. He had done so with Em, certainly. There'd been no risk in that. Em was a stranger who had no idea who he was. He could tell her anything he liked. But the picnic the other day had been the first time he'd shared anything deeply personal with her. She treasured that disclosure all the more for its rarity even while wishing there were more moments like that where the shield was down.

She could see where he got the easy charm from. Both of his parents were charismatic, both of them dark-haired and tall. His father had Cassian's strong, chiselled jaw and his mother, the amber eyes. The Truscotts were a handsome family. The group exchanged pleasantries until a gong announced the arrival of the Hawaiian court. 'Are you ready to see some more of the world?' Cassian whispered beside her as the Hawaiian King, King Kamehameha II, and his Queen, Kamamalu, entered the garden.

Pen's eyes went wide. They were spectacular, dressed in European-styled clothing, which only served to emphasise their majesty. Both of them had thick dark hair and skin, and both stood over six feet tall. Pen had never seen such a big woman before. And the King! He managed to make Cassian's usually intimidating height and breadth look merely average. Some of the newspapers had styled the Hawaiian court as savages come to town, but Pen saw none of that as the King moved from group to group, respectfully greeting dukes and diplomats. He stopped for a long moment with Wellington, sombrely nodding as the hero of Waterloo was introduced to him. He'd done his homework, Pen thought. He understood the import of Waterloo in this part of the world. Impressive.

The royal court approached their group and Pen felt giddy with excitement. She made her curtsy, and, to her surprise, Cassian gestured for two footmen to come forward with two long boxes. 'Lady Penrose has been teaching me about leis and the custom in the islands.' Cassian opened each box to reveal two fresh leis made of roses. 'Lady Penrose tells me the flora on the islands are used for the leis, so I present you leis made of English flora, to welcome you. There is nothing as English as the English rose.'

The King nodded his thanks and the Queen looked touched by the gesture, but no one moved for an awkward moment. Yes, the greeting! She'd read about it once and hoped she'd remembered it right. Pen took a deep breath, eager to avoid creating an international incident with a misstep, especially with the visit off to a difficult start as it was. Pen lifted the first lei from its box and stepped forward. She reached up and put it about the Queen's neck and kissed her cheek. The Queen beamed with pleasure and Pen knew she'd done well. She repeated the process with the King, who graciously bent down to accommodate her.

'*Mahalo,*' the King said. 'That's how we say thank you on the islands.' A little round of applause went up from the onlookers that had gathered, but what pleased Pen the most was the look of approval on Cassian's face.

The Life Guard Band's performance began soon afterwards and everyone drifted inside to take their seats, but Pen was loath to leave the garden. 'Can we stay out a bit longer?' she asked as Cassian made to usher her inside. 'I want to linger in this fairy land a few minutes more.' In truth, she wanted to linger with him. For all the magic the night had provided, nothing compared to the magic of being with Cassian, of having his hand at her back, his words whispered at her ear, the delight he took in introducing her to his friends. They hung back from the crowd, finding their way once more to the fountain where they'd met the Russian Prince. Pen sat at the edge and trailed her hand in the water.

'Thank you for tonight, Cassian. You promised to show me the world and you did. We didn't even have to leave London. Tonight I met a Russian prince and a Hawaiian king.'

'You saved the day with the leis.' Cassian rested a foot on the fountain's edge. 'I had no idea what to do.'

'You brought the leis. That was inspired. Thank you for that.' They'd been specially designed. He'd gone to some effort to see it done. It was further proof that he listened when she talked, that he remembered what she shared, that he made what was important to her important to him.

'We make a good team, Pen.' Cassian gave one of his easy laughs.

There was more she wanted to say, more she wanted to thank him for: for introducing her to his friends, for the chance to meet the Hawaiian royals, for *listening* to her, but Cassian was looking at her in that intent way of his with smoky amber eyes. 'Am I proving myself to you, Pen? That I am more than any man in the room?' His voice was low and intimate as his hand raised her chin up to meet his gaze. 'I have always wanted you as Em or Pen. It doesn't matter. They're both you. Tell me I have a chance? That we're building something new and strong between us here in London. The magic is real, Pen. Believe in it. Believe in me.'

'I do want to tell you that. But it's hard.' Maybe she'd lived with the fear so long it had begun to be part of her without her realising it? Her father's fear had worn off on her. 'Magic spells are often broken, Cassian. Magic comes with costs in all the tales. Everyone gives up something in order to have it, if only for a little while. I'm afraid of what I might have to give up.' But even now she was thinking whatever the cost might be, it would be worth it when he looked at her like that, like he saw the world in her eyes.

'I won't push you, Pen. Tell me when you're ready and I'll speak to your father. It's not the world's most romantic proposal, but perhaps it's the one you need.' Lack of romance aside, the words took her breath away. This man who would lay the world at her feet, who wanted to marry her, wanted to give her every one of her dreams. And yet, he was still a man with secrets, who hadn't shared any of his dreams with her.

The fountain made little splashes in the silence that rose between them. 'So soon? It's only been a couple of weeks and yet you are willing to make an extravagant offer.' An offer as extravagant as the entertainments he'd lavished on her.

'It's been nearly three months since St Piran's Day,' Cassian corrected.

'Do you think you know me well enough to spend for ever with me?' She hated herself for speaking the words, hated the doubt that surged in her despite the feelings she carried for him. How was it possible to care and to doubt at the same time? Most of all, she hated that she couldn't simply accept the miracle that had been given to her.

'Yes.' Lord, how she envied him his confidence. There wasn't a bone of doubt in that whole, hard-muscled body of his. He took her hand and drew her away from the fountain, into the shadows beyond the lantern lights. 'Let me show you how sure.' They were out of the light, at the fence that ran the garden's perimeter. He was kissing her, the hard wood of the fence at her back, and she was burning hot and fast for him. His kisses obliterated all reason. His hand was in her hair, another at her breast, her own hand slipping low between them to cup him through his trousers, to feel the hard, wanting length of him.

Whatever she doubted, she could not doubt this, that there was truth in his wanting. He desired her, his own desire as hot and as rampant as her own. But the stakes were different this time: they could not be anonymous lovers any more. He had said he'd not push her for a decision, but to make love with him now would give him every permission to push her. It would be implicit consent to marry.

Cassian's hand pushed up her skirts, his voice a hoarse rasp at her ear. 'I will not take you against a fence, but I would give us some pleasure tonight.'

'Yes,' she breathed, her teeth sinking into the tender lobe of his ear in her hunger. Then his hand was at her juncture, his fingers seeking her in the tangled thicket of her damp curls. She gasped when he found her, hot, slick at her core, the little nub at her centre throbbing for his touch. He stroked it with his thumb and she cried out as a trill of pleasure took her. She pressed her mouth to his shoulder as another wave took her.

'Let it go, Pen,' he counselled, his voice rough with his own desire, his hips moving against her thigh even as his hand moved against her. 'Scream all you want, no one can hear you except the moon.'

And she did. She arched her neck, turning her face skywards, and cried out her pleasure to the moon as release swept her. She was going to have to decide soon. But perhaps that decision was already made for her. How could she live without this? How dreary her world would become once more without him in it. Did she dare seize the happiness Cassian offered? Did she dare believe in the fairy tale and her very own happy ever after?

Chapter Seventeen

'She's a lovely girl, Cassian. When do you mean to tell her the truth?' his father asked over drinks at White's the next afternoon. They'd made a habit ever since Cassian had come of age to meet once a week during the Season for drinks and talking, catching up on news of the family and their friends.

'The truth?' Cassian prevaricated. 'That I'm crazy about her? I would think she already knows.' White's was still quiet. The late-afternoon crowd hadn't strolled in yet and they had the place to themselves.

His father gave him a hard stare. 'The truth about the land, that you need her acres.' His father tapped his finger on the tabletop in a disapproving tattoo. 'You have to tell her. She will feel betrayed if she discovers it after the fact.'

'She'll feel betrayed if I tell her now. All she

wants is to be loved for herself. If she thinks the land prompted my suit, I will lose her.' The outcome was unthinkable.

His father studied him with hazel eyes. 'I've never thought of you as a sly man, Cassian. Marrying her without full disclosure is dishonest.'

'It is necessary,' Cassian replied, not caring to have his motives questioned in such unforgiving terms. 'For the greater good. I must have that land.' But the rationale sounded more hollow these days than it had in the beginning. At what point was his happiness, Pen's happiness and a successful marriage built on honesty and trust worth more than the greater good? How much longer did it need to be sacrificed?

The duke took a swallow of brandy. 'Would you marry her without the land?'

'If I could, but that's not relevant because I need the land. I must marry for the land.'

'And not for love? Why?' His father would have made a fine barrister with his soul-piercing questions.

'You know why. For the gardens, to help those who lost their jobs when Collin's venture went under, because I promised Richard

Penlerick to restore the Cornish economy. Because the dream demands it,' Cassian ground out.

'What if the dream becomes a nightmare, son? This dream of yours was noble and good at the start, and it might be again under the right conditions, but not now. Now, it is consuming you. That's not what Richard wanted. He would not want you to sacrifice love and personal happiness for this. Nor would he want you to commit to dishonesty. Many men have started down a dark path, thinking to do good, only to discover that they've lost their integrity along the way.'

Cassian stared into his glass. There was nothing quite like being a man of thirty and being called on the carpet by your father. Yet he couldn't shake the notion his father might be right. When had he become the very monster he'd sought to protect himself from—the unscrupulous fortune hunter? 'Are you suggesting I give it up?' He raised his gaze to his father's, looking for clarity.

'If it comes to that, I would certainly consider it.'

'What about Collin? What about all those

people?' Collin's death had devastated his parents; Collin the baby, the youngest of four children, dead at his own hand before the age of twenty-five.

His father shook his head. 'You cannot carry the blame for that. It was not only up to you to stop Collin. Perhaps we all should have been more vigilant. Any one of us could have stopped him and none of us did. He acted rashly, foolishly when he invested in Brenley's scheme. Yes, people lost their jobs. But he would not have wanted us to let our lives be defined by his mistakes. He's paid dearly enough for them.'

Cassian nodded. How differently his father dealt with regret than Redruth or even himself. He'd seen so much of his own reflection the other day when Pen had talked of her father's regrets; of wishing he could turn back time, that he'd stopped Collin. But perhaps his father had the right of it. No one could dictate another's choices. Redruth was trying to dictate Pen's choices. The man wanted to control everyone as a means of protecting them. All the while never seeing how that was hurting the people he loved.

'I worry for you boys,' his father said gently. By boys, he meant Inigo and Vennor and himself. 'You're all so driven. It is a fine line between ambitions and vendettas. Vennor insists on pursuing his father's murderers even though the trail is cold. Inigo insists on finding justice against Brenley. And you insist on atoning for your brother's sins at the expense of your own happiness. Richard would not want that for any of you any more than I do.' His father looked at his watch and rose apologetically. 'I promised to meet your mother. But before I go, I want your word that you will you tell Lady Pen everything.'

'I might lose her,' Cassian warned again. His father's wisdom was sound, but it formed a pit in his stomach. He'd already lost her once.

'You might. But you will lose her for certain if you don't. It will just be a matter of when. What kind of marriage can you have without the truth between you from the start?'

Cassian hated it when his father was right. He was making Pen promises he could keep: a life of adventure, a life of passion. All of it was honest and true. Except for what he'd left out. Would she think his promises nothing more than barter for her acres? Would she once again think his compliments false when nothing could be further from the truth? He would tell her, but when? Perhaps it would be best to say nothing of the land until their relationship was more stable, where they could weather a storm, or at least a light squall, where the smallest of dents wouldn't destroy their hard-won trust in one another. Everything was so new and fresh between them, fragile like a baby. Cassian let out a breath. He would wait to tell her about the land, but perhaps he could start tonight with smaller truths to pave the way. There were other things he could share with her, things that might win her to his side so that when the time came for the land to be discussed, she would understand. Tonight, he would tell her about the park. Vauxhall would be the perfect setting.

Vauxhall dazzled from the first impression of the lights from the Thames as their wherry pulled alongside the stairs, to the concert and supper with the infamous thin-sliced ham. Pen couldn't stop gazing at all the marvels and there *were* marvels around every corner: paintings, lamps in trees, acrobats and fortune tellers.

'This is even better than the St Piran's Day fair,' she whispered to Cassian, careful for the others not to hear. If there was any imperfection on the evening it was that they weren't alone. Her father was there with Phin and her aunt. Cassian's friend, Inigo, was there along with Vennor Penlerick, who was escorting Miss Marianne Treleven and her sister, Ayleth, friends from home. It made for a merry party in the private supper pavilion Cassian had arranged, but it afforded little intimacy.

'Would you care for a stroll, Lady Penrose?' Cassian offered his arm, his eyes suggesting he'd read her thoughts. 'You haven't seen the paths yet and there's just time before the Cascade and the fireworks.' He courteously nodded to her father. 'We won't go far or be gone long, sir.' The other message was also clear. Company was not invited.

Once outside, Pen breathed deeply. 'The stars are even out tonight. They so rarely are in London. I must thank you for another magical evening.'

'You haven't seen the best yet.' Cassian

steered them down a path lit with colourful gas lamps. There were others strolling as well, but they were alone in the conversation. Out here, they might talk about anything. 'There are still great things to come.'

'I think the lights are my favourite part. I can't imagine this many lights and yet here they are.'

'Twenty thousand of them,' Cassian supplied.

'Impossible. How do they light them all?' Pen argued in disbelief. 'I would need all night to light them.'

'Not by hand, I assure you.' Cassian laughed. 'They're lit by linked fuses.'

'Like daisy chains?' She smiled. 'This place is a fairy tale. I had no idea such a place could exist.' Her smile faded. 'I wonder if I will love Cornwall half as much when I return? I think it might be hard for Redruth to compete. I fear it will seem desolate.' It was already June. A month in London had slipped away, a month of freedom and she was starting to dread what that meant. Every day that passed was a day closer to returning to Castle Byerd and every day closer to making a decision on a suitor, committing to be passed from father to husband. Cassian had already suggested he could make the decision an easy one, that he would offer for her.

She slid an unobserved look at Cassian's strong profile. Would it be so bad if that husband was Cassian? Could the fun of being with him be enough to overlook that he'd come wife-hunting despite having declared love for Em just weeks earlier? If she had to marry one of *them*, one of the *ton*'s titled gentlemen—why not choose him? Her father would be happy. She could imagine his face now when she walked into his study and announced she'd accepted Viscount Trevethow. And she would be happy, as long as she protected her heart, as long as she didn't give it entirely, but kept one small part for herself. That way, she couldn't be hurt if her faith in Cassian proved misplaced. It would be a worthy compromise and it might be the best she could manage.

They stopped outside a small building to listen to the Turkish band inside. 'It sounds exotic,' Pen said wistfully. She could imagine hot nights and harems in the sounds, something straight from Arabian Nights. She danced a couple of steps, rolling her hips, and halted, self-conscious. A decent English girl didn't dance like that.

'Why did you stop?' Cassian looked disappointed.

'It's music for veils, not skirts, I think.' Pen blushed. 'But never mind that. I've been waiting to be alone with you all night. We have to finish our conversation from the picnic. You promised to tell me your dream.' She'd not forgotten despite the allure of Vauxhall. She'd spent most of the evening trying to guess, running through theories in her head. What did Cassian Truscott, a man who'd seen the world, a man with a title, a man who would be a duke some day, dream of? What was left to want?

It was his turn to be self-conscious, something she would not have associated with this confident man if she hadn't seen it. They started to walk again, her hand tucked through his arm as if it had always belonged there. Then the words came. 'I want to bring Vauxhall to Cornwall.'

'You mean a pleasure garden at home?' She cocked her head to look at him with curiosity. 'What would it be like?'

'It would be exotic like the Turkish pavilion.

There would be music from all over Europe and food, too, so people could hear and taste other cultures. Each pavilion could house a country, a culture. The Turkish pavilion would have music, carpets and mosaics, and robes. People could eat kebabs and *kofte*. In the evening there could be a show with Turkish dancers and fierce Turkish warriors with their curved swords. In the Russian pavilion there would be Cossacks with their trick riding.'

'Wherever would you find people who could do that?' Pen couldn't get her head around the logistics of acquiring people and supplies. The magnitude of the concept was bewildering, but exciting.

'It wouldn't be that hard. London has managed to find Turks for Vauxhall. Nikolay could help with the Cossacks.'

'It sounds wonderful. It would certainly bring entertainment and education to an isolated part of the world.' Pen was starting to see the vision, the dream. 'People who never leave home could experience the world.' What a gift that would be for those who couldn't travel, people like herself.

'We'd have amusements too.' Cassian was in

his element now. He made an expansive gesture with his hand, encouraging her to imagine with him. 'I want to have a "mountain" like the one in Russia, a coaster. The problem with it is that it doesn't stop reliably. But I studied a model in France, the Russes à Belleville—it's a little cart you can sit in and it has a groove that's inserted into the track that guides it. It can go up hills, down hills, around corners, and at fast speeds so that there's some thrill to it.'

'Just to ride around a track?' Pen wasn't sure she saw the appeal that excited Cassian so much.

'A set could be designed. We could recreate mountain peaks: the Alps, the Matterhorn, Mont Blanc or the Dolomites. People could pretend they were coasting through those locales. It would be a reality fantasy.'

The Alps, the Dolomites, the Matterhorn.

The words were as seductive as the man, as the night alight with Vauxhall lamps. In her mind, she could see each peak, each range, on her maps. But the magic she was caught up in was all him. 'Maybe there could be a river and we could sail down the Nile and see the pyramids, or camels on the shore, or the Egyptian desert by moonlight.' She sighed and leaned her head against his shoulder.

'We could. We could have rivers and boats and a thousand adventures at our fingertips any time we wanted them.' Cassian whispered at her ear.

'When I was young, I had great plans to sail to China.' She laughed softly in the darkness.

'We'll bring China to Cornwall until you can go yourself,' he assured her. 'It's more than entertainment, though, Pen.' His tone was sombre. 'It's about jobs. Amusement gardens don't run themselves. Think of all the musicians and waiters Vauxhall employs, to say nothing of the gardeners and caretakers who manicure the grounds, or the set designers who paint the scenes and the pavilions, who create the fantasies we see tonight, and the acrobats. Admittedly, some of those jobs are very specialised and will need to come from outside Cornwall, but many of the jobs aren't. Gardeners, caretakers, waiters—all of those jobs can be filled by Cornishmen. They can make a decent wage, take care of their families without leaving home. And that's just the direct employment. People with inns, people who can supply the park with food, they'll all benefit too. People with carts to carry the food.'

'And it wouldn't be charity.' Pen was nearly as dazzled by the thought of employment as she was by the park itself. 'There is so much need. People are happy to work, but there are no jobs to be had.' The charity baskets she made weekly barely had an effect on families and what stop-gap they did provide was short-lived. But a project of this magnitude could create long-lasting change. 'I think you must build your park, Cassian. Whatever it takes,' she whispered, looking about her for the first time since he'd begun his impassioned dissertation. 'There are fewer lights here. You, sir, have taken me off the well-travelled path,' she scolded lightly.

'Because I wanted to do this.' Cassian's hands were in her hair, tilting her face up, his mouth on hers, and she welcomed him wholeheartedly. 'No night at Vauxhall is complete without a little seduction on the paths.'

'Hmm.' She licked her lips. 'I think I was seduced well before the dark paths.' She put her arms arounds his neck and let him dance her back to the trunk of a wide discreet tree, claiming more kisses as they went. She ought to be more careful, but tonight she didn't care. Tonight, she could pretend she was Em again at the fair, a woman with nothing to lose.

There was the famed Cascade at ten o'clock, a mechanical cataract that simulated a waterfall most artfully with a verisimilitude that made Pen applaud enthusiastically along with the Treleven girls who were equally amazed and, following that, the sky lit with fireworks in blue, green, red and violet while the band played Handel. Under the cover of the crowd, she was aware of Cassian's hands at her waist where no one could see, aware of the heat of him as her back brushed his chest. She looked over her shoulder at him, watching his face wreathed in enjoyment and contemplation. He was thinking of his park, his dream as he watched the fireworks and the sight of the determination on his face moved her, inspired her. 'I can hardly wait to see your amusement park,' she whispered with a smile. If there was any man who could bring such a thing to Cornwall, it would be him. If there was any man she could marry, it was him, as long as she was very careful not to fall in love with him completely, again.

'I told her about the amusement garden,' Cassian said carefully to Inigo over coffee and toast the next morning. Inigo had made it a habit of joining him for breakfast. Cassian didn't mind. He welcomed the company. It kept him from being alone too long with his thoughts—thoughts that ran almost exclusively to Pen these days.

'How did that go over?' Inigo enquired, buttering his toast and reaching for the marmalade.

'Very well. She liked the idea.' She'd more than liked it. She'd been impressed by it on all of its levels. She'd seen its potential. Her eyes had lit and in turn the sight of her excitement had lit something warm in Cassian. She could share his dream, they could be partners in it. Except for one thing. Cassian tapped his fork on the table distracted, barely hearing Inigo recount the action at White's.

'The betting book is exploding with speculation after last night. Everyone knows you took her to Vauxhall. Your courting of Redruth's daughter has outpaced even the public's fascination with the Hawaiian King.' Inigo lifted his coffee cup in a saluting toast. 'She's falling for you. You should be pleased. You'll have a wife and an ally.'

An ally. At last. But an unwitting ally to be used against her father when the time came. By the time she understood the dynamics, they'd be married and there would be little she could do except reconcile herself to it. The thought sat poorly with Cassian, even more so after last night. When he'd originally thought of courting Redruth's daughter, he'd not planned on falling in love with her, never imagined she'd be Em. The girl, whoever she might be, had been a means to an end, a sacrifice he'd make for the sake of his dreams. But now, Redruth's daughter was Pen, a woman he loved. A woman who could hurt him with her rejection, with her hatred if she turned against him.

'I didn't tell her about the land.' Cassian blurted out the words. There it was, the one thing that had eaten at him after he'd taken her family home last night. 'She doesn't know

I need her land to do it.' His father would not be proud of his decision to hold that back.

Inigo considered this thoughtfully. 'Perhaps she wouldn't mind? If she favours the idea, perhaps she'll want to contribute the land as a partner, not as someone who felt she was courted for the sole purpose. If she trusts you, it shouldn't be an issue.'

That was the crux of the matter, the one thing that held Cassian back. *Did* she trust him? Had she overcome her earlier misgivings about him and his reasons for having sought out the earl's daughter? Had he proven himself worthy of her? Or when she heard what he wanted, would she think not only that he was no better than the other men begging for her attentions, but that he was worse because he'd betrayed her a second time? 'I can't tell her, not yet. We're not strong enough.' But the question remained: When? When would they be strong enough to let his secret out?

'Don't wait too long. Rumour is, Wilmington is displeased. He is looking to discredit you. I would hate for him to stumble across any evidence that might be made to look incriminating.'

'Understood. But there's nothing to worry over. The identity of the owners of the Porth Karrek Land Development Company is iron-clad. There's nothing he can discover. I won't rush my fences for the likes of Wilmington. It's too soon, the relationship is too fresh. I want to dazzle her a little while longer.' But in truth, it was himself he wanted to dazzle. He wanted to bask in the fantasy that Pen loved him before he tested it with reality.

Chapter Eighteen

The Season became a whirlwind of one fantasy after another for Pen with Cassian by her side. The Hawaiian Royals invited them for a day touring the Exeter Exchange and the Royal National Menagerie topped off with an evening in the King's box at Drury Lane for a performance of *Rob Roy MacGregor*. Cassian took her to the British Museum to see the Elgin Marbles where they debated Elgin's right to have plundered them. He took her to the National Gallery, for drives and walks in the Park, he drove her to Epsom to watch the big horse, Cedric, win the Derby. They revisited the Enclosure and rowed on the Serpentine, Oscar howling from the bow. They attended a Riding Night at Prince Baklanov's equestrian school in Leicester Square. Cassian escorted her to balls and musicales without end.

June passed in a flurry of excitement of new activities and new acquaintances. Cassian had promised to show her the world and he had most spectacularly. She was dazzled by the experiences, but she was more dazzled by the man. He'd not only shown her the world, he'd shown her a glimpse of what their life could be together, of what they could build together. They could be partners. His dream slowly became her dream.

Together, they could bring entertainment and economic recovery to Cornwall, give the people an industry to rely on besides mining. Diversification was what the region needed more than anything. A region could not leave itself vulnerable to the caprices of sea-based industry or the industry of mines. Fish migration routes changed over time and mines played out. She could really live, really give meaning to her life through those projects with Cassian. There would be tangible results for her efforts. Pen fairly trembled with the prospect of possibility, it was that exciting to contemplate. But contemplating it required marriage. She had to decide. Cassian was waiting for her to give the word. She'd wanted the right to choose and he'd given her that too. But always, came the whisper of doubt: *What did he want?*

'You seem happy today,' Margery commented, fixing a comb in her hair. 'You've seemed happy for several weeks now, ever since the handsome young viscount has been squiring you about.'

'Yes.' Pen smiled in the mirror. 'He certainly knows how to keep a girl on her feet.'

'Or sweep her off them?' Margery enquired with an impish grin. 'Do you think he'll propose? Everyone downstairs is talking about it, if you don't mind me saying so. It's the most exciting thing that's happened in the household for ages.' She could hardly begrudge Margery and the others their own joy. It was a reminder that she was not the only one whose life had been changed when her mother had died. Her father's choices had affected everyone.

Margery held up a necklace for her approval. 'It's like we're an enchanted castle coming back to life after the spell has worn off. We're entertaining again, Cook is preparing teas and cakes and meals for more than just the three of you and the odd guest. Maids have a reason to polish the silver. *You* have a reason to wear beautiful clothes It's just wonderful, that's what it is, miss.' She made a little frown. 'I don't know how we'll manage to go back home after this. Everything will seem so ordinary.'

Hadn't she thought the same? Yet, she could change that. Cassian had made no secret of it. He was waiting for her. She would have thought *knowing* the outcome would have made things less tense. Instead, knowing had brought a tension of its own. The choice was hers and she wasn't ready to make it, not yet, although the case Cassian built for marriage was a strong one. Would what they could build together be enough to make a successful marriage? He cared for her, but he had never said he loved her. Was passion enough to sustain them in the absence of mutual love? The passion seemed assured, the latter did not. Cassian wanted her, but love and want were two different things.

What happened to them once the passion and the wanting waned, trampled by the wear of real life? What would be left? Would a common cause between them be enough? In some ways the dazzling display Cassian had laid at her feet didn't help the case, but obscured it. What would life be like after the promise of the Season was gone? Would that life be different, *better*, than what she'd have with any of the others? Or was he just a superior salesman? He had plans where others had platitudes. The questions chased themselves around in her head endlessly these days and she was no closer to an answer. Perhaps she never would be. Perhaps she just needed to take the leap.

'What shall you do today?' Margery moved to the wardrobe, laying out a hat and a light shawl to match her dress, a fetching white muslin sprigged with pink flowers.

'Lord Trevethow is taking me for ices at Gunter's.' It was one of her favourite things to do, to sit on the high seat of his phaeton and eat ices. It gave them a chance to talk, a chance to be private even in public and she was so desperate to speak with him today. It was just the outing she needed to clear her head and her heart.

The outing had gone wrong from the start. Cassian had not driven the phaeton after all, but had borrowed Inigo's carriage to squire not only her but the Treleven girls. The girls were pleasant and she enjoyed their company, but she wasn't in the mood for it. Soon, the outing would be over and she wouldn't have had a chance to speak with Cassian alone. She would not see him tonight. Her father had a long session in Parliament, Phin was out with friends and her aunt had suggested it would be good to rest for an evening, so they were spending it in.

Cassian shot her an enquiring look as he finished his chocolate ice—he had, she was not surprised to note, quite the sweet tooth. 'I am in need of stretching my legs. Lady Pen, would you care to accompany me?' It was not the most subtle of gestures. From the knowing smiles on their faces, Marianne and Ayleth were not fooled. Pen took his hand and let him help her down. 'I fear Gunter's has disappointed you,' Cassian said without preamble. 'You're out of sorts today.'

'No, I'm sorry if I haven't been good company.' She turned and faced him, let him see the need in her eyes. 'Is there some place where we can be alone? I need to speak with you. I had hoped to do so today.'

Cassian nodded, his whisky eyes darkening to agate with concern. 'It can be arranged if

278 The Passions of Lord Trevethow

you're willing to take a little risk. Pen, are you all right?'

'I will be.' She managed a small smile and let him lead her back to the carriage.

They took the Treleven girls home and Cassian gave instructions to his driver, 'The Albany, please.' Pen swallowed hard. They were going to his rooms.

'Unless you'd rather talk here?' Cassian asked in the wake of her silence.

'No. What I need to discuss should be done privately.' She worried her lip. 'We won't be caught, will we?' Everyone knew the Albany had strict rules about women on the premises. Her reputation would be ruined. She'd have no choice but to marry Cassian then.

'We won't be caught. I know all the secret passages,' Cassian offered with a laugh, but Pen wasn't assured.

'You've done this before? Sneaking a girl into your rooms?' The old worry surged. Of course he had. He was an experienced man of the world. A man who'd loved multiple women, a man who gave his heart to no one. Hadn't he told her as much?

'I'm no virgin, Pen, and you know it,' he

scolded her. 'That doesn't mean I'm not capable of fidelity and feeling.' He directed the driver around back at the Albany. 'This is the best time of day. No one is back yet to change for the evening and the servants are all at tea.' He led her up a warren of staircases to the third floor and expeditiously ushered her into a set of plush rooms done in pale blue and cream, firmly locking the door behind them. 'We're safe now.' Under other circumstances, he might have winked or made a joke, but his tone was serious.

'These are nice rooms.' Pen commented, suddenly nervous. She had him alone and now she hadn't any idea where to start. Why did she make a habit of wishing for things she didn't want?

'They do well enough. I'm hardly here.' Cassian strode to the console and poured a drink. 'Would you like one? I can't offer you any tea, but perhaps a little brandy might help you relax?' He poured her one anyway. 'You've got me worried, Pen. You're as tight as a bowstring. Come, sit and tell me what's happened.'

She took the glass from him. Perhaps having something in her hands would help. 'June has happened. The Season is slipping away and I still don't know what you want with me, with Redruth's daughter.' She turned the tumbler about in her hands. 'But it must be extraordinarily important when I consider the lengths you've gone to, all the balls and outings, boxes at the opera and plays, Vauxhall, meeting royalty. You've laid the world at my feet. No man does that without hoping for something grand in return.'

'I do hope for something grand, Pen. I hope for *you*. I hope that one day, you will tell me you are ready for my proposal. I promised you I wouldn't push and I haven't.' No, but he'd certainly persuaded. Dear lord, when he looked at her like that, like she could be the sum of his world, it was hard to remember caution.

Cassian took a long swallow of his drink. 'I am willing to dance to your tune, Pen. I know what marriage means to you and I know what I want.'

Her. He wanted her. He could make it no plainer. She'd never been courted so forwardly, so bluntly before. Not that she'd been courted a lot in any way, but she'd grown used to the suitors like Wadesbridge who went through her father, or the young men at the at-homes and on her dance cards who couched their affections in metaphors and clichés, who never spoke to her directly, fearing to upset her sensibilities.

Pen ventured a sip of the brandy, letting it burn clarity all the way to her stomach. 'You are the most single-minded man I've ever met. Why me, Cassian? Why do you want me? Why do you want Redruth's daughter?'

This was the moment of truth. But which truth? 'I've never met anyone like you, your spirit for adventure, your passion for living. Your tenacity to live by your convictions. Whether you've been Em or Lady Penrose, those things have remained constant.' That was the higher truth, the one that transcended all others. He would want *her* even without her thirty-two acres.

She blushed. 'You do know how to flatter a girl.'

'Does the girl believe me?' he whispered softly, his mouth at her ear, kissing the soft space between her ear and neck. 'I've done my best to be worthy of her. She's very stubborn.'

Pen tilted her head, giving him full access to

the length of her neck and he took it, sweep-ing aside her hair with one hand. 'Is the girl beautiful?' She sighed as he kissed her neck, her throat where her pulse beat fast beneath his mouth. 'You didn't mention that in all your flattery.'

His own voice was husky with mounting de-sire. 'She is more than beautiful, more than the sum of her physical features.' His mouth moved to other side of her neck, laving it with equal attention. Their game of questions had evolved to something more dangerous, some-thing that exposed them both at their cores. They were testing deep waters.

'Do you love her?' The question should not have surprised him. Hadn't everything been leading to this?

'I want her, body and soul,' Cassian whis-pered the words against her skin.

'It's not the same,' came the whispered reply.

'It is the same,' he replied hoarsely. 'Does the girl love *me*?' Pen's arms were about his neck, her body pressed close to him of her own ac-cord, her own heart racing against his chest, her green eyes dark.

'The girl wants you, body and soul.' She

kissed him hard on the mouth, fervent and hungry. 'I don't want to ask any more questions, I don't want any more answers. I just want you. Today. No matter how this ends.'

There was desperation in that hunger. Cassian ought to heed it—he was the one with experience here. He knew the pitfalls as well as the pleasures of giving in to the moment. 'There's only one way this ends, Pen. This is not the cottage.'

'It ends in your bed. I know.' She moved against his hips, against his hardness, making reason impossible for them both. How long had he wanted her like this?

'It doesn't just end in bed, Pen,' he cautioned. If he took her this would end in marriage. He was not in the habit of divesting virgins of their maidenhood and discarding them as a casual affair.

'It would have for Em. Bed would have been the end for Em.' She rose from the sofa. She undid the laces of her walking boots and tossed them away. She lifted a leg, resting her foot on the edge of the sofa. She wiggled her toes, her skirts falling back to reveal a length of silk stocking tied with a pink ribbon. 'Shall I untie them or shall you?'

'You.' Cassian's breath caught. Clothes were so much more erotic when they were about to come off. He set aside his glass, his eyes fixed on her as she undid the ribbons and rolled the stocking down. Did she have any idea what this was doing to him? This tantalising show of bare flesh and promise of more?

Stockings off, she lifted hands to her hair and pulled out the pins, one by one, until the rest of it fell. She looked innocent and wicked all at once, her hair falling forward and loose like a schoolgirl's, but her eyes blazed like a woman who knew what she wanted. 'You'll have to help me with the rest.' Her tongue licked her lips in invitation. 'I can't manage the gown alone.'

Temptation whispered between them: *come undress me, come touch me, come be with me as you wanted to be in the meadow on the heath, naked, skin to skin.*

Cassian went to her, working her laces loose, pushing her dress from her shoulders, her chemise, her stays, all discarded until his mouth could feast on bare skin, until he could hold her naked against him, soft buttocks to his hard groin, filling his hands with her breasts, each caress bringing pleasure to them both. His thumbs ran across her nipples and she gave a mewl of delight at the sensation.

He moved his hand lower to her curls, intent on bringing her pleasure as they stood. She covered his hand with her own and turned in his arms. 'Not until you're naked, too,' she whispered against his lips, her hands working his cravat loose and unwinding it. 'Whoever said women wore too many clothes never undressed a man. Cravat, coat, waistcoat, shirt, boots, breeches. There are so many layers between me and the man I want.'

'Be thankful I don't wear smalls.' Cassian laughed against her mouth.

'You think to shock me,' she whispered in feigned horror. 'You forget, I already knew that. I've already held you in my hand, in my mouth, straight from your trousers.' Dear heavens, he'd spend far too soon if she continued talking like that. He was rock hard with wanting as it was.

'Pen,' Cassian replied in a voice that cracked from desire. 'Do you think you could hurry?'

'Waiting is the best part,' she teased, pushing down his trousers.

'No,' Cassian ground out, pulling his shirt over his head and tossing it into a corner. '*This* is the best part.' He drew her close and danced her through the room to the chamber beyond, the one with the bed. It was time for him to take charge of this seduction.

Chapter Nineteen

Pen disagreed. She rather thought that the best part was seeing Cassian Truscott entirely naked, all broad shoulders and muscle narrowing to a lean waist and long, hard legs. His was a body that clearly espoused the benefits of outdoor living. No London gentleman of her acquaintance had physique that even hinted at a body like that beneath their tailored clothes.

A moment later, she rethought her position. Maybe *this* was the best part—the way he pressed her back to the pillows and came up over her, covering her with the power of his big body. His walnut-dark hair fell forward, framing his face, giving him the look of a savage. A trill of excitement raced through her as his hands bracketed her head on either side, carrying his weight. She liked the thought of being his captive.

'What are you thinking, minx? You've the look of mischief about you.'

Pen licked her lips. 'I never noticed how long your hair was.' It wasn't a blatant lie...she had been thinking that too.

'Hmm...' Cassian teased. 'Somehow I doubt that's all that was going on in your head.'

Pen wiggled beneath him. 'I was thinking that I wouldn't mind being your captive.'

Cassian gave low growl of a chuckle and reached for her wrists, drawing them above her head and shackling them with his hand. 'No more talk, captive.' He moved against her in blatant prelude of what was to come, hips to hips, his hardness to her softness, and her thighs opened of their own accord as if his being there was the most natural thing in the world. 'Are you sure, Pen?' he whispered hoarsely. It was a last bid for caution, for surety.

'Yes,' she breathed. At her core this was what she wanted no matter what happened afterwards, this was right. This was what they'd intended at the cottage, what would have happened had her father not taken her away so abruptly. It was as if fate had ordained they would be together. This had not been avoided, only delayed.

Pen felt his hand move between them, low at her entrance, his fingers testing, caressing, intimately, searching for readiness. Oh, he would find her ready enough. She was warm and she was wet, proof that her wanting was in more than words. She wrapped her arms about his neck, and breathed at his ear, 'Cassian, I want you.'

It was all the permission he needed to press forward, to press into her. 'Hold on to me, Pen,' he urged at her gasp, the pain of the breaching catching her by surprise. She felt him still, felt her body stretch to accommodate him so he could press on. Her body learned him as he moved, his pace like a gentle wave on the shore, surge and ebb, surge and ebb until he was there at her core, filling her completely, her body shaping around him until he was part of her.

He moved within her, and she gave an exclamation of wonderment. There was no more pain, just...pleasure. If pleasure felt like something, this was it. She looked up into his face, his eyes dark, his strong jaw set with the tension of passion restrained as he moved, evidence that desire was riding him hard, each thrust driving him towards pleasure's brink as much as it drove her. Wherever they were going, they were going together. She held him to her, with her arms about his neck, her legs about his waist like a vice as if she could lock him in place, keep him within her for ever. Her hips picked up the rhythm, joining him as his thrusts came harder, no more the long, languorous surge and ebb, but shorter, faster strokes full of exigence. They gave themselves over to the relentless urgency of them until they were there at pleasure's cliff, falling into warm abyss.

Pen knew, before she opened her eyes, she was in uncharted territory. This was not a place on her maps. She'd never known anything like it and she'd never find her way back on her own. This was a journey for two and perhaps not for just any two, but a journey specifically for her and Cassian and no other.

Pen opened her eyes slowly, savouring the idea of lying in bed, naked, in the middle of the day, with him. This might be the best part, watching Cassian sleep, his strong face in rare, relaxed repose. She reached for a sheet to wrap about herself and slipped from the bed. She was content to let him sleep, but her own mind was too awake for drowsing. There was too much to think about, to reflect on.

Pen padded out to the parlour, careful not to wake him. She wandered the small room, running her fingers over the small collection of books on the shelf. A person could tell a lot about another by the things they surrounded themselves with. He read books about travel, accounts of far-off places, not unlike herself. She had her atlases; he had his travelogues. The similarity made her smile. The only difference was that these books were sort of a remembrance for him, a way to recall the things he'd seen and done in person whereas, for her, the atlases were all she had. In the corner, leaning against the wall, was a leather cylinder, the kind used for storing rolled-up documents like maps. She left it for now, moving her tour around the room to the little machines scattered on empty spaces.

On a small table by the window sat a vertical wheel that rotated when the handle was turned, not unlike a miller's water wheel, only this one carried little people in its buckets. On the windowsill sat a brightly painted canopy under which a circle of painted porcelain horses could rotate. She picked up the piece, searching for the winding mechanism. Once found, Pen set it back down on the sill and watched the horses turn. They moved not only around the base, but up and down as well to a tinkly little tune. She understood what this and the wheel were; they were hopes for his pleasure garden, attractions he wanted to create for his guests just as Vauxhall had created the Cascade. Her lover was an ambitious man.

Her lover. She liked the sound of that. When she'd awoken this morning she'd not had a lover. But now, she did. Outside, beyond the window, it was still daylight, of course, although it seemed odd. More time should have passed considering the significance of what had happened. She'd made love with Cassian Truscott, lain naked in his bed. What did it mean? Anything? Everything? What did she want it to mean? Her little tour of his parlour had revealed so much to her about this man. He was clever and creative. The park he dreamed of was a work of the heart for him.

Her gaze returned to bookcase and the cylinder in the corner. This time, she didn't resist curiosity's lure. She picked it up and opened the lid, squinting to see inside. There were papers, long thick papers like the type maps were drawn on! Surely Cassian wouldn't mind if she looked. Pen took the tube to the table and carefully removed the rolled papers. She spread them on the table, anchoring each end with a paperweight. Oh, it was a map!

Pen studied it, her finger tracing the neat lettering beneath each object as she whispered each word out loud. Turkish pavilion, the Pavilion of Kuban, and there, right at the edge, overlooking the sea, was the word 'coaster'. Her breath caught as she realised what she was looking at. This was Cassian's Pleasure Garden, plotted out in minute detail. Seeing it on paper made it all the more real. He truly meant for this to happen. This was not an intangible dream, a theory.

She felt his eyes on her before she even looked up. She smiled and turned. Cassian was watching her, dressed in a paisley silk robe that

hung open loose, teasing her with his naked-
ness. She breathed her approval, 'It's beautiful.'

She'd found it. He wasn't sure how he felt
about that. Cassian crossed the room. 'You've
been snooping, minx.' It was part-jest, part-
scold. She'd helped herself to his secrets without asking. Perhaps he wouldn't mind if this
particular secret didn't mean so much to them.
This was the one that could break them and he
didn't want to be broken, not yet, not after this
afternoon, not when, in his mind, there was no
going back.

Her admiring smile wavered. 'Do you mind?
I didn't think you would.' He'd made her hesi-
tant, doubtful of *them*. She'd thought they were
closer than that. He hated himself for it. He'd
worked so hard to earn her trust, her respect,
her admiration, her love, and in a single sentence he'd managed to put a dent in it. Perhaps
it was a sign of how fragile their relationship
still was, how new. He'd been right when he'd
told Inigo it was too soon to tell her, that he
needed to wait for the right time and the time
wasn't yet.

But if not now, then when?

His conscience poked at him. There would come a time when it was too late to tell her. There was such a possibility of waiting too long and that would be just as damaging as telling her too soon.

He wrapped his arms about her and drew her against him, nuzzling her neck. 'No, I don't mind.' It was only a small lie. What did it matter if she saw the map? He'd already told her about it. He was overreacting. His only excuse was that he knew just how close to the edge they skated on the issue. 'I haven't shared my grand design with very many people, that's all. I suppose I'm protective of it.'

And you, he thought. *I am protective of you and us and what we could have together if given the chance.*

She leaned her head back against him, unaware of the internal turmoil this moment caused him. Her smile was back. 'Did Richard Penlerick see it?'

'Yes.' His voice cracked on the word without warning. That she'd known to ask touched him to the core. She'd listened to him, deeply, not just to the story he'd shared, but she'd listened to how much Richard had meant to him.

She turned in his arms and took his face between her hands. 'Then why isn't it built? This is clearly not some wild imagining. You've travelled the world, studied parks and entertainments. You've put considerable time and energy into this, thinking about it, designing it. But not implementing it?'

Another moment of truth. He couldn't seem to get away from them. 'No land, at least not the right piece of land,' he added when it seemed she was going to correct him. Of course, the Dukedom of Hayle had land, but not the land he needed. 'I need centrally located land so I can maximise access to and for a labour force and for supplies as well, yet I need space around it for new businesses to develop, for those entrepreneurs who want to try their hand at innkeeping. The setting must be picturesque, a view worth leaving London for, something that shows Cornwall at its best. And,' he added to his lengthy list of requirements, 'I don't want to displace anyone. It defeats the purpose if we take land away from people, which rules out most of the Hayle holdings. I don't mean to dispossess our farmers and tenants.'

'You're very specific. Have you thought of building near Truro?'

'Yes, and I've discarded that idea since it's too far to help the people at home. The people in the Hayle environs won't be helped by a pleasure garden three hours away in Truro.'

She thought for a moment. 'I see your dilemma.' She ran her nails down his chest and he shivered delightfully. She moved against him, her hips brushing his groin in suggestion. 'Sometimes when I have a problem, I think about something else and, while I'm busy thinking about that something else, a solution presents itself. Perhaps we should think of solving a different problem.' He could think of several problems he was about to have very shortly.

'Like how to get you out of that sheet you're wearing,' Cassian growled playfully. 'I could spin you out of it, or I could lay you down and roll you out of it, or...'

'Or, I could just slip out of it.' Pen gave a single tug to the sheet and it fell to her feet, leaving her gloriously, deliciously naked, like Venus from the sea. There'd not been time before to really study her, he'd been too intent on the bedding, but there was time now, time to take in her breasts, high and firm and yet full enough to fill his hands, the flare of her hips, the caramel hair between her thighs. Oh, she was a delight to look upon and an even greater delight to bed in her eagerness and her curiosity.

'Come back to bed with me—' Cassian swept her up in his arms '—I like solving problems this way.' He settled her on the bed and drew her on top of him. 'Would you like the reins this time?'

'Can I?' Her eyes widened in excitement.

'Most definitely. I think, for the man, the sensation is even greater this way.' Cassian lifted her hips and helped her into position. She eased down his length and swept her hair over one shoulder, looking like the world's greatest temptress. She wriggled, testing the fit.

'I didn't know it could be this way.' She was suddenly shy as Cassian settled his hands at her hips. 'I didn't know people talked about lovemaking like this, as though it's not a duty, but a privilege, a feast for the senses.'

Cassian levered up on his elbows, careful not to dislodge her. 'It can be like this and better.

It can be any way we want. In bed, we make our own rules.'

'I like the sound of that.' She pushed at his chest, knocking him back against the pillows. 'Do you know what else I like the sound of? You taking your pleasure and knowing I was the one to give it to you.' She began to move and Cassian was happy to oblige, pleased to make all the sounds she required.

He let the lovemaking exhaust him, drain him of all strength, of all thought, of all worry. He lived only in the abyss of climax where his body was capable of surviving only moment to moment. He didn't want to think beyond the now, didn't want to contemplate what happened next. Next was complicated. Now was not. Next had consequences, Now did not.

'Cassian—' her drowsy voice broke through his pleasant fog '—I was thinking.'

'You have the strength to think?' Cassian jested. 'I do not.' He played with her hair, idly sifting it through his fingers, his mind not fully functioning, not wanting to. He wanted to lie in this pleasant state for a while longer.

'A little.' Her head was nestled in the hollow of his shoulder and she shifted to look up at him. 'I have land that would be perfect for your gardens. It's part of my dowry. Thirty-two acres on the coast not far from Redruth.'

Cassian's fingers stilled, his mind forced into full awareness of the moment. He did not want to think about the damn land now. 'Is this a proposal, honey?' He tried to play it off with humour, but Pen was in earnest.

'No, you've already proposed. You said you were just waiting until I was ready. I am telling you, Cassian, that I am ready. Propose to me. Go to my father and ask for my hand. I will say yes. We'll be married, we can lie abed all afternoon every day of the week and you'll have your land.'

'And what will you have in exchange, Pen?' Cassian rose up on one arm. Why was he arguing? Wasn't this what he wanted? His land was within reach and Pen was within reach. He wouldn't even have to tell her about the land, about why he'd been courting Redruth's daughter specifically. She was giving it voluntarily—she was his partner in all of this. He hadn't needed to seduce it out of her after all. There needn't be any trickery. It could not have worked out better. So why did he feel dirty? 'You don't think it's too fast any more?' he hedged.

'It's been over a month since my debut, we've been together almost every day since then and, in truth, we've known each other longer than that, just as you said,' Pen insisted.

'But what about your doubts regarding me?' Cassian pressed. He needed her to be sure.

'You said you came to London because there was nothing left to do but pursue your duty. I believe you.' Pen reached for his hand and laced her fingers through his. 'You proved yourself worthy. You've shown me the world and you've shown me what a life with you could be like. This is what I want, Cassian. You are what I want. Together, we are going to make a whole new world.' When she put it like that, they seemed unstoppable.

'Very well, then, Penrose Prideaux, will you do me the honour of becoming my wife?' It was too good to be true. Cassian didn't allow himself to think about the other end of that adage. When Pen whispered yes, tears shining in her eyes, and he rolled her beneath him in celebration, it was easier and much more pleasant to think that love had triumphed against the odds.

Chapter Twenty

Cassian was going to marry her! *Matthew* was going to marry her! What were the odds her true love was also an eligible suitor? 'It's perfect! It's like those stories where the girl kisses a frog and he turns into a prince. Only Matthew was never quite a frog.' Pen gushed to Margery the next morning. She felt giddy and silly. She could hardly contain herself. 'He's coming to talk to Father today. Father will be so pleased!' She grabbed Margery's hands and spun her around the bedroom. 'Just think, Father and I agreeing on a suitor! I would have thought that was impossible.'

Pen plopped down on the bed. 'Now, what shall I wear? The primrose? That gown reminds me of the sun and I feel all sunny inside.'

'I have yellow ribbon for your hair and your

little heart charm too. Today would be the ideal time to wear it, a token of his affections.' Margery picked up a brush just as the sound of a carriage harness jangled outside.

'Is he here already?' Pen rushed to the window overlooking the street. It was only eleven, too early for a call, but perhaps he couldn't wait either. She was sure she'd slept last night only out of sheer exhaustion. Lovemaking, it turned out, was fine exercise.

Pen pulled back the curtain just enough to spy on the street. It was not Cassian's bright blue phaeton parked at the kerb. She shifted her gaze to the door, recognising the straight-backed posture and sombre clothing of the man on the front step. Wilmington. He was an odd visitor at an odd time—perhaps her father had Parliament business with him.

'Perhaps he wishes to propose too, miss,' Margery suggested.

Pen dropped the curtain with a breezy confidence. 'He can propose all he likes. I will accept only Cassian.'

Half an hour later, there was a scratch at her door. Margery opened it, exchanging hushed words with a footman. Pen did not care for the look on her face when her maid turned around. 'Miss, your father wishes to speak to you in his office immediately. Your brother is with him.'

Something was dreadfully wrong. Pen shifted her gaze between her brother and her father and back again, looking for a clue as to what, but all she received in return was the briefest shakes of a head from Phin. Her father's face was stoic and blank. He was ashen with restrained emotion. It took only a moment to realise he was angry. Angry beyond words. She'd only seen him this mad once before, when the news had come of her mother. 'Father, what's happened?' Pen took the one empty chair in the room.

'Viscount Trevethow has asked for an appointment this afternoon. I believe he wishes to discuss marriage. What do you say to that, daughter?'

Pen smiled—perhaps she'd misread the emotion. This should be pleasing news for him. 'I hope he does. I would welcome his proposal.'

Her father's hard gaze softened for the briefest instant, but with sorrow, not happiness.

'Then it is as I feared. We have been played falsely, you most of all, Penrose.'

'How so?' She furrowed her brow and glanced at Phin for clarity. He offered none. 'The Viscount and I are very much in love,' she tried to explain to them, to herself. How could falling in love mean being played falsely?

Her father shook his head. 'Trevethow does not love you. He would have courted you if you'd been an old crone. I have it on authority from Wilmington this morning that Trevethow is only after your dowry.'

'Nonsense, he has wealth of his own. He'll be a duke some day,' Pen argued. It was as if they were talking about a different man. 'You can't take Wilmington's word. He despises the viscount. Wilmington would say anything.'

'It's the land, Pen.' Phin spoke quietly from his corner. 'He wants the land to build a pleasure garden.'

'You misunderstand, I'm the one that told him about the land,' Pen countered hopefully. This was all a misunderstanding. She would put it straight, although she had to do it carefully.

'When?' her father asked.

'Yesterday, on the way home from Gunter's.' It wasn't technically a lie. They'd just made a stop by the Albany first.

'Yesterday? You're sure?' her father pressed her.

'Yes, absolutely.' Pen smiled, feeling confident this solved her father's riddle. But her father was more stoic than ever.

'Then it seems Wilmington is right.' Her father held out a pair of letters. 'Trevethow was after that land long before yesterday.'

Pen took the papers and read them. It was hard to focus with her pulse racing and her emotions high. She could barely comprehend the import of the words. 'This is a land development firm, the Porth Karrek Land Development Company. What does this have to do with me?'

'Read what they want to do with the land,' her father coached. 'And note the date.'

Her eyes scanned the top of the letter. 'This was written last autumn.' She read the letter, past the salutations and expressions of politeness. There it was, in the fourth paragraph after the request to buy the land—the desire to build a pleasure garden. She moved to the second page, her stomach tightening as her eyes moved over the arguments for the park: to boost the economy, to create jobs, to educate people—all the reasons Cassian had given her.

'It's the first letter.' Her father passed her a packet of papers. 'If you like, you can read the subsequent correspondence. It will show that the Redruth estate rejected the first offer and the second. It will show that the development company doubled their offer and was refused. The last refusal was first of March.' Her father held her gaze with angry, weary eyes. 'I know you think your heart's engaged, Pen, that's why I'm showing you this. You don't have to believe me. Believe the proof.'

She set the letters in her lap. 'What is this proof of? That two people had an idea for an amusement garden? What does this have to do with Viscount Trevethow?' But she knew, as she said the words, that the coincidence was too great for it not to be connected. She just didn't know how.

'Pen, Viscount Trevethow and his father own the development company,' Phin explained.

The room spun. As pieces came together, her world slowly unravelled. She stared at the date on the last letter. Absolute refusal had been in March. Word fragments spun through her mind: *'There's a gentleman I wish to purchase something from... He is stubborn...he doesn't see all the good it could do...' 'It sounds like your gentleman and my father have much in common.'* They were one and the same. Her mind was reeling now. When Cassian had spoke of his problem, it was the problem of acquiring land for his pleasure garden. Why hadn't she seen it sooner?

Cassian's first outing of the Season had been her debut ball in May. The society columns had remarked upon it. Dear Lord, he'd come straight after her, whoever she might have been, knowing that marriage was the only way he was going to get that land. Pen swallowed hard. Now she knew what it was he'd wanted so badly. He'd been after her land all along.

Oh, he'd been relentless and crafty. He'd not even mentioned the pleasure gardens until she was well and duly impressed with him, besotted with a man who laid the world at her feet and overcome her resistance in the most spectacular of ways, all the time knowing what he wanted in exchange for his efforts: thirty-two acres on the coast.

She'd made it easy. He hadn't even had to trick her out of the acres. She had offered them to him yesterday, in his bed, thinking she'd come up with the perfect solution, that it was all her idea. Her throat tightened. This was her nightmare come true. Her worries from the start had come to life: that Cassian or Matthew—the distinction hardly mattered— was nothing but a flirt, who would say whatever was required to get what he wanted. In this case, he'd not wanted her, but the land. She just happened to come with it. No, that couldn't be right, that couldn't be all there was to it. She couldn't accept that it had all been a lie. 'He loves me. He wants to marry me.' Pen made the feeble argument.

'He wants to marry you, that's true. But not for love.' Her father was stern. 'At least we know before it's too late. Imagine how much worse this would have been if you'd actually wed him.'

Pen shook her head. 'There is room for love and land, Father. He loves me. I know it. The land is just an extra benefit.' But the sun was going out of the day, her happiness turning to grey doubt. He had come straight from Em to court a girl he'd never seen with the intent to marry her. She'd accused him of it that night at the ball. He'd denied it, but it was exactly what he'd done. Had he truly only courted her for the land, had he not loved her at all? Had he not fallen for her? She thought of yesterday. She'd given him everything. Had it meant nothing? Just a means to an end? Had he meant to compromise her in case he failed to persuade her to marry him legitimately? Pen pressed her hands to her stomach. She wanted to be sick at the thought of such treachery. No, she couldn't give in to such belief. She knew better. She had to fight.

'I don't believe it and I don't think you should either. You should talk to the viscount and hear it from him.' Pen pushed on, frantic to make sense of this turn of events. 'What's so wrong with marrying for love *and* land?' She was desperate now. 'You picked Trevethow yourself, Father. In May you were over the moon about the prospect of me becoming a duchess. I invested in him, emotionally, and now that I've decided on a man I wanted to marry, you are pulling him away.' Pen lowered her voice, determined to not become hysterical. She played her ace. 'You said I could come to London to find a suitor. Well, I have. I choose Trevethow.'

'And I refuse to sanction the union.' Her father's answer was sharp, cold and fast. He hadn't even taken a moment to think. The speed of his answer rendered Pen temporarily speechless. That had been her ace and he'd trumped her without hesitation.

'Father, I choose him,' she repeated dumbly.

'My daughter will not marry a man who seeks to so blatantly mislead her about his intentions. It is one thing to arrange an alliance through marriage, as long as both parties understand that's what it is. It is another thing entirely to feign affection and deceive a young girl with no experience in the world, who was susceptible enough to fall for the first man who showered her with attentions.'

Pen's temper flared and she rose. 'That is not what happened. I am not a young girl. I am twenty-one years old and I am not naive. I might have lived behind castle walls, but I am not ignorant of how the world works.' Tears stung and this time she could not stop them.

'How dare you think I am too stupid to not know the difference between love and cheap flattery. Mother raised me better than that.'

'You leave your mother out of this.' Her father rose, too, bracing his hands on the desk. 'I have had the task of keeping you safe for the last ten years and I will not falter in that duty now. Your marriage to a bounder like Trevethow would disgrace her memory. That's the end of it. We are going home tomorrow. I've already instructed Margery to pack your things.'

'No!' This was Em and Matthew all over again—she was being pulled from Cassian. Would he think she'd changed her mind? Would he think she didn't love him? 'I won't go.' Not until she heard from his lips he didn't love her, that he'd used her. Only then would she believe it had been a lie.

'You will go. We are going home where it's safe. There's measles at the Royal Military Asylum. The Hawaiian court has come down with them, including the King, and there's been talk of a strange vigilante walking the streets at night, meting out justice as he sees fit. These are not conditions I want you exposed to. Besides, Wadesbridge has written once more, expressing his continued interest in marriage. I will accept the offer on your behalf. You'll be settled with a decent man close to home who won't break your heart.' He smiled, trying to soften the blow. 'I know it seems disappointing now, but in a few months you'll see this was the right decision. We'll have a grand wedding at Trescowe among the autumn leaves and you can wear your mother's wedding dress. It will be the biggest party Cornwall will have ever seen.' He was trying to placate her. This time it wouldn't work.

'Pen,' Phin said, trying to make peace. 'Trevethow isn't honourable.'

She shook her head. 'Please, Phin. Don't. You can't make this better. Not this time.' She gathered her skirts and her dignity and left the room. She would not let them see her cry. She would save those tears for when she reached the safety of her room and hope that at some point she would be able to stop. She doubted it. Her heart was breaking, shattering into a thousand pieces. She'd been betrayed not by one man today, but three and all of them claimed to love her. If that was love, she wanted nothing to do with it.

* * *

The hall clock at White's chimed three. Redruth was late, but that did not dim Cassian's spirits, nor had the request that they move their meeting to the club as opposed to Redruth's town house. He was going to marry Pen. He'd meet Redruth at the tailor's if that was what it took.

'You're cheery today.' Inigo sauntered over and took a chair. 'What's the reason?'

'I'm asking for Pen's hand. Redruth is meeting me.' Cassian kept his voice low, well aware of how the news would affect the betting book.

'He's meeting you here?' Inigo was surprised. 'That's rather public for him.'

'It's how he wanted it, but he's late.' Pen had been 'late' once, too, and she'd never come. He was starting to wonder if it was a family trait.

'Well, then, congratulations are in order.' Inigo waved for a waiter. 'We'll have an anticipatory drink while we wait and I'll tell you all my news. All anyone wants to talk about aside from your courtship is the Hawaiian King with the measles and the vigilante—apparently this week hasn't been the first time he's struck, merely the first time someone has put all the pieces together. Interesting, don't you think? A man who goes about dealing out justice on his own?' Inigo took his drink from the tray. 'Cheers, my friend.'

'Is it any different than what we do? Eaton with his school, me with the pleasure garden, you with your loans and investments, all of which are guided by the principle of making Cornwall better? This man apparently wants to make London better, one night at a time.' Cassian mused, one eye on the door. Any moment, Redruth would walk in. A group entered and Cassian's nerves eased only to tighten again. It wasn't Redruth, merely Wilmington and his cronies. Wilmington gave him a sardonic nod as he passed.

'We don't wear masks.' Inigo chuckled at the analogy. He jerked his head towards Wilmington's group by the window. 'What was that all about?'

'I don't know. He's been angry over Pen for weeks.' Cassian smiled and looked beyond his friend's shoulder. 'You'll have to excuse me, Inigo, Redruth is here.' At last. Only a half hour late.

Inigo clapped him on the shoulder. 'Good

luck, then. I'll be over there reading my newspapers if you need me.'

Cassian motioned the earl over and summoned refreshments, playing the consummate host in his little part of the club. 'French brandy is your drink, I believe.' Cassian shook the earl's hand. 'It's good to see you. Thank you for coming.' Although by rights, the earl ought to be the one thanking him for making this accommodation.

The earl was taciturn as he took his seat, ignoring the offer of brandy. 'This won't take long.'

Chapter Twenty-One

An odd little chill crept through Cassian. The earl wasn't known for his social graces: he ought not be unnerved. Still, 'things' were starting to add up: wanting to meet outside his home, a desire to make the meeting brief, no apology for being late, the refusal to drink with him.

Cassian opted to plunge in. Clearly, the earl was no lover of small talk, and probably not a lover of sentiment. 'As you are aware, your daughter and I have become quite close during the time we've spent together. I have developed an affection for her and I believe she's developed one for me.' That was an understatement based on yesterday afternoon. 'One that has led me to want to ask for her hand in marriage and make her my duchess.'

Sharp green eyes with dagger tips met his

gaze. This was not the look of a man who welcomed a proposal for his daughter. He'd seen that welcoming look just weeks ago. Something had changed. 'I am well aware where your affections lie, Trevethow. They are not with my daughter as much as they are with her land and your damnable amusement garden. I will no more consider your suit for her hand than I did your land company's offer for the land.' He ground out the last words.

'I'm sure I don't understand,' Cassian replied coldly. He was frozen inside, paralysed by the revelation as his mind grappled to make sense of it. Redruth knew. How could he have known? But, more importantly, Redruth did not believe his feelings for Pen were genuine. 'Your daughter discussed the land with me yesterday. She voluntarily suggested it as a site.'

'After you turned her head with opera boxes, nights at the theatre and weeks of dancing dazzling attendance on her. She is not worldly, Trevethow. You took advantage of her. You did not tell her you deliberately targeted her for her dowry.'

'She is more worldly than you think. I mean that as a compliment, sir. She is a fine woman, intelligent, thoughtful and kind. You underestimate her.' Cassian kept his voice low. People were starting to look, to wonder. It had been bad enough to know eyes had been on them covertly since Redruth had walked in. This was the meeting the *ton* had been waiting for since the Redruth ball. To have it take place in public was a gossip's dream come true. Cassian had no doubts stories of this would regale dinner tables around London tonight. He'd been jilted just like his brother.

'She is not for you. I do not want that land in your hands, bringing all nature of strangers to Cornwall. You will corrupt our part of the world. You will bring strangers and strange ideas, and violence and crime. Tell me, is Vauxhall a safe venue? You cannot do it. Women are assaulted there…cutpurses roam the paths. It will be the same for you. The venture will fail to produce the results you want. I will not give my daughter to that. Let me be clear. Your association with her is at an end. We will not welcome you at Byerd House or at the Castle. Good day.'

Redruth rose and Cassian rose with him, letting his height remind the slighter man that he was a peer, too, that he could not be dismissed so callously. 'Who told you about the land company?' Cassian asked, barely keeping his emotions leashed.

Redruth gave a brief nod in Wilmington's direction. 'A better man than you.'

Cassian wondered when White's had last seen a brawl. He was going to kill Wilmington. At the moment, Cassian did not mean that metaphorically. A duel suited him. The jealous prig had deliberately set out to ruin him and in the attempt the man had managed to ruin Pen too. Certainly Cassian was seething for what amounted to Wilmington ratting him out on the land company like a snotty-nosed schoolboy playing teacher's pet, but he was positively livid over what Wilmington had done to Pen and the man didn't even realise it although the bastard professed to care for her, to have her best interests at heart.

He could imagine too well the despair Pen must have felt when her father told her. Redruth would not have spared her feelings, would not have sugar-coated what he thought was the truth, that his daughter had been misled by an experienced man of the world all for the sake of her property. It would have triggered all of Pen's old doubts about him, all of her fears about marriage. Pen, with her broken heart, thinking he didn't love her, that he had never loved her, that he'd taken her to bed to force her hand if it came to that.

That beautiful afternoon seemed dishonourable in the aftermath. Now Pen was ruined, her heart broken, her trust in him shattered, her maidenhead gone, given to a man her father forbade her to marry. Cassian only hoped that was all, that their afternoon hadn't left her with a child. He was regretting not taking precautions now. He'd been so sure of himself, of *them*, or he wouldn't have done it. All that surety was gone now. Across the room, Wilmington looked his direction with a triumphant smirk. He knew exactly what had transpired. That did it. Cassian was out of his chair and striding across the room. Wilmington was going to pay for what he'd done to him, but most of all for what he'd done to Pen.

Inigo met him halfway across the room, blocking his way with a hand on his chest and low-voiced counsel. 'Don't do it, Cass.'

'Do what?' Cassian growled.

'Stir up more trouble. You cannot brawl in here. Remember yourself. You are a duke's son. You outrank that *pissant* in every way.'

'This is about Pen, about what he's done to her.' He tried to push past Inigo, but Inigo stood his ground.

'Cass, you cannot brawl in here and you can't duel out there. Duelling is illegal.'

'No one will convict me, assuming I'm caught,' Cassian growled.

'Assuming you aren't *killed*. Cassian, think!'

'By Wilmington? I will not be killed by that rat.'

'Listen to me, you're angry. You're not thinking straight. Let's go somewhere else for a drink and talk it through. You can't duel a man for telling the truth. He didn't tell Redruth lies. Wilmington is a symptom of the problem, he's not the problem. What do you solve by duelling him?'

Cassian heaved a sigh, reason asserting its slow tentacles.

'Let's go back to my rooms,' Inigo suggested, 'it's quiet there.'

* * *

It was too quiet at Inigo's rooms off Jermyn Street. Cassian could hear himself think and he had only one thought. He'd lost Pen. The more he thought it, the more devastating the concept became. He hadn't just lost the land. In fact, he barely thought of the land. He'd lost *her*: her trust, her affection, her laughter, her stories, her passion for living. 'I had a second chance with her and I failed. She will hate me for ever.' Cassian slumped in his chair, his drink untouched. Not even Inigo's excellent brandy could tempt him. 'My father was right. I should have told her about the land.' He'd misjudged everything. He'd tried to take the easy way out.

'Give her the night to calm down. Go over tomorrow and ask to see her,' Inigo counselled. 'If you love her, you can't let Redruth be the one who decides this. Perhaps a show of strength on your part will persuade the earl you love his daughter.'

'He'll refuse me. He told me as much this afternoon. I am not welcome.'

'Then get a note to Pen. She'll be worried

sick over you just as you are worried over her. Do not let Redruth keep you apart.'

His friend was trying hard to alleviate his suffering with solutions. But no solution would matter if Pen had given up on him, if Pen believed what he felt for her was all a lie, a strategy to get at the land. Cassian managed a small grin of appreciation. 'Thanks, Inigo.'

'For what?'

'For not letting me punch Wilmington in the face, or call him out or make a scene. There was scene enough as it was.'

'That's what friends are for. Now, why don't you come with me to the Treleven monthly musicale? Vennor will be there and it will take your mind off things. I don't want you sitting in a dark room brooding. You *will* see her tomorrow.'

That's exactly what he wanted to do: sit in his rooms and sulk, to give over to the pain of loss rocketing through him. He couldn't lose her, not now when he'd just won her back. Cassian barely suppressed a groan. 'Going out is the last thing I want to do, Inigo.'

'That's why it's the first thing you *should* do. Tonight, the best you can do is go out and show the gossips you aren't beaten. I'll send my man over to the Albany for your things. Remember, while they are all thinking this is the end, you know differently.'

He knew he was going to fight for Pen, for *them*, even if meant giving up the land. His father's wisdom came back to him. He could not let the dream consume him, blind him to what was truly important. This wasn't over.

It was truly over this time. Pen watched out the coach window as London gave way to dirt roads and countryside. Cassian had gone out last night. The early-morning papers had reported it just as they were leaving. Her aunt thought the papers would make good reading on the journey. Pen wished she hadn't seen them.

Viscount T. was spotted at Sir J. T.'s monthly musicale just hours after having a tense encounter with the Earl of R. at White's.

Reports say Viscount T. and Lady P. are officially off.

One might speculate that the Viscount is

*already hunting a replacement from among
Sir J. T.'s many unmarried daughters.*

Good heavens, why didn't they just come out
and say it? The column wasn't even trying to
be discreet.

How could she have misjudged Cassian so
badly? Twice? There was no one to talk to
about it, not even Margery. She was riding with
the other servants in the second carriage. Phin
was out riding with her father and she certainly
didn't want to talk to *him*. This was a mess
of her father's making, of Wilmington's making. Men. Wrecking her life again with their
suppositions about what she wanted, what she
needed and there was still Wadesbridge to contend with. Her father seemed more determined
than ever to see that match happen now. She
didn't want to marry Wadesbridge. She didn't
want to marry anyone.

Not true, her heart reminded her. *You still
want Cassian.* That was the beginning of a
very dangerous game she played all the way
until lunch. Would she still marry him, knowing all she knew now, if he pulled up beside
this carriage and asked her to come with him?

Would life with him be worth it? Would it re-
semble at least in part some of the glamour he'd
displayed for her or was her father right? Once
he had the land he would forget about her, see
no reason to dazzle her and she would be forgotten, discarded.

Would it be worth it to defy her father in
order to find out? It was an enormous risk, and
a hypothetical one, given that they'd reached
their lunch stop and there was no sign of Cassian, although there were plenty of reminders
of him. The heath they stopped to lunch on was
like the place the two of them had picnicked
and where Oscar had played himself into exhaustion. She missed Oscar. Would she ever
see her puppy again? The tears started. Better
to cry out here on the heath alone where her
family couldn't see than to hear once more how
Cassian wasn't worth her tears.

She couldn't possibly explain to them the
tears were for the fantasy, for what she'd
thought they'd had. In the moment, that fantasy
had been very real and, in it, she'd been real.
She'd been alive. She'd given her heart, her
body, her soul to it. When she was with Cassian she was alive for the first time. He made

her laugh, made her think, made her feel. The world was brighter, she had purpose. Hadn't he felt the same? He'd claimed to. He'd told her about his brother, about his guilt over his brother's death. Those were not things idly shared. Which was why it was so difficult to believe Cassian didn't love her. Had he really shared those things just to get her land?

Pen sat down in the meadow and plucked a handful of daisies, playing a new game, a more dangerous game than the one she'd played in the carriage: if he'd been real, he wouldn't give up. If he loved her, he would come for her. Perhaps even now, he was at Byerd House, discovering that she'd left. He would know she'd gone home. In this way, things were better than when she'd left Cornwall. He hadn't known where to find her then. He did now. He could come. It was a rather awful test, though, a blunt one that would not allow her to hide from the truth. If it was true that if he loved her he would come, it had to also be true that if he didn't come, her father was right. He hadn't loved her, only the land, and he'd been willing to do and to say anything to acquire it.

She pulled a petal off the daisy. *If he loves*

me, he will come. She pulled another petal. *If he loves me not...* Then he wouldn't. It was as simple as that.

Day one of the journey had passed with no sign of Cassian. Of course, Pen reasoned, he needed time to catch up with them. Day two had passed and she reasoned he couldn't possibly leave the city immediately. He'd have business to wrap up, farewells to make, plans to cancel. She had reasoned the same on day three and day four, and on into the full first week she was home. July was careening to a close, pleasantly warm for Cornwall, the sea impossibly blue from the cliffs of her thirty-two barren acres. Every time she stood there, she thought of Cassian's gardens, of his coaster speeding by and looking out over the water. It hadn't been just his dream. In the time they'd been together, it had become her dream as well.

Pen picked a daisy. *If he loves me, he will come. If he loves me not...*

He might come anyway.

The problem with such games was that they needed a statute of limitations. When the Season ended, Cassian would come home to Cornwall, but it wouldn't be because he loved her. It would be because it was simply time to come home. Her test would mean nothing then.

She tossed away the denuded flower. She was becoming a danger to daisies. Perhaps her game already meant nothing. She would have to give the game up soon and face reality. Wadesbridge was in earnest. He'd driven over with rose cuttings the day before. She was running out of reasons to resist. Why not marry him? If she couldn't have Cassian, what did it matter? At least Wadesbridge was no risk to her heart, yet that poor, shattered organ wasn't ready to give up yet. If she waited long enough, Cassian would come.

But to what end? To break her heart all over again, to make her face an unpleasant truth or to claim her as his own, to push away the last month of pain as nothing more than a misunderstanding fed out of proportion by a jealous Wilmington? She had to recognise that even if he did come, it didn't necessarily make everything magically better, it might just make it worse. She might have to find a way to live with a broken heart. But she'd never know if Cassian didn't come.

Chapter Twenty-Two

Cassian could not leave town. The Hawaiian King had the bad form to die, succumbing to the measles along with his wife, and requiring the pomp of lying in state at the Caledonian Hotel and then burial at the crypt at St Martin-in-the-Fields, a process that took the better part of a week. George IV insisted the *ton* turn out to honour their international guest, perhaps to make up in death for his poor form when they were alive. He never had received them, having put it off until the Hawaiian king had been too ill. There was no question of sneaking out of town even though the burial was temporary. The bones would be sent home eventually, but here he was, along with London's finest, respectfully laying the Hawaiian King's bones to rest.

Sitting in the pew, listening to the service,

Cassian couldn't shake the irony that he was attending a funeral at the very place he'd hoped to be married. And how fitting it was. He'd felt dead since the morning he'd gone to Byerd House and found Pen gone. They were all gone, the knocker off the door and only a few servants left behind to manage closing the house. She'd left without warning, without a note, without any sort of goodbye. He couldn't blame her for it. She would be furious with him and, even if there'd been a scrap of forgiveness in her heart, she might not have had a choice. Her father held the reins, that much had been clear at White's.

He'd written, of course but his letters had been returned unopened. He had no guarantee she'd seen the letters or that the decision to return them had been hers. But there was no hope in that, only the certainty that each day that passed her anger and disappointment in him would be justified. She would think he'd simply moved on when she'd become too difficult of a prize to win.

Nothing could be further from the truth. He ached for her. He wanted to tell her about Kamehameha. She would grieve his passing:

she'd genuinely liked the Hawaiian King and his wife. He wanted to tell her the stories going around about the vigilante, to share the news of the day with her. Or better yet, to walk along the shore at Karrek Sands, or sneak away to their cottage and make love all afternoon. Inigo nudged him. 'Whatever you're thinking, it's not appropriate for a funeral,' he said, half-joking. 'But,' he whispered, 'I am glad to see you smile.'

'I'm leaving for Cornwall the moment this service is over.'

'Regardless of your reception?'

'Yes. I have to know if there's any chance of winning her back.'

'And the land?' Inigo asked, earning a stern look for talking in church from Vennor on his other side.

'It doesn't matter without her. It's time to let the dream go. It's caused so many problems, it hardly seems like a dream any more.' It had changed him, and not in positive ways. He'd let himself be chained by the past. The dream had driven him, but it had not freed him. He was as captive to that dream as Redruth was to the memory of his wife. 'The only way to convince Pen, to convince her father that I court her for love, is to give the land up.' If he were to surrender any claim to it, perhaps there was a chance. That was the only plan he had. He was going to ride to Cornwall, walk into Castle Byerd and declare his suit.

'And your dream?' Inigo asked.

'It's as dead as the King. Pen's my dream now. I'll find another way to help the economy. I hope that wherever Richard Penlerick is, looking down on us, he understands the choice I had to make.'

Vennor reached across Inigo and gripped Cassian's hand. 'My father believed in love more.'

Cassian hoped Pen believed in love. He was gambling that Pen also believed in third chances. He'd chosen love, now he hoped in the end love would choose him, that it wasn't too late.

The end was near. The end of her father's patience. The end of her freedom. The end of her hope. Her game of waiting for Cassian was nearly over. She sat on the stone bench by the fountain in the walled gardens of Castle Byerd, the ever-loyal Wadesbridge beside her, birds chirping, water gurgling, her heart sinking as he sank to one knee in front of her.

No, not now. One more day, perhaps. Sometimes one more day made a difference. Although her wishes were pointless. She'd known this was coming. Her father had informed her it was time to move on. She'd had nearly a month to set aside her feelings for Cassian, to come to grips with his duplicity. He'd warned her, too, that Wadesbridge was coming today. He'd brought more rose cuttings from Trescowe and he'd been closeted away with her father most of the afternoon.

'My dearest Penrose,' he began. 'It cannot have escaped your attention that I hold you in great esteem.' No, it couldn't have. He couldn't have been more obvious. Or more caring or doting. Why couldn't she like him? He was a nice man. He was not the villain here. There was no villain unless one counted Cassian, which her father surely did. There were just people who all wanted different things. Her father wanted her safe and married. She wanted her freedom. Wadesbridge wanted to marry her, but she wanted to marry Cassian. As to what Cassian wanted, she couldn't be sure. Had he wanted only the land? Was that why he hadn't come? Or had something else detained him? Did he think she'd didn't want him now?

'Will you do me the honour of becoming my wife?' Wadesbridge had reached the critical point in his proposal, a jolting reminder of how real things were. She'd come to the point of no return. She had to make a decision. He pressed her hand. 'I won't pretend to think I'm the man you want. I'm older, quieter, I lived a more reserved life than your London beaux. But I can make a good life for you. We can have a family—I'm not so old that I don't want that as well. You will want for nothing.'

Nothing except passion, excitement, freedom. But perhaps these things were overrated. Just look what had happened when she'd embraced them. What did she have to show? A broken heart, disappointment. She had to stop living in the fantasy and *for* the fantasy. Cassian wasn't here. He had not come and she had to move on. She could do worse than Wadesbridge. If she accepted him the search would be over, her father would be pleased and in time, perhaps, she would find contentment. She did not think she'd find more than that, but perhaps it would be enough. Perhaps it would be the first necessary step in setting Cassian aside. How long could she cling to hope before it became ridiculous? Before she let go of a good man for a fiction of a romance that hadn't truly existed except in her mind. She had to accept someone. Why not Wadesbridge?

Her voice trembled. He would think it was from maidenly nerves. 'You do me a great honour. I would be pleased to accept.'

Wadesbridge smiled, relieved. 'Shall I tell your father? What would you prefer for an engagement? I was thinking of two months, with a harvest wedding in October. It will give me time to make the house presentable for a lady, or would you like to do that? Perhaps what I really mean is that it would give you time to make the house ready.' He laughed nervously, eager to please her, and she thought once more what a shame it was that she didn't love him.

'Whatever you prefer is fine with me.' Now that the decision was made, she was numb. She had no stake in this fight. There was no fight, not any longer. There was nothing to fight for.

The French doors opened on to the garden

and her father strode towards them, a rare smile on his face. 'Do you have news to share?'

Wadesbridge smiled at her before addressing her father. 'We do. Penrose has consented to be my wife. I am the happiest man alive.'

Her father shook Wadesbridge's hand and hugged her, his joy over the decision evident. 'We shall celebrate tonight at dinner. There will be champagne and perhaps Cook can find something sweet for dessert. We shall make a party of it.'

Pen managed a smile. 'If you would both excuse me, I'd like to take a walk before dinner.' If she was to begin as she meant to go on, there was something she needed to do first.

'Just around the castle grounds,' her father warned with an eye to the sky. 'There's likely to be rain by supper.'

'Just around the grounds.' It was an outright lie. Pen fully meant to venture beyond Castle Byerd. She grabbed a shawl and stuffed her glass heart into a small drawstring bag. She didn't have much time.

The cottage was just as she remembered it. Even prepared as she was to face memories, the familiar space assaulted her senses the moment she opened the door: the lingering scent of the lavender she'd brought that last day, the ashes in the hearth, the thin quilt on the bed. Every space contained a memory: eating meat pies before the fire, watching Cassian build that fire in the rainy days of spring, later, lying together on the bed, whispering dreams to life. By the window stood the table, still covered with the faded cloth, a chipped vase holding the now-brittle sprigs of lavender. She squinted. Something was propped against the vase.

Pen went to the table and picked it up. For a moment her heart raced. Had Cassian been here? Had he come back? Was he trying to reach her? She unfolded the note and scanned the letter, her hopes fading. It had been written in April after she'd left. He wasn't here. Not now.

Pen sat down on one of the chairs, reading slowly. It was the only letter she had from him.

Dearest Em,

That seemed ages ago—when they were simply Em and Matthew.

Whoever you are, wherever you are, know that you carry my love.

I have gone to London to do my duty, but my heart remains here with you in this cottage.

The tears started and she let them come. She would cry one last time for all she'd lost. He had told the truth then, that first night at the ball. Matthew had loved Em. That was some consolation. Maybe Cassian had even loved Pen by extension. If so, why hadn't he come? Why hadn't he sent word? Or for that matter, why hadn't he told her of the land from the start when he'd realized who she was that first night in London? How different things might have been then. But he hadn't even tried to fight and now it was too late. She might never know. Pen left the note on the table and put her glass heart next to it. The cottage would be their shrine. She would leave her heart along with his. It was better this way, better that she leave it behind instead of torturing herself with the remembrance every day. She had to let go of them both—Matthew and Cassian. She couldn't keep one and not the other.

At the door, she paused. 'Goodbye, Matthew.' Perhaps some day when she was stronger, when there was more nostalgia than hurt associated with this time, she would come back to the cottage and remember. For now, she had to go home. She had her engagement party to attend.

He was nearly home. Cassian had ridden hard, taking advantage of dry roads and good weather all the way from London. It looked as if that was about to come to an end, though. Rain was imminent, and probably more. It appeared they were due for a summer storm. He pulled his hat tight on his head and spurred his horse forward for one last push. Hayle wasn't far, but that wasn't his final destination tonight. He would make for Redruth and Castle Byerd. He didn't want to waste another moment. Enough time had been lost. Never mind that he'd be travel sore and road weary when he arrived. There was one stop he did have to make, though. He'd pass the cottage. He wanted the note he'd left. He wanted it as proof that his heart had always been true.

At the cut-off towards the cliffs, he turned his

horse from the road and jogged down the dirt path until the cottage came into sight. On the horizon, a fork of lightning split the sky far out to sea. He had time until the storm arrived in full. Inside, he strode to the table and stopped short. His note lay open and Pen's glass heart beside it. She'd been here! He picked up the heart, running his thumb over its smooth surface, wondering. Had she left it as a sign? Had she left it as goodbye? Was she trying to purge herself of their association or was she leaving him a message? He had a hundred questions, but beneath them there was hope. She'd come here because she hadn't forgotten.

His mind raced. What if she came back? He should leave a sign as well. Cassian ran outside, a fat raindrop catching him on the nose. He picked a handful of wildflowers and grabbed his canteen from his saddle. Indoors once more, he laid aside the lavender, poured fresh water into the chipped vase and arranged his wildflowers as best he could. If she came again, she'd understand. He stuffed the note and the heart into the pocket of his jacket and set off for Castle Byerd. With luck, he could return them both to her tonight.

* * *

He was soaked and dripping by the time he arrived at the Castle. The rain had begun in earnest. He tossed the reins to a groom and strode up the wide steps to the door. He thumped hard to be sure he was heard over the storm and had his foot ready when the door was answered.

'What do you want?' The footman passed a jaundiced eye over his dripping form. In the distance, thunder clapped. The storm was arriving in force. Cassian raised his voice.

'I am Lord Trevethow from Hayle. I wish to speak with the Earl of Redruth.'

'I am sorry, sir, the family is not receiving tonight.' Cassian got his foot in the door just in time.

'I don't think you heard me. I am Viscount Trevethow.'

'Let him in, but he won't be staying' came a low voice from behind the servant. The door opened wide enough to admit him, and Cassian stepped inside, unapologetically dripping water on the floor.

'Redruth, good evening.'

Redruth ignored the greeting. 'Did I not

make myself plain? You will not be received here or in London.'

'Where is Pen? I have something to say to her and then, if she prefers not to receive me, I'll depart.' This was his boldest gambit yet. This would be the last chance in truth. But Pen had gone to the cottage. It had to mean something.

'She is unavailable at present.' Redruth met his gaze with a steely look of victory. 'Tonight, the family is privately celebrating her engagement to Lord Wadesbridge.'

'I want to see her.' Cassian was reeling. *Engaged?* Pen was engaged? This was not how it was supposed to happen. He'd ridden hard, she'd read the note. They were supposed to be reconciled.

The earl's smile widened without pity. 'You see, you and whatever you wished to say are too late.'

'Milord.' A voice spoke behind the earl.

'Yes?' Redruth snapped, not caring for the interruption. The maid behind him cowered nervously.

'Lady Penrose is not in her room, milord. We've looked for her everywhere. She's gone.'

'What do you mean, gone? Did she come back

from her walk? She was on castle grounds. Did someone look in the gardens?' Redruth's attention was fixed on the maid, his brow creased with obvious worry. Regardless of his often abrupt manner, the man loved his children.

'Yes, milord. She came back, but when her maid went to dress her for dinner she was gone again.'

'Send for her maid,' the earl barked as thunder boomed directly overhead.

The maid recited her tale, her eyes drifting towards Cassian. 'She came back from her walk, milord, but she seemed sad. She asked for some time alone before dressing. She said she wanted to lie down. I left her for half an hour and when I came back she was gone.' Thunder rolled again and Cassian grew impatient. There was something the maid wasn't telling them.

'Was anything missing? Did she take anything from the room?' This would indicate how 'gone' she really was.

The maid looked anxious, torn between protecting her mistress and doing her duty to her superiors. 'I don't know. Maybe.'

'That is not an answer!' Cassian growled.

'Lady Penrose may be in danger in that weather. This is no time to keep secrets. What was missing?'

The maid looked directly at him. 'A cloak and a dress she keeps for walking outdoors. Her jewellery. Her hairbrush. Just small things.'

'Thank you.' Cassian nodded. She'd gone out as Em and she'd taken portable items with her. Convertible items that could be turned into money. She didn't mean to come back. Cassian didn't wait for further instruction. He was already striding towards the door as the next thunderclap hit.

'Where do you think you're going?' the earl called after him.

'Out to find Pen. It's dark and wet out there— you'll need as many men as you can muster. This is the worst storm of the summer and the woman I love is out in it.' There was no time to lose. Cassian called for his horse, barely watered and still tacked. 'I'm sorry, old boy—' he swung up into the saddle '—but she's out there and she's going to need us.' He'd rather have his horse, tired as he was, under him in this weather than a fresh horse he didn't know. Ajax was sure-footed in the mud of Cornwall and solid. He didn't spook at thunder or lightning, and he was strong. He could carry two.

Cassian turned Ajax east and headed to the hills. This was where he'd find her. The hills were her refuge. Hopefully, she'd found a cave for shelter. He didn't like thinking of her out in the weather, soaked to the skin, unable to see the ground. It would be too easy to turn an ankle, to fall. She could be lying in a ditch, unable to get out of the mud. He preferred to think of her in a cave sitting before a small fire, staying warm.

Cassian didn't get far. The hills proved to be almost impassable. There'd been a mudslide, the land giving way under the deluge, and piles of earthy debris made progress futile. He had to rethink his plan. If she couldn't go to the hills, where else would she turn? Surely she wouldn't have kept walking in this storm and she would not have taken refuge with other people if it could be helped. Anyone she stayed with would remember her, would tell her father she'd passed that way. It would be tantamount to giving herself up. He would not waste his time on the villages. Redruth and Wadesbridge would be searching there. It was the first place they'd look. It was possible she might be there. She might not have had a choice. But if she did have a choice, where would she go?

The cottage. She could have made it that far before the storm would have demanded she take shelter. What better shelter was there than the cottage? There was firewood, a bed and a roof that didn't leak. And it was away from the road. Cassian turned Ajax towards the sea and began to ride.

Hold on, Pen, I'm coming, was the litany that thundered in his mind. The cottage would be secure, but getting there was less so. Navigating the terrain in the dark would be difficult. he prayed she would be safe.

Pen pushed streaming hanks of hair back from her face and struggled to get her bearings. Was she still on the road? She should get off it. She'd be too easy to discover. The road and the villages were the first places her father would look once he mounted a search party. But to lose the road would risk losing her way. She had to go on. It was now or never. When she'd seen the dress laid out on the bed, the gown she'd wear to her engagement party, she'd known she couldn't go through with it. If she did, there would be no more choices. Her course would be set.

At the moment, however, that course wasn't set. She was still in charge of her fate. Pen could disappear. She could become Em one last time. Em could go anywhere, be anything. Em couldn't disappoint her father, couldn't disappoint Wadesbridge. Em could roam the world. It wouldn't be easy and it wouldn't be safe. But perhaps she'd had enough of that. There was no time to plan, only to do. If she stopped to think, she might doubt and doubt would lead her back to Wadesbridge and the life that waited for her.

She wasn't sorry. Even in the pouring rain she didn't regret the decision, although she did regret the weather. She would have liked a dry sky and a lovely sunset to walk by. She was making no progress in this muck and her clothes were soaked. She needed to get dry. There was no sense escaping only to catch pneumonia her first night out. She was close to the cottage, though. She could shelter there and continue in the morning.

Pen turned off the road and cut through the meadow, not seeing the rabbit hole until she stepped in it. She went down hard with a yelp, her hands landing in mud, her ankle screaming with sudden pain.

It's not broken, it's not broken, she chanted under her breath as if the words could make it true. She pulled her foot out of the hole and gave it an experimental wiggle. It hurt, but she could move it. It was only sprained, or perhaps twisted. Still, getting off it was imperative, an imperative that was doubly difficult to satisfy now. A twisted ankle impeded her progress to the cottage significantly as she hobbled towards shelter.

By the time she reached the cottage, she was exhausted. If there was a condition beyond soaked, she was that too.

Inside the cottage, she set about the tasks of seeing to her needs. She lit the lamp and laid the fire, trying to remember how she'd seen Cassian do it. Cold, hurt and exhausted, the chores of preparing for the chore of taking care of herself seemed endless. She'd not realised how much work went into taking care of oneself.

With the fire going, Pen stripped out of her

clothes and wrapped herself in the quilt from the bed. She dragged both chairs before the fire, laying her clothes over one and sitting at last in the other to see to her ankle. It was throbbing and swollen. It took enormous effort to pull her foot out of her boot. What could she do for it, though? She hadn't anything to wrap it in. A bucket of cold rain water might help with swelling, but she didn't have a bucket. Even if she did, it would take time to fill.

She leaned her head back against the chair and closed her eyes. Her adventure was poorly planned and supplied. She had no medical supplies, no food, no spare clothes. She'd thought to buy those things once she got to Penzance, somewhere far enough away where her jewellery would not be recognised. She'd not accounted for any emergencies that might befall her before she reached her destination. Who would have thought an emergency would occur three miles from home?

It wasn't until she'd rested a bit and got her spirits back that she noticed the table. It looked different in the dim light of the cottage, or was that just the shadows playing tricks? She got up, using the chair as a makeshift crutch, and thumped her way over. She froze at what she saw. Someone had been here and not long ago. She'd just left the cottage hours before. But her glass heart was gone. The note was gone. She'd been foolish to leave them, thinking they'd be safe. The idea of a shrine had been fanciful and now her keepsakes were lost. She glanced around the room, her nerves on edge and what the missing keepsakes might mean. Had someone been watching the cottage? How would they have known to come and look around? Were they watching the cottage now?

Fear tickled her spine with a cold finger. What kind of a fight could she put up with a bad ankle and no weapon except for the poker by the fire? She supposed she could smash the vase and use a sharp shard like a knife. The vase. Her gaze went back to it. She noticed the lavender laid aside, dry and brittle. The flowers in the vase were new, fresh. Wildflowers from the meadow. Whoever had taken the keepsakes had picked the flowers.

Cassian. She breathed his name and fear released her, replaced by something more powerful: hope, ridiculous, irrational hope. Cassian had been here mere hours ago. Perhaps she had just missed him that afternoon. The question was, would he come again? Did she dare wait that long to find out? Pen trudged back to the fire with her chair crutch and sat down, eyes closed, weary with an odd sense of peace. Cassian was here, somewhere. The thought made her feel safe, safe enough to sleep.

She must have dozed. The pounding at the door woke her from her awkward sleep with a start. She gasped, half-startled, half-fearful. In her panic, she rose too quickly, forgetting about her ankle. She cried out as she fell.

'Pen! Is that you? Are you in there?' a voice hoarse from yelling called out. 'Can you raise the bolt? Can you open the door? Pen, it's me, Cassian. Let me in.'

Sweet relief swept her. Of all the people that could be on the other side of the door, that was the one she wanted. She levered herself up, grabbed her chair and made for the door. She was in his arms the moment it opened, ignoring the rain running from his clothes, ignoring the blanket that fell to the floor. She hadn't enough hands to hold him and the quilt too. Given the choice, she'd much rather hold him.

'Pen, thank goodness I found you. I was so worried. I went to the hills, but there were mudslides.' He was pressing kisses to her hair. 'You're hurt?' She stumbled against him, unable to keep her balance.

'My ankle. It's twisted.' She'd barely uttered the words before he'd swept her up in his arms and carried her to the bed.

'I like this, being met at the door by a naked woman,' he teased, setting her down and going back to retrieve the quilt.

'You should get undressed, too,' Pen said as he tucked the blanket around her.

Cassian arched his brow. 'Is that an invitation?'

Pen blushed, realising how it sounded. 'You're soaking wet. Lay your clothes by the fire. With luck, we'll both have something dry to wear by morning.'

He strode to the fire and began to strip out of his wet things. Even a perfunctory undressing was titillating when it came to Cassian. She couldn't take her eyes from him as his waterlogged coats came off and his sticky shirt was peeled from his body. But she could not let her thoughts stray in that direction, not until things were resolved. If they simply jumped back into bed with one another, nothing changed. She still wouldn't know where she stood with him. What was true? What was a game?

'Why didn't you come back sooner?' she asked the first necessary question. His hands stalled on the fall of his breeches.

'We are to play twenty questions, is that it, Pen?' It was softly said, kindly said.

'I'd rather play twenty answers, Cassian. I'm tired of having doubts about you, about us. Questions imply the existence of the unknown and there is too much of that between us.' She wanted surety, even if it hurt.

Cassian finished with his breeches and came to the bed, gloriously naked, distractingly so as he sat on the edge. He reached for her hands, the tenderness of the gesture unnerving her. It was the type of gesture one made when one had bad news to impart. She didn't want bad news. 'Then we will play the game, Pen, one last time and you can decide once and for all if I am worthy of you. First, let me tell you why I didn't come, why I couldn't come.' He paused, bracing her for his next words. 'The Hawaiian King has died, Pen, and his wife. When they sickened and there was a real possibility they wouldn't recover, it was impossible to leave the city. King George was adamant that, should it come to it, the *ton* must be on hand to give him the funeral he deserved. He was laid in state, his bones were laid in the crypt at St Martin-in-the-Fields. There was all the requisite pomp and ceremony. I couldn't leave. My father is gone from London at the moment. I had to represent the family and, as a new, close acquaintance to the Hawaiian King, George felt I should be there especially.' He sighed. 'Telling you now, it seems like such a little thing, a poor reason to leave your side, to not run to your rescue.'

Pen nodded. 'I understand.' She caressed his hands with her thumbs. It felt good to be touched by him again. She'd given up hope of feeling that touch. It would have been easy to give in to it, to let his body persuade her all was well between them. But his explanation didn't answer every question she had. She could not relent yet. 'You had your duty and we left suddenly.' If only they'd delayed their departure by a few hours, then her father, too, would have been forced to stay. She could have confronted Cassian personally. 'I'm glad you were there. He seemed like a nice man, a man interested in the world. It's too bad the world played him false.'

'His wife died first. After that, he seemed to lose the will to fight it. He had no immunity and no strength.' She felt the pressure of Cassian's grip tighten on her hands. The king's death had touched him. 'My friend, Eaton, had the measles when he was young. We almost lost him to them too. It's a powerful disease.'

'But you're here now,' Pen prompted. 'Why?'

'Can't you guess? I am here for you. I left London half an hour after the funeral and rode as hard as I could. I rode straight to Castle Byerd. I wanted to hear from your own lips that you were done with me. Your father was quick to tell me you were engaged to Wades-bridge, but it's hard to be engaged when one party has disappeared.' Cassian drew a deep breath that moved his chest. 'So, Pen, are you through with me? Will you give me a chance to explain? Or have you decided it's to be Wades-bridge?'

It was hard to think with that chest of his on such blatant display, but she had to think. This was about more than a handsome, half-naked man wanting to bed her and she him. This was about her future with a man she could trust. 'Tell me the truth, Cassian. Was it always about the land? Is that still what you're here for?' This was the only question that mattered and her heart was in her throat at the asking of it.

'You know it was not always about the land, not since the moment I saw you in London and realized you were Em.' He left her and crossed the room and retrieved his coat from the hearth. 'You saw the note I wrote.' He pulled the paper out, soggy at the edges and returned to her. 'You know I loved you before I met you in London. To see you that night at Byerd House and to know you were my beloved Em was like a miracle to me. In that one moment everything was perfect.' His knuckles skimmed her cheek. 'I should have told you sooner about the land, I was just too afraid I'd lose you. There was already so much doubt between us without that. Then, that day when you found my drawings for the park, I should have told you then, but you volunteered the land and I took the easy way out. I lost you over it. I will always wonder, if I'd told you sooner, would it have made a difference? Or would you have pushed me away? Would I have lost my chance altogether? You were not in a listening mood that night in London.'

He loved her. It had not been a lie. She could see it in the regret, in the pain, in his eyes and in the wanting, too, that was still there. How difficult their journey had been. Losing one another, then finding one another again, only to have her doubts keep them apart. He'd worked hard to overcome them, to make a space for them where he could tell her about the land without recrimination. He had almost succeeded if it had not been for Wilmington's disclosure. She was not going to be thwarted in love by a jealous man's trump.

Pen searched Cassian's face. 'Who says you've lost me?' she whispered. 'I've missed you every day since I've been back. I wondered why you didn't come. Was it that you didn't love me? That my father was right? I only said yes to Wadesbridge when I felt the best I could do was protect myself from being hurt again by putting myself beyond your reach, beyond love's reach. I said yes because I was out of hope.'

'Where there's love, Pen, there is always hope. Will you hope with me?' he whispered against her skin, pressing her back against the mattress.

'There is still my father to contend with. He was your stubborn gentleman, was he not? I figured it out when my father showed me the land company's letters.' She gave a soft laugh.

Cassian didn't chuckle. 'I am sorry for that. I would not have chosen for you to find out that way. When I thought of you hurting, of what you might be thinking, my heart broke anew. I would never choose to cause you pain in anyway, Pen.'

'It is in the past, now. All has been explained and forgiven.' She stroked his brow with a gentle hand, her own desire starting to heat, her body starting to burn. 'But my father must be considered. His resistance hasn't changed. He will not sanction the marriage. There is also still the issue of the land and the park.'

Cassian moved over her, his mouth brushing her lips. 'No, there isn't. He needs to know how much I love you, that I will do anything to have you, to be with you. The land is nothing. I will tell him tomorrow when I take you home. I will give it up for you.'

The announcement sucked the air from her. 'Cassian, I can't let you do that. You would come to hate me if I was the reason you lost your dream.'

'You are my dream now. Together, we can find another way to build the park.' He bracketed her head with his hands, his finger smoothing back her hair, his mouth kissing her softly. 'I wasn't sure I'd ever get to do this again with you, Pen.' His body moved gently, reverently against hers, letting her feel the press of his arousal. 'I had three long days on horseback to think about what I truly wanted and what I want is you, more than I want the amusement gardens, more than I've ever wanted anything in this world.'

'And I want you, Cassian. More than anything else in this world.' Enough to risk marriage, enough to risk her father's ire.

'You shall have me.' He took her then in a swift thrust of homecoming, and she gloried in it as he filled her, joined her. They were together now, their doubts set aside. As long as they stood together, it didn't matter what her father thought. She and Cassian would find a way.

Chapter Twenty-Three

The world was rosy after a night of storms, after a night of lovemaking. If only it could stay that way, Pen thought as they approached Castle Byerd. She sat before Cassian on Ajax, wrapped in Cassian's arms, held tight against his chest and between his thighs, last night's intimacy lingering. Her night had been far more pleasant than her father's. She had to remember that. While she'd been safe and dry in Cassian's embrace, her father had spent a restless, unfruitful night, searching for her. He would be worried beyond measure and reliving the horror of losing her mother all over again, thinking perhaps he'd lost her as well and under similar circumstances.

Guilt poked at her, marring the rosiness of the morning. She'd not meant to be cruel. She'd merely meant to live her own life. But she saw the cruelty in her decision now, the pain her choice would have brought him. 'My father will be angry.' She looked up at Cassian.

'He has every right to be, but we'll see it through,' Cassian assured her. She wished she possessed his confidence. But Cassian had never seen her father mad.

In the stable yard, their appearance brought all activity to a halt. 'Someone fetch the earl!' a groom called out, issuing instructions. 'Someone help with the horse.' Hands reached up to help her down. Cassian dismounted behind her, issuing instructions of his own to take care of her ankle, which had been useless this morning. He'd carried her to the horse.

'My lady, come this way,' someone offered, but Pen refused, reaching for Cassian's arm. She didn't want to be separated from him, didn't want anyone ushering her away from the decisions that would be made. They were her decisions. She needed to be part of them, she needed to fight for them.

Her father appeared in the stable yard, drawn and pale from a sleepless night, Phin and Wadesbridge with him. Phin rushed to her and hugged her. 'I'm glad you're back.' To Cassian he said, 'Where did you find her?'

'Safe and mostly sound at the gamekeeper's cottage between Hayle and Redruth,' Cassian answered. 'She's twisted her ankle, nothing more.'

'Nothing more?' Redruth strode forward, all fuming, barely restrained anger. Pen squared her shoulders and felt Cassian's hand close around hers as the storm of her father's wrath broke. 'You're out the entire night with my daughter and you say nothing more? Step away from him, Pen. This blackguard has intentionally thought to compromise you.'

Cassian took a half step in front of Pen, just enough to shield her, not to hide her. She would not want to be hidden. She would want to be supported. 'I found her. She was in no condition to travel and the weather made travel more dangerous than staying in place. To return home would have risked our health and the horse's. Her ankle is proof enough of that. I appreciate that you spent a night in worry over her, but she is home now.'

'She is disgraced now! A night spent with a man?' Redruth sputtered.

'I fully intend to marry her, to renew the proposal I made in London.' He glanced at Wadesbridge apologetically. Wadesbridge was an innocent bystander caught up in the contretemps. 'I should think my proposal overrides any other offers on the table since I did make it first.'

Redruth scoffed. 'You were refused in London and now you think to compromise her, to give me no choice. This is exactly what you want.'

Cassian gave a dry laugh. 'I don't think this is about your choice, sir, but your daughter's. After all, I'm not proposing to you.' That brought a round of nervous laughter from the stable boys before they were glared into silence. 'Might we go inside? Perhaps more privacy would be appropriate for this discussion?' Cassian suggested. He could practically feel Pen's cheeks burning beside him and her hand was crushing his in its grip. He didn't want to make this fight harder for her than it had to be.

Redruth nodded and ushered them inside, Wadesbridge diplomatically declining to join

them on the grounds that this was a family matter. It was the most minute of agreements, but
it was a start. If they could agree on this, perhaps there were other things they would find
agreement on. Phin poured out drinks while
Cassian took up his position at the right shoulder of Pen's chair. 'My lord, we both agree we
want what is best for Pen,' he said. If Redruth
could realise they agreed on that, it would be
a monumental step forward.

'And you think you're best for her?' Redruth
was cool as he took a glass from Phin.

'I don't think that's my decision to make at
all,' Cassian corrected. 'Or yours. Pen should
decide what's best for her.'

'She should be guided in those decisions by
the people who care for her the most.' Redruth
did not back down.

'I have been,' Pen interrupted, reaching for
Cassian's hand. 'Mama taught me to embrace
life, not to fear it. I do not want to live my life
behind walls. Last night, when I was out in the
storm, I was frightened. I was soaked, I was
hurt, I had no help to rely on except myself.
It would have been easy to turn around. But
while I was afraid of being out in the storm,

I was more afraid of what would happen if I came back and committed myself to a marriage that would be lukewarm at best. Wadesbridge deserves better. I deserve better. You *and* Mama showed me that. You loved each other every day of your lives. I left because I couldn't live without that in my own marriage, nor could I live with your disappointment in me if I refused Wadesbridge.'

'Pen, you've never disappointed me. Challenged me, perhaps, but I love you. You can't disappoint me. We'll find you another husband. It doesn't have to be Wadesbridge.' It was the softest Cassian had ever seen Redruth. He squeezed Pen's hand, knowing how difficult this was for her. She had done her part, now it was time for him to do his.

'I want to be that husband. I believe Pen loves me and I love her. I would be here asking even if last night did not demand my honour required it. You know this to be true. You know I came to you in this very hall last evening to renew my proposal.' Cassian locked eyes with the earl.

'I want him, Father. He is my choice,' Pen offered in support.

Redruth shook his head. 'Any man but him, Pen. He only wants your land. That hasn't changed. He'll take that land and he'll corrupt it with his plans. I can't give my daughter to a man who only means to use her. He courted you with the intention to deceive me out of the land I'd refused him outright.'

'Then I give up the land. I renounce all claim to it and to her dowry in toto,' Cassian announced. 'I only want her.'

The interruption stymied Redruth. 'If this is a bluff, you will lose, Trevethow. I will not relent.'

'Neither will I. We'd prefer to have your blessing, but we will wed without it because that is the strength of my love for her.' There was satisfaction in seeing Redruth stunned, at a loss for words. Cassian seized the opportunity to press his case. 'With the issue of the land settled, there is no reason to reject my suit. I am a peer of the realm—I will inherit the Dukedom of Hayle in due time. My estate is not far from yours, so you will have plenty of opportunity to visit your daughter and your future grandchildren.'

Redruth's gaze went to his daughter, the

last of his arguments refuted, leaving him no grounds for resistance, as Cassian had intended. 'You're sure, Pen? You have no doubts?'

'None.' Pen's single word filled the room, and Cassian's heart swelled.

'Then I suppose I cannot withhold my blessing.' It was as close as they'd get to the earl's approval. Cassian would take it. He understood a man had his pride and his limits.

'I'd like to wed as soon as possible.' Cassian knew he was pushing his luck. He'd just gained the man's permission and he was already making another demand of his father-in-law. But he'd been pushing his luck in other ways. Who knew—Redruth's grandchild might already be taking root. 'I want to marry as soon as I can get my family here and Pen can walk down the aisle.'

As soon as Pen could walk down the aisle turned out to be two weeks later in the middle of August. It might have been three weeks, if they'd chosen a larger church. But the aisle at the Castle Byerd chapel was short and Pen assured him she could manage. What she could not manage was another night without him in her bed. Cassian agreed. When a man has the rest of his life to enjoy the woman he loves in bed, he is determined to make the rest of his life start as soon as possible.

He waited impatiently for the rest of that life to start at the front of Byerd's stone chapel. The interior was cool inside, the altar simply decorated with a pristine white linen cloth and a vase of summer wildflowers. Pen had not wanted anything lavish and neither had he. In his opinion, the love between a man and a woman was a private matter for them to celebrate alone with their closest friends. To turn it into a circus cheapened it. The guest list was short but meaningful, limited to Pen's family and his. His parents sat in the front pew across from Phin and Pen's aunt. Behind his parents sat Inigo and his father, the Duke of Boscastle, followed by Eaton and his family—his wife, Eliza, and her daughter, Sophie—Eaton's father and mother with them. Behind them were Sir Jock Treleven and his wife along with their oldest daughter, Rosenwyn, her husband Cador Kitto and their new infant son born in March. Nearly all of Cassian's friends and mentors were there. Only Vennor was missing. But Cassian understood. When Ven was ready to celebrate life again, he would return to the fold.

At the corner of the altar, the five unmarried Treleven girls sat with bows poised to provide music. With a nod from the vicar, the girls began a beautiful rendition of a Vivaldi piece on their violins and cello. Cassian had chosen the piece as a remembrance of the night at the St Piran's Day fair and the Venetian glassblower.

The heavy oak doors of the chapel opened and Cassian's heart began to pound. His bride was coming. And she was there, standing in the doorway, framed by sunlight; an angel, a Madonna, *his*. Another perfect moment, the beginning of his life. Pen made her way down the short aisle, slow and dignified on her father's arm, dressed in her mother's wedding gown, a pale blue slip overlaid with an overskirt of white lace, a high waist like the ones worn at the turn of the century, a wide expanse of blue ribbon under her breasts, her mother's pearls at her neck, her mother's veil of old lace covering her hair. But at her wrist, tied in a blue ribbon to match, was the glass heart he'd given her that first night. Blue for truth. Blue for loyalty.

She'd not worn gloves today, had insisted on it, in fact, saying she wanted to feel his hands when he held hers, skin to skin, in prelude for the night to come.

Pen reached the front, her father placed her hand in Cassian's and Cassian nodded his thanks. He knew what an effort this was for Redruth. In some ways, the earl was losing his daughter, setting her free into a world where he couldn't protect her. 'I'll take good care of her, sir,' Cassian said in low undertones as Redruth stepped away.

Eaton had told him he wouldn't remember any of the service, that it would all be a blur. Eaton was wrong. Cassian imprinted every moment of it on his mind: the way Pen looked as she took his hand, the way tears had glistened in her eyes as he'd said his vows, promising to worship her with his body, the tremulous smile on her face when he'd slipped the ring on her slender finger, the feel of her warm lips when he kissed her. He would remember all of it. Most of all, he'd remember the hope in her eyes when she looked at him. Together, they would dream new dreams, see new places and build a new world. Starting tomorrow. Tonight was to be spent in the gamekeeper's cottage and tomorrow they'd begin their honeymoon— a year-long affair of travel. He would take her to Italy, to Venice and Rome, they'd yacht the Mediterranean and see the Grand Bazaar of Istanbul and the great temples of Greece.

'This is the best day of my life,' he whispered as he led her down the aisle and out into the sunlight and the cheers of those assembled.

She laughed up at him. 'Only until the next one.' He drew her close and kissed her hard, much to the approval of the crowd. She was right. There would be other best days: the day she'd tell him she was expecting their first child, the day she had their first child, the day she told him she was expecting their second child, and their third and their fourth. There'd be every morning he woke up next to her and every night he went to bed beside her and those would be the best of days too. He had meant to show her the world, but, deep at his core, he knew that she'd been the one to show the world to him, a secret, private world of the heart.

He recalled the words she'd spoken to him

that first day in the cottage. *'You are my adventure in the very best of ways.'* Yes. Every word of it was true.

Epilogue

Late summer, 1825

Cassian stood at the ship's rail, his arms wrapped about his wife as the Truro Quay came into view. They were home. Very shortly they'd be on Cornish soil after nearly a year away, a year spent on a travelling honeymoon, a year spent watching his wife's eyes light in joy at the wonders of Venice, of the Turkish bazaar. More than that, it had been a year of discovering love, a love that enabled him to forgive himself, to find peace with his brother's memory, to let go of dreams that had weighed him down instead of setting him free. He might not be building a pleasure garden, but he was more than that. He understood that now. That dream did not define him. He would find other ways to help promote economic recovery.

Pen looked up at him. 'Are you happy to be home?'

Cassian grinned. 'I've been home all year. I've been with you, haven't I? Wherever you are, that's where my home is.'

'I think it will be nice to sleep in one bed for a while.' Pen laughed. They waved to the figures on the dock, growing closer. Inigo was there, with his new bride, a veil covering her face. He'd sent word to one of the ports that he'd married. 'I wonder who she is? He was so mysterious not telling us.'

Cassian wasn't quite as interested in Inigo's new bride as he was in his wife. He was pleased to be home despite his comments. After all, he had responsibilities to see to and one could not rely on stewards for ever. But he would miss the rhythm of the road, of not having to share Pen with anyone. On the road his time was all hers. 'It was a grand adventure, though.' He nuzzled her ear with his mouth. 'We'll be unpacking our souvenirs for weeks.' His wife had proven to be an insatiable shopper and a shrewd bargainer. The hold of the ship was full of carpets and silks and gifts for everyone.

Pen turned in his arms, her smile coy. 'Some

of the souvenirs might take longer than that, up to nine months even.'

It took him a moment to fully comprehend, but when he did, a broad smile took his mouth. 'You're pregnant? Are you sure?'

'Three months. I am pretty sure.' Pen smiled. 'Are you happy? It's not too soon? We won't be wandering again any time soon.'

'It's not too soon,' Cassian assured her. 'It looks like Inigo won't be the only one with a surprise to share.' He was counting backwards in his mind. Three months would mean Venice. They'd spent the spring there in a palazzo overlooking the Grand Canal.

'I think it was the night we took the gondola ride.' She laughed.

'That only narrows it down slightly. I have fond memories of many gondola rides. Too bad England doesn't have more canals.' Cassian kissed her, long and hard, as the anchor dropped. Pen had already given him so much: her love, her trust, his life back. And now, she was going to give him a child. He could want for nothing.

'I have something else for you.' Pen reached into the pocket of her travelling skirt for an envelope. 'I don't want you to be bored here at home, so I thought this might keep you busy.'

'What is it?' Cassian eyed his wife with mock suspicion as he unfolded the paper inside. His brow furrowed. It looked very legal. He read slowly, carefully, not daring to believe what his eyes saw.

'It's a deed for the land my father refused you,' she explained. He was aware of her eyes on him, of the hesitance in her voice. 'Do you like it? I thought it was what you wanted.'

'I do like it.' Cassian folded the deed and put it back in the envelope. He tucked it away with reverence, overwhelmed. She'd found a way. He was going to build his amusement garden. No, correction. *They* were going to build *their* amusement garden. He'd let that dream go willingly, and it had come back to him. 'But make no mistake, Pen. You are what I wanted always. I won't say that thirty-two acres of empty land between Redruth and Hayle doesn't excite me. But rest assured, nothing will excite me as much as my wife and thought of our child.' He took her face between his hands. 'How did you convince your father to release the land?'

'Love works in mysterious ways.' Pen

wrapped her arms about his waist. 'I told him you were worth it.'

'And he believed you?'

'Yes, but I think in the end it was you he believed, a man who would give up his dream for the sake of love. Your actions spoke to him far louder than any words ever could. You showed him love was worth fighting for.'

'Well, it is.' Cassian drew her close for a last kiss as the boat thumped against the pier, or maybe that was the thump of his heart. He was home and all of his dreams were within reach because one good woman was in his arms; because love had found a way.

* * * * *

LET'S TALK
Romance

For exclusive extracts, competitions
and special offers, find us online:

f facebook.com/millsandboon

⊙ @millsandboonuk

🐦 @millsandboon

Or get in touch on 0844 844 1351*

For all the latest titles coming soon,
visit millsandboon.co.uk/nextmonth

*Calls cost 7p per minute plus your phone company's price per
minute access charge

Want even more
ROMANCE?

Join our bookclub today!

'Mills & Boon books, the perfect way to escape for an hour or so.'

Miss W. Dyer

'Excellent service, promptly delivered and very good subscription choices.'

Miss A. Pearson

'You get fantastic special offers and the chance to get books before they hit the shops'

Mrs V. Hall

Visit millsandbook.co.uk/Bookclub and save on brand new books.

MILLS & BOON